# The Birth of
# *The Orpheus Circle* . . .

Nathan Cassierer's thin, veined hands tightened around the cane on which they lightly rested. His eyes held Thompson's with a dark intensity.

"Put yourself in the place of these Prussian aristocrats, these young SS men in the summer of 1944. Their world is collapsing. . . . At the very least their lives will be blighted forever by the stain of SS membership. How can they escape? They can leave, of course. . . . Do what Barbie and Mengele did. Hide and run in the jungles of South America, hunted animals. . . . Or they can become servants of the Arabs, training their armies and police. . . . No. These men wanted more. They wanted to die and be reborn, cleansed to participate in the renaissance of a New Germany. . . . I want you to find them, Dr. Thompson. Give me their names. I will do the rest. . . ."

# The Orpheus Circle

A Novel by

## Edward McGhee

PUBLISHED BY POCKET BOOKS NEW YORK

Another *Original* publication of POCKET BOOKS

POCKET BOOKS, a division of Simon & Schuster, Inc.
1230 Avenue of the Americas, New York, N.Y. 10020

Copyright © 1987 by Edward McGhee
Cover artwork copyright © 1987 Peter Caras

ISBN: 0-671-64097-6

First Pocket Books printing October 1987

10 9 8 7 6 5 4 3 2 1

POCKET and colophon are trademarks of
Simon & Schuster, Inc.

Printed in the U.S.A.

For Mary Lee

# The Orpheus Circle

# Chapter 1

"THE SS CAME IN FOUR ARMORED CARS. ABOUT forty in all. They spread out through the village, blocking the streets, methodically emptying all the houses of people and driving them toward the market place. Nobody was afraid. Things like this had happened before. Document checks. Searches for people without papers. It was June 1944. The Allies had landed in Normandy. Things were going badly in Russia. The Germans were nervous. We were not afraid. In the square they separated the women and children from the men and marched them off in the direction of the church. We were told to form up in three lines. I was in the back row with my back almost up against a house. Then without any warning the machine gunners in the square aimed their weapons and began to fire, sweeping the line from right to left at about the level of a man's navel. Bodies were crumpling in front of me. I turned and ran, opening the first door I saw and throwing myself inside. The officer began shouting. I raced through the house, that of Pierre Delville, and jumped through a window into the garden. I ran down an alley and into an empty street until I came to the fields. I climbed a small hill and hid among the trees. The machine guns stopped. Then they started again from the direction of the church. They fired a long time. Two, three minutes. Then the church started to burn. They forced the women and children back inside and shot them. Then they burned the church. A woman appeared at a small window. They shot her as she jumped. Another threw her baby out and started to follow but the bullets forced her back. They killed everybody in the village. Six hundred and forty-two people."

I leaned back in the ancient Thonet chair and rubbed my eyes. I'd been at it for four hours without a break. The files were beginning to blur and run together. One more and I'd call it a day. I pushed aside the testimony of the French witnesses at the Berlin trial of Untersturmfuehrer Heinz Barth and flipped open the SS officer's personal records. Born Gransee, Prussia, October 15, 1920, son of a railroad worker. Joined Hitler Jugend, June 1932. Drafted into German army February 1939. Transferred June 9, 1942, to Sicherheitspolizei in Prague, Czechoslovakia. Entered officers' training school, September 1942, commissioned Leutnant der Sicherheitspolizei January 27, 1943. Transferred May 1943, to Waffen SS 10th Division with rank of Untersturmfuehrer. Chest wound December 1943. Transferred to Waffen SS Division "Das Reich" in France, January 1944.

The file was incomplete. By late 1944 not even the Germans were bothering to keep up records. The cities were in ruins and the Russian and Allied armies had reached the German borders. Food was giving out. It was only a matter of time before the Third Reich collapsed. Heinz Barth, commander of the unit which utterly destroyed the French village of Oradour-sur-Glan on June 10, 1944, went underground in the chaos and disappeared for thirty-five years.

I returned to the East German trial transcript. Barth

had obtained false papers in the last days of the war stating that he was a simple policeman. He worked as a laborer in the first postwar years before returning to his home town seventy miles north of Berlin in 1948. There he worked hard, studied nights, became an accountant and, finally, manager of a food distribution organization. He joined the Communist Party, was made a member of the local government, married, fathered three children and was preparing to retire when his name surfaced in a trial of war criminals in France. A routine inquiry through Interpol located him. At his trial Barth protested that he had never taken the initiative. He had always followed orders, like a good soldier.

"I was very ambitious and eager to fulfill my orders conscientiously and to the letter. Orders and duty were my life. I was ordered to kill those who acted against the law. It was war. The first time, when Reichsprotektor Reinhard Heydrich was killed in Czechoslovakia and we were told to execute the villagers at Lidice, I did not volunteer like some of my comrades. But when I was ordered to join the commando, I could not refuse. So I did what the others did. I became part of an execution team. We killed in groups of three. They told us to shoot for the head or the heart. I wanted to get ahead, to be an officer. I only did what I was told."

I turned back to the SS file. "Barth shows a healthy ambition and true comradely feelings. Both on and off duty and vis-a-vis his supervisors he is always a model of military correctness. He understands the National Socialist world view and, following his participation in recent events, is ready for a reserve officer training course."

Barth seemed genuinely puzzled during his East German trial. "I was only following orders," he protested under cross-examination. "The French resistance were killing our soldiers from ambush. It was

3

war. We took hostages and destroyed their villages to make them stop. What else were we to do? We killed them and burned their farms, but only to persuade them not to attack our columns. It was a bad time. We were surrounded by a hostile population. No one dared to drop behind. Anyone not with his unit was cut off and executed by the resistance. It was war. I was only following orders."

A big hand slapped down on my shoulder. "How's it going?"

"Huh? Oh. Christ. Great. I'm accumulating the biggest collection of mass murderers and all-purpose monsters since Mary Shelley invented Frankenstein."

"Come on. We're closing up. I'll buy you a beer at Willy's."

"You know something, Hugh?"

"What?"

"I've been working on it for ten years now. And I still can't figure it out."

Hugh LeRoy, in his early fifties, was director of the Berlin Document Center, the central Nazi archive, captured and administered by the American occupation authorities. He flipped the light switch, darkening the windowless, low-ceilinged room, and we moved out into a wide corridor, leather heels echoing off the walls.

"You ought to quit after this book. Find another specialty. Get out of this hole." He gestured toward the stark cement walls. "Christ, you've got to be a masochist to spend your vacations in a Nazi archive, two floors underground, buried among the files of mass killers. What the hell ever got you interested anyway? You look like a healthy, reasonably sane young male."

"Viet Nam mostly. I saw a lot of bizarre behavior out there when the pressure was on. Besides, war is fascinating. Nothing comes close to it for excitement. Hell, you were in a couple. You know what I mean."

"Yeah. Only this place hasn't got much to do with

4

war. Killing maybe, but not war." He led the way up a narrow staircase, two stories into the light. "Anyway, you ought to let up."

"I can't, Hugh. I'm broke. The grant runs only six weeks. I'll never get the research done as it is. I need at least three months. Probably more."

"So you come back next year."

"It's getting tougher to get research money. Nobody's interested in history anymore. I was thinking of asking you to let me work here nights."

"No way, Alec. Absolutely out of the question. I'm already giving you the run of the place. If anybody found out I was letting you work here on your own, I'd be out on my ass instantly. It's just too fucking sensitive."

"When are you going to turn it over to the Germans? I read somewhere the microfilming would be finished soon."

"It is finished. The computer team will wind up in a couple of days. Everything in here is on microfilm. You punch out the codes and you can call up any file we've got."

"Great. Just ten years too late to do me any good. So when do the krauts take over?"

"They don't. No interest."

"You're kidding. They don't want to get their hands on the personnel files of the Nazi Party and the SS? Why not?"

"Easy. We can keep this stuff under lock and key. Open it only to accredited scholars. Stiff journalists and curiosity-seekers. You give it to the Germans and they'd have to open it up to the public. No way the Greens and the rest of the left-wing kooks in the country would let them hide anything. And you know what that would mean."

"A lot of embarrassed people."

"More than that. Some of them would be in the slammer. Nobody wants to rake it all up again. Look at Barbie in France. The French didn't want him back. Somebody fucked up. They'd just as soon he died of old age down in the Bolivian jungle or somebody knocked him off. Now he's going to blow the whistle on who collaborated with the Germans in World War II. And, worse, he's going to prove that the resistance wasn't all that heroic. If he ever gets to trial, that is, which I very much doubt."

"There aren't that many really bad ones still kicking around, are there? I mean, the war's been over for forty years. You'd have to have been at least twenty-five at the end of it to have had any real responsibility. That means anybody under sixty-five is reasonably clear."

"People live longer today, Alec. There are one hell of a lot of ex-SS men in big jobs in this country today. Don't kid yourself. Hell, there's a guy who does nothing but look for them."

"Simon Wiesenthal?"

"Him, too. I'm thinking of somebody more important. He's trailing some really big fish. Nathan Cassierer."

"That's a famous old Berlin family. Jewish bankers. Made their money under Bismarck."

"Yeah. He's in his eighties. Got out in 1933. Became a British citizen. Fought in the limey army during the war. Elegant old bastard. He came back to Berlin a few years ago and started looking for a bunch of SS men who disappeared at the end of the war."

"He won't find them here. They slipped out through Italy and Spain to South America or the Middle East. Egypt, Syria, Libya. He wouldn't have to look hard. The cafes, souks, and cemetaries of Bagdad, Damascus, and Cairo are full of them. Plus the guys like Mengele and Barbie in Paraguay."

We emerged into a flat-roofed, one-story building shaped like a horseshoe. Black ventilation ducts scarred the uncut lawn. A stand of trees partially blocked the view of a twelve-foot wire-mesh fence around the perimeter.

"There were others, Alec. People who changed their names, assumed other identities, had plastic surgery, then just disappeared."

"In Germany? They couldn't get away with it, Hugh. You know it better than anybody. Look at these files." We were passing through a room filled with row on row of ancient wooden filing cabinets. "Everybody who ever joined the Nazi Party is in these files. On neat little cards with a picture and vital statistics. Down in that underground tomb where I work there are half a million SS files plus three hundred thousand marriage application folders."

"And two million special files on ethnic Germans who came back from outside Germany. So what are you saying?"

"I'm saying this place isn't like America where anybody can walk into city hall with a name, get a birth certificate, go down to the Social Security Administration, show the certificate, come out with a card, get a driver's license, and apply for a passport. He gets a job, opens a bank account, establishes a credit rating, and he's in business with a new identity. Unless he gets booked for a felony and his fingerprints are on file with the FBI, he's safe. Not here. Every German has to have an identity card with his picture on it. When he moves he reports to the police. His *Akte,* his personal file, is kept by them. When he graduates from school, it's noted. When he marries, in it goes. His children, his jobs, everything up to what happened to his ashes if he's cremated."

"You're right, Alec. It's a very methodical system. And you know something?"

"What?"

"That's the easiest kind to beat because it's so

7

predictable. Everybody feels secure. Nothing can go wrong. It's sort of a warm bureaucratic womb. And everybody in Germany is so fucking law-abiding. Once you're in the system, nobody would think of questioning you. Plus, you've got to remember the postwar period. Total chaos. Records destroyed. Families scattered. Millions of displaced persons. It was an ideal environment to disappear into and resurface a few years later with a new name, new face, new history."

"And Cassierer is looking for a couple of Nazis who did this?"

"More like a couple hundred. High-ranking SS men who knew the war was lost in mid-1944 and set out to save their asses."

"How does he know?"

"Ask him."

"What?"

"I gave him your name. His researcher just died. Remember the old boy with the funny little Flying Dutchman beard?"

"Yeah. Haven't seen him lately."

"Cassierer hired him. He was a retired professor. Got killed in a car accident a couple of weeks ago. Cassierer asked if I knew anybody who could take his place. I suggested you. He pays well. Give you a couple more months to work."

"Thanks, Hugh."

"No problem. I figured you'd be less of a pain in the ass than some new character who doesn't know his way around."

"How do I find the old boy?"

"Here's his number. It's a cutout. He's cautious. Somebody tried to kill him a couple of years ago. Or he thinks they did. How about that beer?"

He was an old man sitting very erect at a corner table in the Cafe Moehring. Thin, almost translucent, hands resting lightly on a cane. He stood and bowed slightly when I came up to the table.

"So good of you to come, Dr. Thompson." His English was British with just a hint of an accent. "Hugh told me nothing but good things about you and your work."

"He thinks I'm part of the furniture out there, I've been doing research for so long."

"Yes. Did Hugh tell you what I'm looking for?"

"Not in detail. Something about finding one of the organizations set up after the war to allow Nazis to disappear."

"There were many, as you know. *Die Spinne,* the web. The Atlas Group. The *Kameradenschaft.* Skorzeny's network operating out of Madrid. Large numbers of the top Nazi leaders escaped and have been living lives of luxury in South America and certain Arab countries ever since the war."

"And you've got information on some of them?"

"Not on individuals. On the Orpheus Circle, an organization set up some time in the summer of 1944 to enable a restricted group of SS officers to assume false identities and submerge into postwar Germany."

"Almost a year before the war was over? How could they get away with it without the Gestapo finding out?"

"The Gestapo was part of the SS, Dr. Thompson, as you well know. Some of the leaders of this group were high-ranking police officials. They were," he stopped, "are, I should say, highly intelligent men who had realized that the war was lost after the successful Allied landing in Normandy in June. Germany's defeat was only a question of time. They were shocked into action by the attempt on Hitler's life. Had it succeeded and a regime of right-wing but anti-Nazi generals taken over, they would have been shot out of hand. And they knew it. So they moved very quickly to put into effect plans which had been formulated shortly after Stalingrad. Plans designed to assure that the system would survive a defeat by protecting a nucleus of leaders who would lead a future resurrection."

I studied the old man as he talked. Slim, elegantly tailored in an ancient but superb lightweight British tweed, immaculate in the way some old men are, he was the picture of an aging Prussian aristocrat, with piercing blue eyes, a sharp beak of a nose, and a thin, hawklike profile vaguely reminiscent of von Rundstedt.

"Funny I've never run across the group in my researches."

"Not really, Dr. Thompson. They figure in no official histories. They left no documentary tracks the way so many of the stupid petty officials of the Nazi empire did. And they were and are an exceptional group of men. Intelligent, well-educated and, most important for their survival, all members of the Prussian aristocracy."

I fiddled with the coffee cup in front of me. I'd met a lot of obsessive people while researching the Nazi period. The traumas of some would never heal. One man who had haunted the Document Center for a time told me he had watched from hiding as his wife, mother, sister, and six children had been dragged away to disappear in the Auschwitz gas ovens. He had tried to confirm their fate with a compulsive intensity for fifteen years. It seemed unlikely that an organization as widespread as the one Cassierer was describing wouldn't have surfaced in the forty years since the war. The old man was chasing nightmares, trying to exorcise the past.

"You doubt my information, Dr. Thompson? You think I am an old crank, approaching senility, seeking revenge with trembling hands, a prisoner of old hatreds and the nightmares of age?"

"No. It's just that the whole thing seems a little

unlikely. Not that people didn't try to change their identities. Some probably succeeded in 1945. But it's hard to believe that such a big organization could have been kept secret for so long. Somebody always splits, drinks too much, boasts. Or somebody is broken. Like Eichmann."

Cassierer raised his eyebrows, thickets of white hair which almost met above his nose. "Then you do know something?"

I must have looked blank.

"The first information on the group came from the Eichmann interrogations."

"You must be mistaken, Herr Cassierer. I've read every line of those interrogations, and there is nothing in them about such a group."

"Tell me, Dr. Thompson. Are you willing to work with me on this project? Hugh tells me you need money to continue your research. I will pay you a thousand marks a week for the remaining time you can spend in Germany. Two months, I believe, before you must return to your university. For this I would expect that half of each day be expended on my needs. The rest you would be free to use for your research."

"That's more than three hundred dollars a week, Herr Cassierer. You can buy three young researchers for that price at the Free University."

"Yes. I know. But Hugh was kind enough to show me your dossier. Also, I read your book on the SS. A fine piece of scholarship. More important, you show an indispensable *Fingerspitzengefuehl,* feel, I believe you say in English, for the psychology of the SS, which is rare. I need a man not only of intelligence but of insight, who can make the jump from facts to truth, Dr. Thompson. For some reason not wholly apparent from your dossier it is clear that you have the ability to enter the mentality of these men, to divine their motivations and, to some extent, forecast their actions. I

11

suspect it has something to do with your Polish mother and the Celtic fanaticism of your father. You may have it in your blood."

"How the hell do you know about my family?"

"This is a most delicate matter, Dr. Thompson. I was almost killed two years ago when I began working on this project. I am fortunate to have a modest fortune, and following the attempt on my life I engaged a bodyguard." He nodded toward a neighboring table where a compact, dark-skinned man of thirty or so sat impassively staring into a coffee cup. "I do not take chances. I have access to your academic record through Hugh. Your army personnel file and security clearances were made available to me by friends in your government. You are an impressive young man. Superb scholar. Ruthless war record. The son of a southern union organizer and a Polish immigrant's daughter. That marvellous genetic combination of Celtic lyricism and Slavic phlegm obviously combined in you to produce a unique blend of realism and idealism. As such you bear an uncanny psychological resemblance to these young Nazi fanatics from the Prussian aristocracy who sought to recreate the German superman in their own image. A perverse idealism, but idealism nonetheless."

"Yeah. Well, I hate to break it to you, Herr Cassierer, but my idealistic father went to jail for stealing union funds, and my mother was about as phlegmatic as a vial of warm nitroglycerine. As for my great insights into the Waffen SS," I shrugged. "Yeah, I can understand some of the warrior mystique. Anybody who's been in a war can buy into that. But the rest of it is pure foggy Teutonic horseshit."

Cassierer smiled. "Dr. Thompson, I've read your military file." He extracted a green folder from the briefcase at his side. "Perhaps you'd like a copy. I doubt that you've ever seen it. I think you'll agree when you've read it that it indicates an uncanny if limited similarity between you and the men I seek. You will forgive an old man's arrogance, but I think you are the man I need. Given your straitened economic situation, I assume you will be willing to take on the job?"

"Yeah. I need the money. But I doubt that I can come up with anything useful. Tell me specifically what you want."

"It begins with the interrogation of Adolf Eichmann, the Nazi war criminal. I was instrumental in assisting the Israelis in his kidnapping through a branch of my family's bank in Argentina. I participated, mostly as an observer, in his interrogation. The transcripts you have read are only a partial record of those sessions. There is also a secret file of his examination under scopalomine and sodium pentathol. He was also placed under extreme psychic stress in order to break his spirit. I regret to say that none of these methods were totally successful. Despite his lack of education and petty-bourgeois mentality, Eichmann was a man of great shrewdness and inner strength, a man convinced that he had done no wrong. Such men are hard to break short of the most extreme and extended forms of physical torture, which we were unwilling to use." The old man stopped and stared into the distance. "Perhaps in error, given the information he took with him to the gallows."

"Did you try succinylcholine?"

"That's a torture drug, Dr. Thompson. It causes convulsions and excruciating pain. No, we did not."

"What did Eichmann say?"

"I will give you a xerox of the relevant transcripts provided you agree to work with me. And, of course, give me your word not to reveal their contents."

I met the old man's eyes momentarily and looked

away. I couldn't remember anybody asking me for my word on anything since the sixth grade. He was truly naive. But he was right. I wanted the manuscript. I decided to string him along.

"I know what you are thinking, Dr. Thompson. The transcripts would represent a real coup for you to publish. Please. Do not even consider it. The entire Israeli government and scholarly establishment would swear they were forgeries and you would be discredited as a scholar much as was the man who recently forged Hitler's diaries."

"What did Eichmann say?"

Cassierer took a file out of his briefcase and passed it over. "I've given you the original German rather than the English translation so you can get the flavor of the man and his exact words. He mentions an organization composed of high-ranking SS men, mostly quite young, who belonged to the Prussian nobility. As you know, the SS, particularly the so-called Waffen or Armed SS, attracted large numbers of fanatical Prussian nationalists in the thirties. Many were men who had nothing but contempt for Hitler and the Nazis but hoped to use them to further a resurgence of Prussian power.

"Once involved in the movement, most were gradually seduced by the dream of a greater Germany, a Germany from the Urals to the Channel, a Germany with Europe at its feet. They also received rapid promotions, access to the highest circles of the party, genuine power. They foresaw a time when they would oust the vulgar arrivistes around Hitler and take control themselves. Gradually then became increasingly corrupted. It is an old story, Dr. Thompson. Greek hubris leading to destruction. A fatal character flaw."

The old man was quintessentially German. He couldn't just spit out what he wanted. He had to envelop it in a philosophical and psychological context, give it ideological weight. Otherwise it wasn't real.

"What do you want from me?"

"Read the Eichmann interrogation. Attempt to put yourself in the place of these young SS men in the summer of 1944. Their world is collapsing. Many, though not all, participated in the murder of millions of people. They will be persecuted and hunted after the war. Some will be executed or imprisoned. At the very least their lives will be blighted forever by the stain of SS membership. How can they escape? They can leave, of course. Have the SS tattoo in their armpits surgically removed. Do what Barbie and Mengele did. Run and hide in the jungles of South America, hunted animals, always looking over their shoulders for the Mossad hit team, or an individual bent on revenge. Always at the mercy of venal local police and politicians or some bounty hunter. Or they can become servants of the Arabs, training their armies and police, stultified by the desert heat, cut off from their beloved Germany. No. These men wanted more. They wanted to die and be reborn, cleansed, to participate in the renaissance of a new Germany. And, I regret to say, there is evidence that they have succeeded in doing just that. I want you to find them, Dr. Thompson. Give me their names. I will do the rest." The old man's thin, veined hands tightened around the cane on which they lightly rested.

"What have you got beyond the Eichmann interrogations?"

"One specific piece of information. I am not persuaded of its value. However, it is all we have. But first, are you interested?"

"I'm interested in the money, Herr Cassierer. Frankly, I think you're wasting your time. If this group has managed to stay underground for forty years without any of them surfacing, then they are a very bright

15

bunch of people. They must have covered their tracks superbly. After so much time, the trail would be so cold that it would take a miracle or a piece of wild luck to find them."

Cassierer nodded. "I'm not a religious man, Dr. Thompson. I do not believe in miracles. As a professional historian, however, I am sure you will agree that luck plays a crucial role in the affairs of mankind."

"Yeah. In Viet Nam we got obsessed with it. Even the most rational of us. So you had a piece of luck."

"In a manner of speaking. Two years ago in London, you will recall, there was a massive conference of economic leaders from the five most important Western countries to discuss what to do about the problems of the developing world. It lasted ten days. Almost a thousand people, including experts, attended. More than two hundred German industrialists, bankers and economists took part. It was a failure, of course, as all such conferences are. Too many people discussing too many concerns. Small working groups which could not reach decisions resulted in controlled chaos at the plenary session."

Cassierer lifted the heavy porcelain coffee cup with the Cafe Moehring crest on it and sipped, clearing his throat with an old man's dry cough. He was obviously tired. "Among the participants was an American Jew, Abraham Passent, a native of Kiev in the Ukraine. In 1942 Passent was a tailor in Lubny, a small town near Kiev. On November 12, SS Einsatztruppe B under the command of Hauptsturmfuehrer Fabian von Bursian entered the town, rounded up all the Jews, took them to a field on the outskirts of the city, forced them to dig a long trench, and shot them. There were three thousand Jews in the village, mostly poor farmers. Four escaped. Passent was one of them. He dove forward into the trench just as the machine guns began to fire and was covered by the body of another victim. The trench was shallow. He edged his way toward the surface as the few remaining Jews were forced to cover the bodies with dirt, before being killed themselves. Passent constructed a small opening between two bodies, a pocket of air, and as darkness fell he dug his way upward through two feet of loose dirt and escaped."

"Jesus!"

"Hardly." Cassierer smiled. "Abraham Passent was a rather unpleasant, overbearing, courageous man with a brilliant financial mind and an unparalleled instinct for survival. He made his way south behind the German lines to Rumania where the Jewish community hid him until he could be smuggled aboard a Turkish freighter. From Istanbul he went to Egypt where he fought with distinction in the Jewish brigade of the British Army. In the postwar period he was a leader of the so-called Stern gang and was, I believe, personally responsible for shooting two British policemen in the back in street assassinations designed to force the British to recognize the existence of an Israeli state."

"Sounds like a charming fellow."

"One could make excuses for Abe, of course, but I suspect that his experiences in that death trench only confirmed his natural character. Ruthless, predatory, efficient. In any event, he made his way to the United States and became a highly successful manufacturer of quality woolens which he sold in his own stores across the country. He was at the conference not to solve the problems of the third world but to lobby for the protection of the Western nations' woolen trade from the cheaper goods from the underdeveloped world. He was then in his early seventies. Short, dynamic, irascible and suffering from congestive heart disease. In the lobby of the Dorchester Hotel, where several subcommittees of the conference were meeting and many of the participants lived, Abe suddenly saw an apparition."

17

"Von Bursian?"

"You are quick, Dr. Thompson. Von Bursian. Forty years older. Graying, lined. Somewhat heavier but unquestionably von Bursian."

"You'd think it's something that would have happened more often over the years."

"Not really. You have to realize that very few survived the massacres. Also, after forty years, most people are unrecognizable. Von Bursian is an exception. According to Abe, he looked very much as he did as a young man."

"What did Passent do?"

"He almost died of a heart attack. Literally. He began to run after von Bursian, rage flowing through him. In the middle of the lobby, the increased strain on his heart became too much for him and he was stricken by a massive coronary occlusion."

"He died?"

"Not then. He called me from the intensive care unit of a London hospital two days later when he had partially recovered and demanded that I come to his bedside."

"Why you?"

"He was a sergeant in my platoon during the German siege of Tobruk. I was badly wounded on a reconnaissance mission in the German rear one night. He carried me back to the British lines. As you Americans say, I owed him one. Abe always collected his debts."

"He wanted you to find von Bursian?"

"Yes. He gave me all the details he had and died two days later."

"Did von Bursian see him in the hotel?"

"Abe thought not. There were hundreds of people milling about. Von Bursian was already at the door. In any event, the German would not have remembered him. Abe was only one of thousands of faceless prisoners being led to the slaughter. He would not have made the connection."

"Did Passent describe von Bursian?"

"Yes. Unfortunately the description fits almost any aging, upper-class German. Tall, slim, graying, blue-eyed, handsome, regular features, a classic Nordic type."

"No distinguishing marks of any kind?"

"None that Abe remembered. You must realize he saw him only during the march to the execution site, quite close but a long time ago. Also he was very sick when I talked to him. Almost incoherent in his eagerness to find and kill the man."

"Is that what you intend to do?"

"My intentions do not concern you, Dr. Thompson. I am hiring your scholarly skills. Nothing more. Do not burden your conscience with questions."

"My conscience wouldn't bother me. He sounds like a perfect candidate for the executioner. I just don't see how the archives can be of much use to you. First, about a third of the SS files are missing. But even if he's there, they won't help you much."

"I have a copy of his file. You also have here the notes of Kresche, my previous researcher. Nothing very useful, I'm afraid. However, the Berlin Document Center has a great deal more than individual SS files. It contains a vast array of information on the Nazi period, the entire party files, the names of ten million members, 600,000 SS men, dossiers on two million Volksdeutsche, people of German origin who were brought back to Germany from eastern European countries. If you were looking for a foolproof way to disappear and melt into the chaos of postwar Germany, it would have been here that you would seek a new identity. Somewhere in that building is the key to finding and destroying the Orpheus Circle. If you can find von Bursian and discover how he submerged himself using another identity, then we can track down the others."

I watched the old man walk down the Kudamm, followed by his unshaven shadow, and picked up the green folder. I wasn't interested in my war record. Nobody knew it better than I did. Still, the army sometimes came up with some pretty bizarre stuff. I opened the file, and suddenly I could smell it. The sweet sour perfume of the jungle, the foul stench of the bodies of men whose bowels had emptied at the moment of death, the smell of battle. Over it all the fear.

SECRET

<u>Memorandum to:</u> Judge Advocate General, Fort Bragg, N.C.

<u>From:</u> William G. Bailey, Lt. Colonel, commanding 112th Special Forces Battalion

<u>Subject:</u> Inquiry into Special Forces Patrol No. 11 March 13–April 25, 1972, Ia Drang Valley

Special Forces Patrol No. 11 was activated March 10 after receipt of information to the effect that the command post of North Vietnamese Army Third Corps was located in a complex of tunnels on Hill 116 in an area bordering the Ia Drang Valley. Patrol 11 was tasked with finding the headquarters and, under cover of darkness, destroying it with napalm firebombs and explosives placed in the tunnels.

Captain Alec Thompson and the four enlisted Special Forces troopers were transported by helicopter to within five miles of the site on the night of March 13. After observing the camp for forty-eight hours Captain Thompson led his men in an attack in the predawn hours of March 15, placing five-pound shaped charges in some twenty tunnel entrances, following neutralization of the above-ground guards. Simultaneous detonation of the charges which ignited the napalm firebombs created a firestorm in the tunnels resulting in a deoxygenation effect causing suffocation to personnel in deep bunkers unaffected by the fire and explosions. Two light machine guns sited on the perimeter of the camp eliminated survivors. ARVN intelligence information indicates that the entire headquarters complex including commanding General Vu Gien Ho and three hundred of his staff were liquidated in the attack. There were no survivors. No prisoners were taken.

Captain Thompson led his command, which suffered no casualties in the initial attack, through enemy lines, and returned to base on April 25. One member of the team was killed in an attack on an NVA position to obtain supplies. A second died during a firefight. The command regards the charges brought against Captain Thompson as unjustified by the facts, and the result of extreme stress brought on by combat.

Captain Thompson has been recommended for the Silver Star for courage under fire behind enemy lines and exemplary tactical leadership.

I turned the page of the folder.

**SECRET**

<u>Memorandum to:</u> Judge Advocate General, Fort Bragg, N.C.
<u>From:</u> Dr. Morton Klein, M.D., Psychiatric Unit
<u>Subject:</u> Psychological Evaluation of Captain Alec Thompson, Special Forces Battalion

The following evaluation is based on in-depth interviews with Captain Thompson and the two surviving members of Special Forces Patrol 11, Sergeants Craig Wilson and Lester Morgan.

Thompson, Wilson and Morgan, as well as the two deceased members of the patrol had been in virtually continuous combat behind enemy lines for eleven months prior to the final mission. The Special Forces patrols were tasked with carrying guerrilla war to the enemy through ambushes, behind-the-lines attacks in supposedly secure rear areas, terrorism of the civilian infrastructure loyal to the NVA through assassination and interdiction of supply routes. Thompson, known as "The Indian" because of his ability to move silently in the jungle and an uncanny facility at extricating his men from seeminly hopeless situations, was a charismatic leader. He had, however, by the time of Patrol 11 been traumatized by a series of disastrous losses to his unit.

The Special Forces Missions, enveloped in the secrecy necessary to their effectiveness, bivouacked separately from other units and conducting what amounted to a separate war, were a law unto themselves. In late February 1972 fifteen men from Thompson's unit were lost in a patrol in the Ia Drang Valley. The survivors brought back two prisoners. Captain Thompson and Sergeant Craig Wilson, both graduates of the Monterey Language Institute and fluent in Vietnamese, interrogated the prisoners at length without success. Thompson then, according to Wilson's testimony, took the two prisoners in a helicopter to two thousand feet and threw one through the open door of the helicopter after unsuccessfully attempting to elicit information from him. The second prisoner, held outside the helicopter by his heels for several minutes, upon further interrogation revealed the location of the NVA third Corps Command Center.

Captain Thompson proposed a small force operation to take it out. The initial phases of the operation proceeded as described in Colonel Bailey's covering memorandum. The Vietnamese were not expecting an attack so deep behind their lines by such a small force. Total surprise was achieved.

I stopped reading the fading xerox and stared off into the pastel Berlin sky. We had started at two A.M. when Charlie changed the guard, coming out of the tunnels near the hutches, stretching and chattering and joking. The hutches were real. Families of Vietnamese lived in them, a dozen or so. From the air it looked like any of thousands of mountain villages. The tunnel network extended into the mountain, expanding into hollowed-out rooms containing communications gear, command centers, and living quarters. Light and ventilation were provided by generators carefully camouflaged and built into the mountain.

We had done it all before. Me, LeBlanc, Morgan, Wilson and Jones. It wasn't difficult. The guards were half asleep anyway, standing next to the hutches, leaning on their Kalashnikovs. We worked from outside in, taking one as he wandered off to the urinal, another as he bent to readjust the hatch to a tunnel through which some light still shone. You put a knee in their back, left arm around the throat, then the knife in one quick slice cutting off any sound. Charlie was small and delicately boned, not very strong, although possessed of incredible endurance. The first phase had taken ten minutes. Then we placed the charges, a little plastic explosive on one end of the pipe to ignite the main napalm charge and blow it into the tunnels. We'd found only twenty tunnel entrances. Morgan armed the other ten bombs and laid them against the hutches.

The two machine guns were set up at oblique angles on either side of the jungle opening. When the napalm blew, the roar of the explosives was muffled by the tunnels. The hutches, enveloped in flame, went up like torches. You could feel the air being sucked in by the fire, making it hard to breathe.

Somehow we'd missed a couple of tunnels. Fifteen or twenty Charlie came stumbling up, outlined against the flames. Morgan and Jones cut them down with the machine guns. We hadn't brought much ammunition, so the bursts were short and choppy.

"Hey, Captain. How long we gonna stay?"

"Until we get them all."

I turned back to Klein's report.

Captain Thompson led his men back through the jungle to the helicopter landing area, but by the time they reached it, the jungle was alive with Viet Cong. They went to ground for two days, concealed in the deep jungle, and began their walk out. The trek coincided with an offensive by the NVA Third Corps, only marginally delayed by the destruction of its headquarters staff. The patrol was forced repeatedly to wait for the passage of large numbers of regular NVA units. It became unsafe to move except at night. Foraging for food in the jungle was time-consuming. The men were weakened by hunger.

On April 5, according to the testimony of Sergeant Morgan, Thompson decided to collect supplies in a Vietnamese village. They surrounded four huts in a small clearing and moved in. The peasants, all women, children and old men, bowed and offered food. Two ate while three stood guard, one replacing another in echelon. Sergeant Mervyn LeBlanc, according to the testimony of Craig Wilson, took aside one of the young women and entered a hutch with her.

Thompson looked up from the file and ordered a brandy. The girl's screams had brought him from the perimeter on the run.

"What the fuck is going on, Jones?" The big black sergeant had sat spooning rice into his mouth. He had looked up and shrugged. "That fucking honky LeBlanc's getting his ashes hauled, Captain." He nodded toward a hutch in front of him. The villagers were huddled in a group staring at the piece of cotton flapping over the entrance.

LeBlanc came out, zipping up his fly, grinning. The girl appeared immediately behind him, long slender knife in a tiny hand. It flashed upward three times into LeBlanc's lower back and he went down. Thompson shot her then, the Uzi stitching a line across the black pajamas. Behind him the team had moved in one fluid motion, M-16s on full automatic. The seven villagers crumpled in a heap as they hit them with short bursts.

"Oh, shit," LeBlanc had said. "I ought to fucking well know enough not to turn my back on the bastards."

Jones had stared down at LeBlanc as the blood surged into his mouth. "He done bought the farm, Captain. Let's get the fuck out of here."

I turned back to Klein's report, remembering the contempt and abrasive arrogance with which he had conducted the interrogations. Tall, slim, impeccably tailored, dark hair curling over his collar, he nibbled on black-rimmed glasses during the sessions, smoothing a western gunslinger's drooping moustache when irritated. Three days into the sessions, Wilson and Morgan asked me to meet them in a bar outside the base, a fake thirties diner decked out in maroon plastic booths, colored neon lights and mockups of ancient jukeboxes. They were into their second pitcher of Coors when I got there. Wilson wasted no time.

"This shrink is trying to send us up, Captain. If we aren't careful, we'll be pulling two to five in Leavenworth."

"Yeah," Morgan said, "He looks at me like I'm some kind of bug."

"What do you want me to do?"

"Play games," Wilson said. "He's a shrink. Shrinks buy into guilt complexes. We tell him we're full of neuroses induced by what we were forced to do, torn up by the traumas of combat. All that good psychological horseshit."

"He's got an IQ in the stratosphere, Wilson. And he's used to being hustled by experts. He won't buy it."

"He'll buy it, Captain," Wilson said. "All they're looking for is an excuse to turn us loose. Morgan knows a master sergeant in the Colonel's office. They don't want another My Lai incident, all that fucking bad publicity ruining the image of their heroic combat veterans. But if we tell that asshole the truth, they'll hang us by the balls. So we give them some poor ignorant combat-weary mothers who went a little nuts under pressure and they'll eat it up."

I looked at Morgan, who grinned, blackened teeth a slash in his pale, pock-marked face. "Don't worry about me, Captain. He thinks I'm just naturally psycho. The army screwed up giving a loony like me a gun. Ain't my fault, no way."

Wilson took a sip of beer. "You know what this asshole told him? Accused him of hiding out in graduate school to avoid combat."

Morgan grinned and winked. "Now he's got a guilt complex, Captain."

26

LeBlanc was killed by the young woman after he had raped her, and in revenge the patrol wiped out the village. Some ten days later, the patrol was caught between the lines in a firefight between a unit of ARVN paratroops and NVA regulars. Sergeant Washington Jones was almost fatally wounded. As the NVA and the ARVN withdrew, Captain Thompson was faced with attempting to bring out the wounded trooper, at the risk of losing the entire patrol, or leaving him to be taken prisoner. At Jones's request, Thompson shot him in the head.

The above description of the patrol coincides in all its principal elements with the individual testimony of Wilson, Morgan, and Thompson. While there are unquestioned legal grounds for the prosecution of Captain Thompson for his conduct of this operation, it is my view that legal sanctions are meaningless in conditions of unbearable combat stress which lead men to commit actions which, in normal times, they would consider only with revulsion and horror.

The Special Forces patrols were imbued with an elitist ethic which the military has used in all modern wars to inject shock troops with that final dash of fanatical abandon which leads to victory. The German *Stosstruppen* of the First World War, the *Jaegerbataillon* and Waffen SS of the Second and our own Marine Corps tradition attest to the effectiveness of such units. The obverse is what I would call the "above God and man" syndrome which leads groups to develop an ethic, a group dynamic which excuses any excess to preserve the unit. Thus Morgan replied when asked why he was in Vietnam: "To kill gooks." How he killed gooks or which gooks he killed was a matter of indifference. Killing had become a raison d'etre in and of itself.

All three survivors of the patrol have reacted with classic stress protection mechanisms to the horror which they were forced to undergo. Lester Morgan, a man of little education and less subtlety, accustomed from birth to the violence of the Tennessee mountains, has become desensitized to all human emotion. An incipient psychopath before entering the army, he will be in need of extended psychotherapy before he can safely be released into society. Craig Wilson, a college graduate who was drafted when his application for graduate school was turned down, is marginally manic-depressive with definite suicidal tendencies. He must be institutionalized until he has recovered from massive feelings of guilt and loss of self-esteem. Captain Thompson would appear on the surface to have suffered the least. His high intelligence, athlete's self-assurance and ability to rationalize his actions have enabled him to adapt with seeming normality to peaceful military routines. The wounds to his psyche are, however, deep and probably incurable. While his superficial adjustment may hold up in normal situations, hidden wells of violence exist within him which, under provocation, could lead to dangerous anti-social acts. He is a walking bomb with a relatively long fuse.

While it is not within my province to recommend whether to prosecute Captain Thompson or his men for violation of the articles of war, I feel sure that extenuating circumstances exist—unbearable stress and danger for long periods of time as well as the tacit acceptance by higher authority of the types of activity indulged in—which would make prosecution difficult if not impossible of success.

SECRET

Memorandum From: Judge Advocate General, Fort Bragg, N.C.
To: Colonel William G. Bailey, commanding, Special Forces Battalion
Subject: Request for Honorable Discharge of Captain Alec Thompson

Request approved.

# Chapter 2

THE ORPHEUS CIRCLE.

I doodled the name on a yellow lined pad I'd liberated from Hugh's office, writing it in the strange elongated Corinth script of German nineteenth-century documents, printed it, drew it in Gothic embellished with curlicues. A week in the archives had produced nothing. Except frustration, neglect of my own research and an increasing obsession with Fabian von Bursian and the shadowy figures around him. I flipped open the beige folder containing the young SS officer's request for permission to marry. An almost endless low-ceilinged windowless room was filled with three hundred thousand such files, meticulously kept in their original German covers, neatly tied with brown string.

Each folder opened with a handwritten one-page autobiography done by the applicant. Next came two pages of three photographs each: one full face, one in profile, and one at a slight angle. The ideologue of the Nazi Party, Alfred Rosenberg, had decreed that only thus could hidden Jewish traits be instantly distinguished.

Facing the young officer were pictures of his bride-to-be. Both gazed back at me from paper yellow and fading with age. Two unexceptionable young people, the man slim and conventionally handsome, the girl about ten pounds overweight, if her slight double chin were any indication. I turned the pages, unfolding the two genealogy charts and running through them quickly. A litany of names and dates gleaned from family bibles and the Koenigsberg city archives traced the young officer back to one Hans Bronia, smallholder, in the Kreis of Allenstein, East Prussia.

I stopped for the tenth time at the page outlining his short SS history. "Fabian von Bursian, born April 12, 1918, in Allenstein, East Prussia. Graduated Goethe Gymnasium, June 1936. Matriculated, Gneisenau Kadettenschule, Koenigsberg, September 1936. Graduated June 1938. Commissioned lieutenant, 9th Regiment, Potsdam, July 1938."

I made a note on a three-by-five card before reading on. The 9th Regiment was a famous unit of the German army. In it had served most of the young nobility of Old Prussia. The prestige of its graduates in postwar Germany was immense. At least one president had begun his career in its ranks, along with a dozen or so of the highest ranking figures of the present regime.

"Seconded to the Leibstandarte Adolf Hitler (LSAH) Untersturmfuehrer." A volunteer, obviously. Nobody had been forced to join the SS in 1939. Why had this young Prussian aristocrat with impeccable military credentials chosen to leave the regular army and join what amounted to the bodyguard of a vulgar, lower middle-class political leader who had mesmerized Germany?

"September 12, 1939, wounded at Wloclawek in attack on strongpoint protecting bridge over Vistula. Cited for bravery. Awarded Iron Cross Second Class. Promoted October 15, 1939 to Obersturmfuehrer. June 1940, wounded Charleville, cited for conspicuous bravery in repelling French armored counterattack at Montecornet. Awarded Iron Cross First Class."

Montecornet. I'd visited the place once. An unexceptionable little French provincial town. It was here that a tall French brigadier general had led the French Fourth Armored Division in a quixotic attack against the coiled might of the German army. Charles de Gaulle had won a minor victory, taking 500 German prisoners before being driven back.

I moved down a page dense with citations for bravery, notes of wounds and medals, until I came to an entry dated October 1942. Von Bursian had been severely wounded in the chest in an attack in the Caucasus and have been invalided home to Allenstein. Medically unfit to return to the front, he had been temporarily assigned to a rear echelon SS unit, Einsatztruppe B, by now with the rank of Hauptsturmfuehrer, equivalent to a captain in the regular German army. He served as deputy commander from October 5, 1942, until December 15, 1942, when he rejoined his unit in time for the abortive thrust aimed at relieving von Paulus's army, surrounded and being decimated at Stalingrad.

I checked for the fifth or sixth time the xeroxed record of the Nuremburg trials describing the activities of Einsatztruppe B from June 1942 through October 1943, when it was disbanded and folded into the Waffen SS.

"Einsatztruppe B was responsible for maintaining civil security in an area encompassed by the towns of Lubny, Sumy and Nezin northeast of Kiev. The area contained approximately 150,000 individuals of the Jewish faith. During the period of its responsibility, SS Einsatztruppe B's records show it liquidated, either by shooting or execution in mobile gas vans, 113,043 Jews, 750 Gypsies and 483 ethnic Ukrainians for crimes against the occupation forces. Some thirty thousand names of those executed were listed by the unit until its operations became so widespread that exact records were no longer kept."

I returned to the von Bursian file. "Wounded March 12, 1944, battle of Kursk. Promoted Obersturmbahnfuehrer April 12 and awarded Iron Cross with Swords and Oak Leaves May 1, 1944. Assigned June 12, Kadettenschule Bad Tolz. Partially disabled by leg wound complications. Certified fit for duty November 1, 1944. Assigned 12th SS Hitler Jugend Panzer Division November 15, 1944. Killed in action Bastogne, December 28, 1944. Buried, Frankfurt Central Friedhof, Plot 12, Section 14, Area 1."

I yawned and headed up through the empty whitewashed corridors to the small coffee room at ground level. Six tables lined a glassed-in corridor overlooking the inner courtyard. Hugh LeRoy sat nursing a large ceramic coffee mug embossed with a priapic Greek god. I poured a coffee and sat down.

"Not doing so well, huh?"

"Cassierer is wasting his money, Hugh. There's nothing to go on."

"The Eichmann stuff is useless?"

"It's fascinating. They put him under with some sort of knockout drops and injected sodium pentathol. Truth serum. They weren't looking for anything special. Mostly just trying to test his conscious answers to see if he was lying. He was an odd duck, Eichmann. Product of the system carried to a kind of extra dimension. Obedient, hardworking, tenacious, loyal, even courageous in a bizarre kind of way. And totally amoral."

"He was a fucking psychopath," Leroy said.

"That's an easy way out. Anyway, Eichmann isn't the problem. Von Bursian is. He's out there somewhere. Probably rich, powerful, respected. A pillar of the community. And he hasn't left a trace."

"What about his family? Even if he changed his name, he'd probably stay in contact."

"Mother and father died in the fifties. Two older brothers were killed in the war. One sister disappeared in the exodus of four million Germans from East Prussia. Another killed in an air raid in 1945. His wife simply disappeared."

"How are you going about finding him?"

"I'm looking for people who served with him. The files have lists of officers, transfers, unit numbers. Only trouble is von Bursian moved around a lot. He was a golden boy. They kept pulling him off assignments and promoting him. That's how he got that job with Einsatztruppe B. The men were rebelling against shooting women and children. They brought him in to re-establish discipline."

"And he did?"

"Yeah. In spades. He personally shot a sergeant and two other ranks in front of the assembled unit. They didn't give him any more trouble."

"Nice fellow."

"Funny thing is, he comes across as a pretty decent type when you read his record. Ambitious, hard-driving, brave to the point of being nuts, but his men, except for that Einsatztruppe, seem to have loved him."

"Lovable SS men are not my cup of tea," Hugh said.

"He moved out between the lines, during the attempt to break through to Stalingrad, to bring one of his wounded machine gunners back under murderous fire." I shrugged. "Give him his due. He was a good soldier."

"You sound as if you're beginning to like him."

"He's a chilly bastard, Hugh. Probably have made a good scientist in peacetime. Or maybe a banker."

"You realize they were mostly non-Germans, the Einsatztruppen," LeRoy said. "Ukrainians mostly. Criminals a lot of them."

"Careful, Hugh. You're starting to sound like an apologist for the Nazis." The two men laughed. The Berlin Document Center didn't breed Nazi apologists.

"Jesus Christ, look at that," I said, nodding toward a young woman walking toward the coffee room across the uncut lawn. She was big, with broad shoulders and the muscled body of a natural athlete. Bright red hair in a pageboy bob bounded rhythmically as she moved toward us with the grace of a young lioness.

LeRoy stood up as she entered. "Hello, Kathy. Good to see you again. What brings you to our little zoo?"

"Same old stuff. Grubby research."

"Alec Thompson. Kathy Chapin. You're in the same business."

"What are you working on?" Thompson asked, inventorying the young woman's expensive blouse, skirt, shoes and indefinable air of preppie arrogance.

"I did my diss on the role of brothels in Bismarckian Germany, but right now I'm working on a women's thing. Comparing the lot of women in the late empire to the Nazi era. What's your field?"

"Nazis."

"Oh. Of course. You're the Thompson who wrote the SS book. Good stuff. Stein liked it."

"You studied with him?"

"Yeah."

It figured. Manfred Stein was the leading U.S. authority on Nazi Germany. He held court at Princeton like a medieval potentate. His graduate students were the cream of the crop. "What are you doing now?"

"More SS. Profiles of the leaders."

"Sounds grim."

"It is."

"Yeah, well. Nazi women aren't exactly the stuff of musical comedies either. Christ, I sometimes think they were better off under the Kaiser."

35

"Gotta get back to the tomb," I said, lifting out of the chair, wincing as I did so.

LeRoy grinned. "You still working out in that kraut gym?"

"Yeah."

"Those kids will put you away one of these days. You're too old to wrestle."

"Wrestle?" The girl stared at me with a look of mild disgust.

"Dregs of adolescent macho," I said, instantly regretting the note of apologetic aggression in my voice. The goddamn rich preppies had begun to get on my nerves lately.

I held on to the guard rail going downstairs until my back unstiffened. I'd been trying to train the big muscle-bound kraut in how to escape from being bottom man in the referee's position, the humiliated, almost defenseless, wrestler on his hands and knees with his opponent, with all the advantages, on his back working for a pin. I'd exploded back into a low squat, looking for power and mobility, simultaneously trying to break the handlock around my waist. It was a classic move. Only as I'd started up, concentrating on getting maximum power and balance in my thighs, my right foot had slipped on the mat, filthy with sweat and slick with age. The big kid had picked me up and slammed me, landing on top, two hundred pounds of eager, untrained bone and gristle. I should have quit right then. At thirty-five, outweighed by thirty pounds, I'd been a fool to continue after I felt the muscle go. It had taken another three minutes to pin the clumsy clown. By the time I'd showered I could hardly walk.

I flipped open the Eichmann file and began to read.

<u>Interrogator:</u> Who ordered the evacuation of the French Jews to Litzmannstadt?

Eichmann: Himmler. But that wasn't enough. We had to get the cooperation of the Vichy government to round them up. Then the transport ministry for the cars. And the army, of course. It was all very complicated. One had to be efficient.

Interrogator: Did everyone know what was going on?

Eichmann: Yes. I told them. I told them when they asked me why it was being done. And I didn't lie. I'm the kind of man who cannot tell a lie. For example when I was in Hungary, Dr. Kastner, the spokesman for the Hungarian Jews, said: "Herr Obersturmbahnfuehrer, stop the extermination machine in Auschwitz." I said to him: "Herr Dr. Kastner, I can't stop it because I didn't set it in motion." And when he said it another time I said: "Herr Kastner, I can't, I can't, I can't. It's not my province. I have no powers. It's the same as if you tried to stop it. You stop it. I can't. I'm too small. I have no means. It's not in my power. The extermination machine is under Administration and Supply Headquarters, Gruppenfuehrer Pohl. That's what I told Dr. Kastner in Budapest."

Interrogator: Rudolf Hoess wrote this about you in his *Commandant of Auschwitz:* "I became acquainted with Eichmann after I received orders to exterminate the Jews. He came to see me in Auschwitz to discuss the details of the liquidation process with me. Eichmann was a lively, active man in his thirties, bursting with energy. He was always hatching plans and always in search of innovations and improvements. He could never rest. He was obsessed with the Jewish question, and the order had been given for its final solution. He had to give the Reichsfuehrer SS direct, oral reports about the preparation and implementation of the various actions. Eichmann was convinced that if he succeeded in destroying the biological foundation of Jewry in the East, Jewry as a whole would never recover from the blow." Do you want to say anything?

Eichmann: Basically I reject all that as untrue. Totally untrue. I'm covered with guilt, Herr Hauptmann, I know that. But I had nothing to do with killing Jews. I've never killed a Jew. And I've never ordered anyone to kill a Jew. And I know no one can ever produce a document proving that I've done such a thing. Maybe that's what gives me a certain peace of mind. I wasn't responsible for the detailed implementation . . .

I skipped through the file and stopped at the part Cassierer had marked in red for me.

Interrogator: When did you realize the war could not be won?

Eichmann: After Stalingrad, I thought the best we could hope for was a stalemate. That the Fuehrer make peace with the British separately and then with the Russians and we could keep the boundaries of 1939. That's what I hoped anyway.

Interrogator: When did you know the war was lost?

Eichmann: Oh, after July 20, 1944. I suppose everybody knew it was just a matter of time by then. That's when people started to make plans.

Interrogator: Plans?

Eichmann: You know. To escape.

Interrogator: Did you make plans?

Eichmann: I tried. But you understand, Herr

Hauptmann, I was a small cog. A very small cog in a very big wheel. People like me were not important. There was one group I tried to join, but I was rejected. They were using DP identities.

Interrogator: What group?

Eichmann: (with contempt) Some young aristocrats. Waffen SS mostly. They began to organize to go under, you know, to hide, in Germany after the war. Fools. Nobody could do it. You had to leave. Go to Egypt or South America where they like and respect Germans.

Interrogator: You knew this was going on and did not report it?

Eichmann: Report it? To whom? Everybody was looking for a lifeboat, I can tell you. By December [1944] everybody had something going. No, I didn't report them. They were protected by some very high people in the Gestapo. They had false papers, new identities. The Orpheus Circle never amounted to anything, however.

Interrogator (insistently): Tell me about the Orpheus Circle.

Eichmann: No. I can't. It's too dangerous. They would kill me. I don't know. I don't know. I tell you, I don't know (voice rose to a scream as the drug wore off).

I thumbed through the rest of the file. The interrogator had repeatedly come back to the Orpheus Circle, and each time Eichmann had panicked, some ingrained fear overpowering the inhibition-releasing effects of the drug. There was nothing there, really, except the name. I glanced up as two workmen edged through the narrow door carrying a Hahn computer, letting it down gently on a long table between the files. Another followed with the screen.

I walked over and watched as they connected the machine, and a white-coated technician sat down at the keyboard and began to play, fingers a blur of confident motion.

"What sort of capacity has it got?" I asked.

39

"Capacity?" The German looked up, puzzled. "This is an industrial machine, sir. Every piece of information in this archive has been stored on the machine. Ask and it will answer."

"Can it give you a list of every SS man born on April 25, 1918?"

"Of course." He touched a dozen or so keys and the screen lit up with a list of names. I leaned over and picked out von Bursian from among the flickering green symbols.

"Pretty incredible," I said. And useless. I already had the files. The machine was just an expensive toy. I had to find some new angle to approach the problem. Hardware wasn't going to solve it.

"Thanks," I said, collecting my briefcase and heading up the empty, ghostly corridors of the old building. Hugh LeRoy was gone. The archive was closing down. I walked out into the warm summer evening and hooked my satchel to the back of an ancient bicycle I'd bought a decade before and left from year to year in the archive garage over the winter. The guard saluted as I wheeled through the gates and down the deserted street which dead ended at the archive. I rode between the forest on the right and the fenced Document Center compound on the left, heading down Wasserkaefersteig to Quermattenweg and the room I rented from the widow of a German engineer. The car was parked facing me on the wrong side of the street. An old Mercedes, boxy and rust-spotted, with a crushed left fender. They stopped me as I swerved out into the center of the narrow road, blocking my way.

"What's up?"

"We want to talk to you. Over there." The one doing the talking motioned toward the woods. "Get off the bike."

I dismounted slowly as the two approached on either side. It couldn't be happening. Not in Berlin. This was Europe. Nobody got mugged in Europe.

They were dressed like punks. Black leather pants stuffed into motorcycle boots. Tank tops. Mohawk hairdos. The one on the left was big, with the bulging, high-definition arm muscles and prominent veins of a bodybuilder. As he turned, I saw the black swastika tattoed on his bicep.

It all happened in slow motion. The big man grabbed me by the shoulder, pushing me toward the woods as his smaller companion pulled the bike away, lifted it and slammed it against a tree. I reacted more or less automatically, crossing my right hand to grip the big man's wrist. My left came up and found his elbow. Holding the wrist and twisting upward I brought forward pressure to bear on the elbow, leaning my weight into it in a smooth twist, at the same time slamming my left foot into the back of his knee as his body turned, pitching him forward, all the weight coming down against the rigid arm. His shoulder separated with an audible crack almost drowned out by his scream.

The smaller man stood momentarily transfixed, then bent slightly and brought a knife out of his boot. As he straightened, I kicked him in the balls, feeling my heavy walking shoe bury itself in the black leather. I chopped down on his arm, feeling the pain shoot up my arm as it connected with bone. I picked up the knife, an ornate switchblade, suddenly aware of the headlights of a car behind me. The girl came forward into the beams of the headlights, and I moved out of the crouch, folding the knife and slipping it in my pocket.

"Need some help?" She was holding a tire iron and grinning.

"A ride maybe. Looks like Rosinante has bought the farm. Only first I'd like a word with my two buddies. You want to pull down the road while I talk to them?"

"Can't I watch?"

"Sure." The big man was rocking back and forth on

the ground, nursing his dislocated shoulder. "Okay, George. Who sent you?" I used a gutter Berlin dialect.

"Fuck off."

I stepped back and kicked the dislocated shoulder under the armpit. This time the scream was a choking gurgle of shocked pain.

Hunkering down I met the big man's eyes. "I've got all night, George. Nobody lives around here. It's just you and me and Harry here. You'll pass out eventually but it'll take some time. Now you want to tell me who sent you or do I cut four balls off, one at a time?"

"Weber."

"Who's Weber?"

"Used car dealer. Berlinerstrasse. Auto Weber."

"What were you supposed to do?"

"Rough you up. Tell you to lay off the research you're doing on the Nazis. Get the fuck out of our country."

"What's the swastika on your arm for?"

"None of your fucking business." He scrambled back against the old Mercedes as I stood up.

"Shall we get the hell out of here?" the girl said.

"Sure." I unhooked my satchel from the debris of the ancient bicycle, noting the license number of the Mercedes, and slipped into the little sports car's bucket seat, wincing as my back froze up.

"What was that all about?"

"Christ knows. They couldn't have been trying to rob me. I hear they beat up little old ladies for kicks. Maybe they thought I was a little old lady."

"You were pretty impressive. I mean, you handled them like a pro."

"They weren't looking."

"Hugh says you teach wrestling at a German gym. He says you're a little nuts."

"Hugh is not trying to live on an academic salary and pay his way to Europe every summer to do research on books that sell five hundred copies each to a bunch of nuts whose only aim in life is to find a screwed-up footnote."

"Where can I drop you?"

"What about dinner? I mean if you're free?" I couldn't believe I'd said it. I had no money, no time and no real interest in this handsome, somewhat chilly, preppie redhead.

"Academic rules?" Academic rules meant dutch treat. All academics were poverty-stricken.

I inhaled the leather upholstery of the car. She had about four times as much invested in it as my net worth. "Sure. Where do you want to go?"

"I just remembered. I can't go to dinner with you. I promised a couple of friends I'd meet them at the Einstein. Why don't you come along?"

She drove like a young Fangio, wheeling the green Morgan through the evening rush hour traffic with ruthless efficiency, leaving in her wake a trail of white-knuckled, horn-blowing Germans. "You in a hurry?"

"No. But I'm sick of krauts saying all Americans are pussies in cars. So you're taking over Kresche's job with Cassierer?"

"Kresche?"

"The old boy with the Lenin beard and beret who was working for Cassierer until he got killed."

"I thought it was supposed to be a secret."

"Hugh sounded me out about the job earlier."

"And you weren't interested?"

"I was. Cassierer wasn't. He'd already heard about you. Kresche had talked to him, I think."

"Yeah. We had coffee a couple of times. I'd forgotten his name."

"Cassierer wanted you because you'd done the SS book. Do you think there's anything in it? The Orpheus Circle?"

"Hard to say. Oh, sure. There have got to be some SS types who traded identities and survived. Whether they're organized and whether anybody can winkle them out is something else again."

"Have you got any leads?"

"Not really." She drove down Clayallee at about a hundred and twenty klicks an hour, weaving in and out of the slower traffic expertly, turning left onto Teplitzerstrasse and heading for the center of town.

"Have you ever thought about the East? They've got Nazi records too."

"My contacts with the STASI are a little out-of-date." The STASI, or *Staatssicherheitsdienst,* was the East German successor to the Gestapo. Rumor had it that a lot of its personnel had been taken over from its predecessor. "Anyway, I'm just being paid to grub around in the archives, not play James Bond."

She drove down the famous Kurfuerstendamm, the pulsating main artery of Berlin. The whole city radiated from the garish four-lane boulevard which was divided for most of its way by a parking strip. It wasn't the Berlin of the twenties, but it still had a touch of the raw dynamism, cultural vitality, sensuality and corruption which had made it a magnet for all Europe in the years after the First World War. She cut over beyond the great ruin of the Memorial Church, left as it stood after the bombing, and cut right on the Kurfuerstenstrasse, squeezing into a parking spot in front of a peeling old mansion.

The Einstein was a cafe, restaurant and night club run by Viennese emigres. It occupied the first floor of the mansion of a prewar actress, one of the few buildings in the center of the city to survive the bombing. Nothing much had been changed. The walls of the entryway were plastered with art exhibit posters. The bar, a plastic and glass monstrosity, was on the right as you entered and the rest of it was fin-de-

44

siècle shabby, old Thonet chairs and tables, maroon plush benches against the walls and a raised stage with a piano in the main salon. Up front, a circular wood-paneled room, with a telephone booth indented into one of the walls, looked out on the street.

The evening clientele was self-consciously intellectual. Young men in turtlenecks and beards, young women in tight jeans and floppy sweaters or the weird baggy pants and Peter Pan boots Europeans were affecting this year.

"Over here, Kathy." We slipped through the crowd to a tiny table in the corner, collecting a couple of unused chairs en route.

Two bearded males in their thirties stood. Kathy kissed them impartially. "Alec Thompson, Inge Wohlgemuth, Paul O'Brien and Ludwig von Wrangel. Alec is doing research on the Nazis. Paul works for the American mission and Ludwig does something with the Federal Republic's office here."

"God, Nazis," the dark-haired girl said in disgust. "Can't you Americans ever give up? Why don't you write about Viet Nam or your own racial problems and leave Germany alone? It's been forty years. I'm sick of hearing about it."

"I'm an historian. It's history."

O'Brien had made room for Kathy next to him on one of the plush benches. His hand drifted over and began to stroke the inside of her thigh. "What are you working on?" He had a slight British accent, an affectation of many American diplomats.

"Some young SS men traded identities with other people at the end of the war and submerged. I'm trying to find them."

"They must be all dead by now," Inge protested.

"The war ended forty years ago. Most of them were between twenty-five and thirty. A lot are still around. Some probably in positions of power."

45

"You're working in the Document Center?" von Wrangel asked.

"Yes."

"I would have thought that it would already have been stripped of anything interesting." His English was excellent. Pompous, but excellent.

"There are a couple of new pieces of information. I might be able to put something together."

Kathy blocked O'Brien's hand automatically as it moved toward her crotch. He stared at me with a kind of unconscious insolence which, along with a thin patina of oil on all visible surfaces, seems to be a universal characteristic of the rich. "I thought German records were so meticulous nobody could get away with changing identities. I mean to say, there are pictures and measurements and documents about everything. How could they do it?" His phony British accent deepened as he failed to complete paragraphs.

"The SS ran the police at the end of the war. It wouldn't be hard to fake the files on people who got killed in Russia. Missing in action. You alter the forms, change the pictures and pick up the dead man's life."

"What about his family? Friends?" O'Brien shook his head. "Sounds a little far-fetched to me. You'd practically have to find a bunch of orphans. Even then the risk of discovery would be pretty high. You'd have to pick people with no real history."

"Jesus, can we change the subject?" Inge asked. "I'm sick of this morbid shit."

The conversation picked up around me. They were going to a party given by a French journalist. I stared into the brandy. Somewhere there seemed to be a connection between what O'Brien had said and the mass of material I'd been wading through, but it eluded me.

"François is expecting us. We'd better toddle along," O'Brien said. "Coming with us, Thompson?"

"No, thanks."

We shook hands all around. As they left, Inge turned to Kathy. "Is he a new one on your string?"

"No."

"Oh. Yeah. I forgot Chapin's first law. No more than one lover in the same town at the same time."

# Chapter 3

I WANDERED INTO HUGH LEROY'S OFFICE THE NEXT morning and dropped into his overstuffed sofa.

"You look beat."

"Couldn't sleep."

"You're getting obsessed with this Cassierer thing. Well, listen, don't get discouraged. Sometimes stuff falls in your lap."

"Yeah. Only after some big bird just flew over. What are you so excited about?" LeRoy was practically jumping up and down with glee.

He tapped the file in front of him. "You know the consulates in West Germany run routine checks on anybody who was old enough to be in these files asking for a visa?"

"So you told me."

"Well, about a month ago, we came up with a beaut. Guy named Schiwy runs a ball bearing factory down in Bavaria. Wants a visa to visit some customers in Indianapolis. Sixty-seven. His file comes up and we run him through the mill. Guess what?"

"Bingo."

"You better believe it. Turns out he was a member

of Einsatztruppe A in Lithuania. They killed half a million Jews in a year. So you know what the dumb bastard does?"

"No."

"When the consul confronts him, he gets depositions from three friends attesting to the fact that he had nothing to do with the killings. Worked as an administrator back in Warsaw."

"And?"

"We checked out the three friends. Turns out they were in the same unit. The West German government arrested all four of them yesterday. They'll be lucky to get out of the slammer by the time they're eighty." He got up and unlocked one of the row of metal cabinets along the wall, refiling the three-by-five visa search cards.

"Hugh. Suppose you wanted to take on a new identity in 1944. Where would you go?"

"Death lists of people killed in combat. Pick somebody my age, height and with the same general physical characteristics."

"Yeah, but he'd have a history, family, friends, bosses. People would know he'd been killed. It's too risky."

LeRoy nodded. "You're right. It's not ideal. So what would you do?"

"Eichmann mentioned the Displaced Persons files. How many have you got?"

"Two million, give or take a hundred thousand. Why?"

"They're Germans from all over the East who were repatriated. Pockets of them were everywhere. Rumania, northern Italy, Poland, Russia. They'd lived there for centuries, some of them. When they left, they must have come out with nothing but the clothes on their backs and a couple of suitcases."

"Pretty much. But they all had papers. All these countries were nutty about records. Also, to get accepted as Germans they had to prove they were pure aryans. So they were well documented."

"I've been looking through some of the files. There were a lot of single men."

LeRoy nodded. "Yeah. They came out first, a lot of times planning to look things over and bring out the rest of the family later. Then they'd get drafted into the army first thing." Hugh leaned back in his chair. "I see what you mean. If you're looking for somebody without a past in 1944, what could be better than one of those guys? He comes out of nowhere, gets killed, has no family in the West, is buried in a mass grave. Wiped off the face of the earth."

"He'd be taking some risks of course. Family members in the East who were driven out after the war ended might notice the name of a lost relative and check up."

"Not very likely," LeRoy said. "They would have been informed that he was dead by the military authorities. They'd assume it was somebody with the same name. Especially if they got a look at him, and it wasn't their lost relative." LeRoy leaned back, put his feet up on the desk and stared at the ceiling.

"So it's simple, all you gotta do is separate the Orpheus Circle out of these two million names. How you gonna do that?"

"With that computer of yours. When will it be working?"

"Couple of days. What have you got hold of?"

"Tell you later, Hugh. Maybe nothing."

I used the pay phone at the end of the hall. "Herr Cassierer?"

"Yes."

"Thompson. I think I may have an idea. But I need some information. That conference where Passent spotted von Bursian. Would it be possible to get a list of all the German participants?"

"I have it, Dr. Thompson."

"I'll pick it up tomorrow. Would three o'clock be convenient?"

"Yes."

Kathy Chapin leaned against the phone booth as I came out. "How about a coffee?"

"Sure. How was François?"

"French. If you've seen one Berlin intellectuals' party you've seen them all. A lot of self-conscious posturing, puerile spitballing and outrageous anti-Americanism. Still, the city is kind of interesting. I mean, you run into everybody. British, French, Americans, Russians, Germans. It's really kind of like 1945 preserved in amber. Paul keeps saying we're here by 'right of conquest.' "

"What does he do at the mission?"

"Political officer. He and his wife and I were at Princeton together. He took the foreign service exam and quit short of his doctorate. How's the research coming?"

"It's not. I'm going to take a break. Go look at used cars."

She looked puzzled for a second. "Oh, you mean Weber. Is that smart? Do you know who he is? I mean, it could be dangerous."

I shrugged.

"You want a ride?"

"Sure."

Auto Weber was about fifteen minutes away on Berlinerstrasse. There was a showroom up front and a workshop in the back. "You want me to come in with you?"

"To hold my hand?" I relented. "Kathy, keeping the enemy off balance is everything. He's not expecting me to come after him. He won't know what kind of backup I've got." I got out of the car and leaned in the window. "Thanks for the ride. I'll call you." I watched

51

the Morgan disappear in traffic and went into the showroom. A big man with the scarred eyebrows and flattened nose of an ex-boxer was on the phone.

"Ja, Herr Doktor, we will do our best to have it ready. Ja, Herr Doktor. I guarantee the fuel injection will work perfectly. Ja, Herr Doktor." He hung up and looked up at me. "What can I do for you, sir?" He spoke English with a stage German accent.

"I'm looking for Herr Weber."

"And you are?"

"Thompson."

"Herr Thompson." He looked me over curiously, a faint grin deepening the scars around his mouth. "Herr Weber is out in the garage. If you will come with me, please?" He led me through the parking lot and into a garage packed wall to wall with half-dismantled cars, turning as the heavy door closed behind me, and landing a short right hook to my gut. He must have weighed about two-forty, most of it muscle, and the punch might have broken me in two if he hadn't taken something off it. I dropped to my knees wondering if I were permanently paralyzed.

"Sucker punch, Herr Thompson, no? That is what you call it, no? I remember good my English from days I boxed your soldiers right after the war. You want to get up? The floor is full of oil here. You will ruin your pants. Here I help." One big hand caught my coat and lifted me, pushing me against the wall.

"Hey, Anton. Willy. Over here. I've found a friend of yours." He turned his head to call out, and as it came back around I stuck a short right into his throat, trying for the Adam's apple. I missed by an inch and got a column of muscle. He laughed and moved in, looking more and more like a truck. I tried for his eyes with my left and he blocked easily, slamming a right hook to my ribs. I grabbed and held, trying to tie up his arms. It was like trying to immobilize tree trunks. I drove a knee up into his groin and got his attention. But as I tried to move off the wall, he pushed me back and drove that right into my gut again, following it with a left hook which caught me behind the ear. After that it was downhill.

I came to on the floor, my nose buried in a shallow puddle of gasoline. "Tie him up, Anton. Put him in the trunk of the Audi. Take him out to the canal behind the brick factory and get the ropes off. Don't hit him any more than you have to. I don't want him marked up. Just before you dump him, hit him here." He fingered the base of my skull. "Not too hard. I want him out cold but breathing when he goes into the water. The police have to find water in his lungs. It has to look like an accident. I don't want any screw-ups like with the old man. Now get him out of here. The crew will be coming back from lunch soon."

I was crumpled up in the trunk when I finally came out of it, my head jammed against the spare tire, hands tied behind my back. I tried to move, find something sharp to cut the ropes, but my knees were crushed against my chin. There was no way to turn. I must have passed out again, coming to just before the trunk opened.

"Hurry, Anton. Someone will see us."

"Relax, Willy. The place is a ruin. Nobody can see us. Besides, I want to work the bastard over a little before we dump him."

"Goddamn it, Anton. Weber will kill us if we fuck this up. Get it over with." I felt the ropes come off my wrists as I was pulled to my feet. My right eye was half-closed and blinded by oil. I could barely see the sliver of water off to the left as the big guy turned me around. His right arm was strapped to his side with a tan bandage.

"Shut up, Willy," he said.

I saw the kick coming, taking it on my hip instead of

in the balls, falling back and flipping toward the canal. "Oh, shit," the little guy said, diving for me. We went over and into the water together, him hanging onto me. I took a full breath before we hit and pulled him down and under, shutting off his cry, locking an arm around his neck and letting the current pull us along, slowly expelling air to stay under. He fought for about ten seconds in total panic, sucking water into his lungs as I alternately loosened and tightened the hold. Once I almost lost him, then he began to flail, arms losing strength, body finally going limp with a sort of shuddering sigh. I let him go and clawed my way to the surface, fighting the weight of my clothes. I was thirty yards farther along the canal, passing a fence dividing the deserted brickyard from a small company manufacturing wooden beer kegs. A stairway descended to the water, and I pulled myself up onto it. The big man stood at the fence, unable to get around a semicircular spiked metal guardrail which extended over the canal.

I pulled myself up on the steps and headed for the gate. A couple of workmen stopped amd stared but nobody said anything. Out on the street I turned toward the brickyard. I was still ten yards away when Anton's car came through the opening in the wall, skidded into a rocking turn and disappeared.

"Good God. What happened to you?" Kathy Chapin had pulled the little Morgan over to the curb.

"I forgot to duck. What are you doing here?"

"I followed you. After I left you at Weber's I thought you were sure to get in trouble, so I drove around the block and parked. You didn't show. Then I saw those two thugs from the other night come tearing out, and I followed them on an impulse. When they drove into that deserted brickyard, I called the police from a booth up the street."

"The police?"

"I called Paul O'Brien and he's sending the American military police. Where's the other one?"

"In the canal."

The MPs roared up in three jeeps about five minutes later, piling out with drawn guns. Two German police cars were right behind them. A sedan from the U.S. Mission, with O'Brien and a paunchy, gray-haired older man, who looked like a retired Boston cop, pulled up behind them.

"You okay, Kathy?" O'Brien asked, ignoring me.

"Yes. He's not in such good shape, though."

"What happened, Thompson?"

I told him in about four sentences. It was hard to talk. One of Weber's punches had partially paralyzed my diaphragm. Also my lungs were still half-full of water.

"Why did these two attack you?"

"I don't have a clue."

"You should have gone to the German police," the fat little man said.

"Yeah. I think you probably have a point."

"We'll have the Germans pick up Weber and bring him in for interrogation."

At that point they found the body and the whole thing got a lot more serious. It was close to midnight when the Germans were through with us. Weber had disappeared, as had Anton.

"If you can think of any reason for these men attacking you, Thompson, call me at this number," O'Brien said as we stood on the steps of the police station. "Can I offer you a ride?"

"I'll drop him, Paul," Kathy said. O'Brien looked annoyed. "Give my love to Beth and tell her I'm sorry we kept you out so late."

"Who's Beth?" I asked as we drove away.

"His wife. My roommate at Princeton."

"Oh."

55

"Not really," she said, laughing. "Paul and I had a thing going for a while, but it broke up. He married Beth. I was her maid of honor." She giggled. "I mean I went down to the city hall with them."

"And now he wants both."

She shrugged. "He's a man. Are you hungry?"

"Yes."

"I know a Greek place in Kreuzberg that may still be open. You up to it?"

"Sure." The cops had dried my clothes and pumped me full of weak German coffee, but I hadn't eaten since breakfast. I was beginning to shake as the tension slipped away.

"You'll look just right in this place. It's in Little Turkey."

I leaned back in the sports car and tried to will away the various aches and pains. "What did you say O'Brien does at the Mission?"

"Political officer."

"Spook, you mean."

She glanced over. "What's that?"

"CIA."

"Paul?" She laughed. "Why do you say that?"

"I knew a lot of them in Viet Nam. It's tattooed on his forehead. What's he interested in me for?"

"He came because I called him, Alec. The other guy, the little fat one, he's in charge of the police in the American sector. Paul just came along as a favor."

"Yeah."

The Greek place had no name. It was deep in the middle of a Berlin district taken over by middle eastern guest workers, primarily two hundred thousand Turks. The proprietors had taken an old German *Kneipe*, added fishing nets full of plastic fish and lobsters, bad wall-paintings of scenes from antiquity, fake amphorae and wine bottles encrusted with candle wax on each table. We ate *tzetsiki* and *souvlaki* and drank a bottle of *domestica* before I returned completely to the land of the living.

"You know why they're after you, Alec?"

"No, why?"

"Don't be dense. It's the research you're doing for Cassierer. Somebody must think you're getting close."

"Yeah. Well, I've got news for them. They're wasting their time. I haven't found a goddamn thing. I must admit, though, I'm beginning to think the old boy must have something. Otherwise they wouldn't be so eager to shut me off. It's also beginning to look as if Kresche might have stumbled onto something I missed when I went through his papers."

"Like what?"

I shrugged. "A line on one of the members of the Orpheus Circle. Maybe something he didn't realize was important."

"You look like death warmed over, buddy," Hugh LeRoy said when I walked into the coffee room the next morning. "I heard what happened at the Mission staff meeting. Sounds like you might have lucked out."

"Depends on the way you look at it. Right now I'm not sure drowning wouldn't have been better."

"You know why they did it?"

"No. Tell me, Hugh. How did Kresche, the little guy working for Cassierer, die?"

"Massive cerebral damage according to the doctors. He got hit by a car. Why? You think it was something else?" He put down his cup. "Are you onto something, Alec? Have you got a lead?"

"No. I've got zilch. But the little guy might have had something. Something he didn't even know he had."

"You went through his papers, didn't you?"

"Yeah. He seemed to be trying to work toward von

Bursian through former friends and relatives. But from his notes, he hadn't gotten very far. I'll take another crack at them."

It was mid-afternoon when I ran into the marginal note on a xeroxed copy of a Bund der Deutschen Maedchen file on von Bursian's older sister, Margarethe. "Teresianer Kloster, Rothenburg" and a question mark. It wasn't much. According to the records Margarethe von Bursian had died in a bombing raid in Dresden in April 1945. I'd ignored the note originally. Now I went up to Hugh's office and consulted his secretary. After a couple of minutes with the impenetrable German phone system she had winkled out the name and address of a nunnery in Rothenburg-ob-der-Tauber run by Teresian sisters. Five minutes later I had the mother superior on the line.

"No, Dr. Thompson. We have no sister Margarethe in the order at this time. May I ask why you're enquiring?"

"I'm doing some family research for a friend in the United States. His cousin was listed as missing during the war, and I came across some information that she might have entered your order."

"I'm very sorry, Dr. Thompson, but the only Margarethe we have at the Kloster is Margarethe von Benedickt. She is not a member of the order but lives here in retreat."

"Thank you, Sister."

I found the name two generations back in the autobiographical file attesting to von Bursian's aryan origins. His great-great-grandmother's maiden name was Elke Margarethe von Benedickt.

My appointment with Cassierer was at three. He lived in an old building in Zehlendorf, a village which had been enfolded into the sprawl of Berlin in the nineteenth century. The bombing hadn't reached this far out. His apartment was on the second floor of a private house, large and airy, furnished with eigh-

58

teenth-century antiques and German Expressionist paintings. A Nolde head, stark and overpowering, dominated the salon.

"Tea, Dr. Thompson?"

"Sure." The old man poured it out of an antique silver kettle, very simple with an acorn design on top.

"What do you have?"

"Two things. First I think I may have found von Bursian's supposedly dead sister." I explained the name in Kresche's notes and the woman living in the Rothenburg Kloster.

Cassierer listened, tenting his fingers. "And the second piece?"

"Weber. I looked him up in the SS archive. He had quite a career. Born 1918 in Breslau. Entered the army in 1936. Transfered to the SS in 1937. He fought in just about every campaign of the war and wound up a master sergeant working for Skorzeny, the guy who rescued Mussolini. He was also a member of the same Einsatztruppe as von Bursian in the fall of 1943." I told him what had happened when I visited Weber.

"I was not mistaken in my choice, Dr. Thompson. My congratulations. What do you propose to do now?"

"I'd like to go down and see Margarethe von Benedickt."

"Yesterday's incident indicates they intended to kill you. Are you sure you want to continue with this?"

"Yeah. I want to continue. Only I'm broke. I'll need expense money. Also, I'm going to have to have a weapon. They cost money."

"Tell me your needs."

I walked out with five thousand marks and the feeling that Cassierer had gotten me cheap. He'd also given me a list of the German participants in the London Economic Conference where Passent had seen von Bursian, or his ghost. It was a little early, but I took a cab to a bar I knew on Kantstrasse, run by a retired army sergeant who'd married a German woman and stayed on in Berlin. It was a hangout for black soldiers, prostitutes who catered to them, and the usual groupies turned on by rumors of their sexual prowess. I got there just as the cleaning women were finishing up.

I'd known Scottie in Viet Nam. The consummate hustler. He'd joined the Special Forces because the discipline was lax to nonexistent and the opportunities for minor larceny endless. In camp his floating crap game never stopped. In the field he was a survivor, the possessor of some sort of sixth sense for danger, never taking a chance unless he had to. The other grunts thought walking next to him was life insurance.

I'd been on patrol with him a few times, three-man hunting teams behind the Cong lines. Nothing much had ever happened. We always seemed to just miss them. Then one day we went out on sniper duty. Just the two of us. Scottie and me with the M40-A1 bolt action single-shot killing guns handmade in the Marine Corps gun shops. It wasn't normally a Special Forces job, but Scottie and I had punched the sniper ticket and battalion had come up with another of its brilliant ideas.

We were supposed to vector in on a point where infiltration routes from the north and west converged. ARVN intelligence had pinpointed a small camp set back from the crossing where the slope brass met for strategy sessions before moving down into the war zone. It was too well concealed for the planes or choppers to get at. We were supposed to find the place and stake it out, waiting until some important Cong officer showed up, then knock him off. The idea was, if you wasted a general officer here and there deep behind their lines it would shake them up. Knock them off balance, keep them from settling into the comfortable routines the military love so much. It was deep penetration. Twenty miles behind the Cong lines, across a couple of low mountain ranges.

We split a mile or so short of the trails. Scottie moved west to a ridgeline overlooking the bivouac area. I scaled a small knoll looking down on the camp and climbed an ancient mahogany tree reaching upward from the surrounding forest. You threw a rope over the lowest limb and climbed twenty feet or so, careful not to touch the trunk or rough up the bark, then used the steel climbing spurs issued to telephone linemen to go the rest of the way. I quit about eighty feet up at a fork and slung the fine mesh sleeping hammock from a limb to the main trunk. Once up, you stayed up. We were scheduled for five days unless a target appeared earlier. Normally you shoot, hole up, wait for the search to die, then slip back through the lines. Patience is everything. Sniping was different from combat. Guys who, in battle, would cut down fifty or a hundred Cong without turning a hair couldn't pull the trigger at five hundred yards, looking into the guy's eyes through the scope.

I clamped the high-powered Zeiss telescope on a limb and focused it on the target area a quarter of a mile away. It was empty except for a couple of unarmed slopes asleep next to one of the hutches.

For two days nothing happened. Small groups of young officers hunkered down occasionally around the central hutch drinking tea as their troops rested on either side of the jungle-covered trail. But nobody important showed. I alternated looking through the telescope and reading Thucydides's *Peloponnesian War*, folding into the hammock as the light failed, enveloped in a mosquito net, larded with insect repellent, conserving the iron rations and five-gallon canteen of water. Then, late on the third day, there was a flurry of activity. Movement along the trail stopped. Patrols moved out toward the western ridgeline. An hour later half a dozen Cong came back dragging a bloodied figure towering over them, hands bound behind his back. I focused the glass and recognized Scottie under the blood and mud.

They stripped off his shirt and tied him by his wrists to a pole slung between two trees. His toes barely touched the ground. The slopes took turns standing in front of him, questioning, then beating him with long bamboo canes. The interrogation went on until dark. I slept a couple of hours, collected my gear and repacked it, leaving nothing behind. Then I took the gun down, oiling every part, rubbing the cool metal with a chamois cloth, greasing the shells, laying out a dozen in a hollow space in the tree, fixing a tripod on a limb, shaking the tension out of my arms.

The light came around five, quickly, as it always does in the tropics. I screwed the bulky noise suppressor onto the end of the barrel and set up the shoot, scanning the camp for sentries. There were two, both nodding half-asleep over their weapons, backs against the hooch. It was an easy shot. A little over five hundred yards. No wind. I'd vectored it down to the inch. I took the one on the left first, putting the slug a couple of inches below his throat. His body jumped inside the loose black pajamas as the slug hit, slamming him against the bamboo walls of the hutch. His companion turned. I could see the puzzled look on his face dissolve as the steel-jacketed shell caught him at a slight angle.

Scottie had lifted his head, glancing at the two Cong, then turned to stare in my direction, eyes seeming to bore into me. I took my time. It was a tough shot. The rope was hemp, about an inch thick. My chances of hitting it were zilch. I went for the pole, using an explosive shell. The first shot was a little high, ripping off splinters of wood near the rope. The sound would bring the Cong on the run. It took three more shots to weaken the wood enough for Scottie to pull it and break it, slipping the rope off. He moved quickly to the dead slopes and picked up one of the Kalashnikovs, spraying the black figures spilling out of the hutch, then turning and fading into the jungle.

Two days later he met me at the perimeter, giving me the high five, grinning. "Hiya, loot. I was beginning to worry about you. Gonna get some of the boys together and come looking for your bones."

"How'd they make you?"

He shrugged. "I had me a little dope. Guess they got a whiff of it. Or maybe some wiseass saw the smoke. You shoot real good for a white boy, loot."

"Is Scottie around?"

One of the women, a Turk built like a tank, motioned toward the office in the back. Scottie was now in his early fifties. He'd retired at thirty-seven with twenty years in. Over the years he'd won the Berlin military racketball tournament five or six times, and he was still in excellent shape, a tall, elegant, chocolate-colored man with a small military moustache. We played racketball now and then on the army courts, but I hadn't seen him lately.

"Hey, man. Long time no see." His accent still had the smallest trace of the south. "How's your hammer hanging?"

"Limp. Buy you a beer?"

"Coffee. Got to watch my paunch. Hilda's been giving me a lot of shit about getting fat."

Hilda, who worked in the financial section of a bank days and kept his books nights, looked a little like Marlene Dietrich and had a Master's in economics. Scottie always looked a little dazed when she was around. She was a woman who knew what she wanted and had it.

"How's she doing?"

"Making us rich, man. That is one smart chick." He poured us coffee from one of those German machines which resemble the propulsion mechanism of an intergalactic rocket, and motioned me to a chair. "You look like you had a disagreement with a truck and lost."

"Ran into a door."

"Yeah. Door with a pretty good left hook. You look like you here on business. What can I do for you?" Scottie didn't deal. As far as I know the only thing he had going for him was the bar, which was moderately profitable, and his pension. But the word was you could get anything you wanted at his place if you tapped the right button.

"I need a piece."

"Say what?" He was from Mississippi or west Tennessee, but he did the ghetto bit to perfection.

"A piece."

He looked me over for about thirty seconds, face very still. "This ain't New York, man. Piece is hard to come by over here."

"I hear some of the boys find one lying around the range once in a while."

He smiled. But not much.

"Okay. Tell you what. You come in around ten tonight. Bring five bills. I'll see if I can find a man to help you. Understand. This ain't my deal. I'll talk around and point you to him. I never heard of you or no piece."

"Okay."

"How about a game someday?"

"I've got to go out of town for a couple of days. When I get back."

I ate a wurst and drank a beer at one of the street stands and headed back to the archive. I'd started down into the bowels of the building when one of LeRoy's minions stopped me and asked me to follow him to the director's office.

"Hello, Alec. You know O'Brien. This is Frank Xerxes. Dr. Thompson." Xerxes was a big man in his fifties, running to fat. His stomach pouched out over his belt, and his body strained against the stretch of an expensive pin-stripe. Elegant handsewn loafers with tassels made it possible for him to get into his shoes without bending over to lace them. He had a striking mop of thick white hair, coal-black eyebrows and a dark Mediterranean skin set off by deep green eyes.

"Happy to meet you, Dr. Thompson. Hugh tells me you're doing some work in the archive for Herr Cassierer which has rattled somebody's cage."

I shook his hand.

"It seems clear that Weber's goons intended to eliminate you yesterday, after trying to deliver a warning out here that evening." He glanced down at finely manicured hands. "Unfortunately, both Weber and the man called Anton have disappeared." He looked up. "And the other one was drowned in the canal. We have persuaded the German police to consider his death an accident. The record will show nothing of your involvement."

"Thanks."

Xerxes smiled faintly. "In return for that little favor, I'd like to know why Weber's goons are going after you."

"I don't know."

Xerxes frowned. "Dr. Thompson, I'm not sure you understand how serious this is. You've become involved in a very delicate situation, one with heavy implications for our relations with the German government. I must ask you to be completely frank with us."

I looked at Hugh LeRoy. "You told him about Cassierer?"

LeRoy nodded.

"Then you know as much as I do. The old man is looking for some Nazis who submerged after the war. He asked me to help. A couple of days later two clowns tried to beat me up. Then Weber tries to get me killed. Maybe they think I'm onto something. Or maybe I'm getting close and they want to shut it off."

"You know the name Klaus Barbie, Dr. Thompson?

65

The SS man who murdered several hundred people in Lyon during the war, including Jean Moulin, the hero of the French resistance?"

"Yeah. He was extradited from Bolivia after hiding out for forty years."

"Exactly. Well, his presence in France is causing a lot of heartburn. For openers, one of our predecessor organizations, the OSS, used Barbie after the war. Some of their people helped get him out of Europe. As a result our government has apologized to the French government."

"I read about it."

"Quite a bit hasn't surfaced yet. Some of it very nasty. Barbie has been talking. Talking uninterruptedly. And in the process he has implicated large numbers of currently respectable Frenchmen in his operations. A lot of them are dead, but some are quite high-ranking figures in French political, intellectual and business life. It is a most difficult situation."

"Why don't the French just knock him off? Shoot him while escaping. Poison him."

"Very funny, Dr. Thompson. Very funny indeed."

"What's Barbie got to do with Cassierer's group? Was he a member?"

"Not as far as we know. But the chances seem excellent that if you are able to isolate and identify the members of the Orpheus Circle at least some of them will be in high positions in German society."

"Yeah. That sounds reasonable."

Xerxes extracted a Gauloise from its distinctive blue packet and lit it. His fingers were stained dark yellow by the black tobacco. It smelled as if he were smoking horse manure. "You understand the problem we face in this, Dr. Thompson?"

"No."

"Don't act disingenuous," O'Brien said, his British accent noticeably muted.

"Our German friends would be thoroughly unhappy

to have it revealed that, forty years after the end of the war, a couple of dozen high-ranking financiers, diplomats and God knows who else were prominent members of the SS.''

"That's their problem, not ours.''

"That's a very admirable stand, Dr. Thompson. One on which you are to be complimented.'' He looked me in the eye. "However, it is not a position which fits your history like the proverbial glove.''

"Look, mister. If you want me to quit working on this for Cassierer, say so and I'll consider it. However, I've contracted with the old boy. I've taken his money. And spent it. Also the project interests me. It's right in line with my own research. So if you want me to quit, you're going to have to be goddamn persuasive. And the problems it's going to cause for a bunch of murderous ex-SS men who've decided to go straight won't do it.''

"We could withdraw your research privileges at the Document Center,'' O'Brien said.

I looked from him to Xerxes to LeRoy. The information in the scruffy old building represented a very large chunk of my scholarly capital. If I were barred from it for any reason, ten years of hard work would go down the drain.

"We are not suggesting that you drop your investigations, Dr. Thompson. In fact, we are most interested in finding any members of the Orpheus Circle who still survive. Particularly any in positions of power. I think you can appreciate why.''

"Yeah. You'd have them on a string.'' A thought occurred to me. "What if the East got hold of this information? They could squeeze pretty hard.''

"So could we, Thompson,'' Xerxes said. "We have reason to believe that some of them are in East Germany. So all we are asking, demanding if you like, is that we get the undertaker's look at anything you come up with.''

"Undertaker's look?"

"Sorry. An old Greek expression meaning you get a look at all the other bids before making your own. Wholly unethical, of course, but highly effective. Are we agreed?"

"I come to you with anything I can dig up and show it to you before I give it to Cassierer?"

"And we decide whether he should have it," O'Brien said.

"What's in it for me?"

"Satisfaction at being an American patriot. And, of course, continued access to the archive."

It was an offer I couldn't refuse. "Okay."

"Now, once again. What have you got?"

I told them about Weber being in von Bursian's unit, about the probability that the Orpheus Circle had used names from the Displaced Persons file. I ran through what Cassierer had told me. And I said nothing about Margarethe von Bursian and the Rothenburg Kloster.

"Christ, we've got all that shit," O'Brien said impatiently. "There's got to be something else. They wouldn't try to kill you for that."

The archive was closing when they wound it up. As I walked out, Kathy Chapin came up from the file rooms in the basement. "Well, well. You look almost human. Are you free for dinner?"

"Sure." She was wearing a simple cotton dress which clung as if by accident in just the right places, giving off a kind of lascivious innocence. I realized that she was the kind of woman who, looking good in clothes, would look stunning without them.

We ate in an Italian place across from the Egyptian museum, spending some of Cassierer's money. "You must have struck gold," she said, as the manager led us to a table.

"Sold an article on Sepp Dietrich," I lied. In fact the article had just come back from the tenth or eleventh magazine. The waiter held out the usual platter of dead fish and various unappetizing calf organs. We ordered mixed pasta, lemon veal and a white wine with the picture of a lobster on the bottle.

"My god, that's a beautiful wine."

"Aragosta. Means lobster. Don't ask me why. I ran into it once when I was hitch-hiking through Italy."

"What are you going to do now, Alec?"

"Well, my first priority is to seduce this preppie redhead sitting across from me."

"With that swave and debohnur approach you're assured of success."

"It's known as the Joe Harrington gambit."

"And who was Joe Harrington?"

"Guy I knew in Viet Nam."

"And what was his gambit?"

"Ask any ten women to sleep with you, and one is sure to say yes."

She looked exasperated and then started to laugh. "You made it up."

"The gambit. Not Harrington." I lifted my glass and touched hers. "To Joe."

"He's dead, isn't he?"

"Yeah."

"How?"

"Measles."

"You're in fine form tonight, Dr. Thompson."

"He brought his helicopter into a landing zone at Khe Sanh under fire six times one afternoon to take out wounded. The seventh time they turned the bird into a ball of flame just as he took off with ten half-dead grunts on board."

We gossiped about academia and traded biographic information over dinner. She had graduated from Smith, doing her junior year at Goettingen, and gone on to Princeton for her doctorate. After spending three years at Harvard on a junior fellowship she'd been hired by Stanford and was a year away from tenure.

"Permanent attachments?"

69

"I almost married a guy at Harvard, but he wanted me to trail around in his wake like a good little wife. I couldn't see it, so we finally split." She shrugged. "I'm like all highly educated women of my generation. I want it all. Both and. So I take it as it comes. And you?"

"I had a wrestling scholarship to USC. Joined ROTC to pull in a little more money. The army took me one day after graduation. A year at Monterey learning Vietnamese. Eighteen months in Nam. Doctorate in German history at Columbia."

"Married?"

"I was."

She waited. She was good at waiting.

"She was twenty when I met her. Running a computer for one of those polling organizations. Making peanuts. Turned out she was some sort of genius. Five years later, when I got my doctorate, she was making fifty thousand a year heading a section specializing in consumer tastes. The only place I could get a job was at Santa Cruz in California. We agreed I'd take it for a year while I tried to get a job near New York." I stopped.

"And?"

"After a year she was making seventy-five and there were no academic jobs in the east. We drifted into a divorce.

"She split a couple of years ago and set up her own company. It just went public. She's probably worth a couple of million by now."

"And your poor little male ego is crushed?"

"I've got to meet a man in a bar. You want to come along?"

"Sure."

Scottie's place was crowded. The bartender, a one-time competitor in the Mr. America contest, moved smoothly up and down the long wooden rectangle, filling glasses and making chatter, his hair sticking out from his head in short, thick braids. Scottie spotted me and left his table to come over.

"Hey, Alec. You doin' good, man. Who's the pretty lady?"

I introduced them. "Come on over. Meet some of the boys." German bars all have something called the *Stammtisch,* a table reserved for the regulars. At Scottie's it stood along the wall next to the high desk where Hilda presided over the money. "Jerry, Bob, Clarence, meet a couple of friends. Alec and Kathy."

They were all close to Scottie's age, one obviously still active military, given the length of his hair and muted clothes. "Hey, man, I hear they tried to waste you out on the canal yesterday."

"Where'd you hear that?"

Scottie grinned. "Clarence is in the CID. You shoulda told me you had some people around town didn't like you. We could have handled it all real quiet."

We had a beer for form's sake, and I took Kathy over and introduced her to Hilda. Scottie excused himself after a couple of minutes and talked to a tall, slim black standing at the bar. "Why don't you leave your lady with me for a while, Alec? Got somebody wants to talk to you."

I shook hands with the tall man. No names were exchanged. We moved to a wall table near the juke box where the noise level was most intense. "Hear you need a piece, man."

"Yeah."

"All I got is a .45 automatic."

"What kind of shape?"

He grinned. "Still in the cosmoline, man. Ain't never been fired. They gon trash it when that new Baretta come on stream."

"How much?"

"For some clown off the street, five hundred." He grinned. "For a buddy of Scottie's, five hundred. I'll

71

throw in twenty rounds, an extra clip and a shoulder holster."

"You got a deal. When can I pick it up?"

"You got the bread?"

I passed over an envelope. "It's in marks."

"Hell, man, I'll take yen. You wait here." He joined a table of three blacks and a flashy blonde with a gold tooth who passed over a plastic shopping bag. I followed him into the john. He handed me the bag and motioned toward one of the cubicles. "Check it out, man. Move it a little. This place get raided now and then. You wanna get your ass outta here soon's you can with that thing. German slammer ain't no place to vacation in."

He was right. The heavy automatic smelled of cosmoline. I freed it from the holster and pulled back on the slide mechanism, flipping a cartridge into the breech, ejected the clip and the cartridge, snapped the trigger a couple of times, reloaded the cartridge into the clip, slipped it back in the gun and jammed it into my waistband, stuffing the extra clip and cartridges into the side pocket of my jacket. I handed him back the holster.

"You got a deal."

"Have fun, captain. Don't knock down no houses with that cannon." I gave him a minute. He was gone when I came out.

"Let's go," I said to Kathy who was dealing a stud poker hand to the four men when I came up.

"Hey man. The lady's winning all our coins," Clarence protested, eyes settling on the bulge in my waistband. Kathy, green eyes full of mischief, started to protest until Scottie's hand on her arm tightened.

"Sorry, fellows. Some other time," she said, scooping up a pile of one-mark coins. "You ought to quit trying to fill inside straights, Jerry. Best way I know to go to the poorhouse."

"They're interesting men," she said as we got into the Morgan. "I don't get a chance to talk to people like that much. Who was the skinny guy you bought the gun from?"

"A thief. You're going in the wrong direction."

"I thought you made me a proposition earlier."

# Chapter 4

I WOKE WITH A CRAMP IN MY ARM. SHE LAY CURLED against me in the single bed, legs intertwined with mine, hair a tumbled red mass on the pillow, looking about fifteen. She lived just around the corner from the Cafe Einstein in one of the row houses that had somehow survived the bombing, sharing an apartment on the second floor with Inge and a German school-teacher and his wife. The place was huge. You came in through a glass entrance door protected by a wrought-iron grill and climbed a massive set of stairs to the apartment. The rooms gave off either side of a long hall. Three bicycles and a mass of laundry hung from the fifteen-foot-high ceiling, suspended from a set of Rube Goldberg pulleys and ropes. A framed Beethoven T-shirt, a pornographic Grosz print, three Picasso-designed Spanish plates and an enormous poster of a grotesque pregnant woman advertising a Hundertwasser exhibition covered the walls.

She had two rooms at the end of the hall overlooking an inner courtyard. I had taken her coat and pulled her toward me as we entered what was obviously her study. Papers were neatly stacked on every surface, boxes of index cards marched in ordered rows, and a portable typewriter sat neatly covered. "Can we have a brandy?"

"Sure."

She poured us two slugs of Asbach Uralt and dropped onto the long sofa, looking vulnerable. She knocked the brandy back in one quick motion and came into my arms. I made the usual moves. I mean, what else can you do?

"Listen. I've got an idea," she said, stopping my hand. "Come on." She headed toward the bedroom shedding clothes as she went. I was still taking off a sock when she lit a small candle and leapt into the bed, a flash of red signalling that she was indeed a redhead if I'd ever had any doubts.

Her mouth was frantic on mine, going after me with a manic hunger. I stroked her and tried to quiet her, running my hands over her body gently. We fit perfectly, her big muscular body folding into mine as if moulded.

"Hey. You kiss good. For a boy," she said, giggling.

I ran my hand down her stomach and stroked her, enveloping her between my fingers, feeling her harden through the folds.

"Oh, lover, lover, lover," she said, lips pulled back over her teeth. I let myself slide down over her body, running my lips over her breasts and stomach, feeling the curly red hair scratch my chin. Her body arched as she responded to the caress, little cries coming in gasps. We made love then, she coming to a climax, me stopping a sliver short, waiting for the passion to subside, starting over, then, finally, losing control, moving into the final frenzy.

"Jesus Christ," she said, propping herself up on one elbow and staring down at me. "I underestimated you, Herr Professor. Here I was expecting a friendly academic screw and you come up with an oriental wet dream." She slipped back into my arms. "Where'd you learn that stuff?"

"Doing what comes naturally," I said, mimicking the song.

"God, it's good," she said burrowing into my shoulder. "I could absolutely do without men if it weren't for this. You're all such crude, insensitive oafs."

"Ann Landers ran a poll recently. Most women aren't interested in sex. All they want from men is a little cuddling and sensitive attention."

She looked up at me, running a hand over my chest, twining her fingers in the mat of hair. "You're a woolly beast. Anybody ever tell you that? Have you got a girl?"

"No. Have you?"

"A girl?"

"Whatever."

She laughed. "No. Oh, a diversion here and there. Nothing permanent."

"So I'm a diversion?"

"You want to live happily ever after?"

She had fallen asleep in my arms finally, inserting herself into the crevices of my body until she was comfortable. I tried not to awaken her now, slipping my dead arm out from under her head. She moved in protest, fitting her hips against me. The bed was too small for me to move away from her, and it didn't take long for the inevitable to happen. All of a sudden it was overpowering.

"What are you doing? No, Alec, don't."

I turned her on her stomach, feeling the surge of desire as he went all the way in. It didn't last long. Her body arched beneath me in a long shudder as she bit the pillow and grabbed my hand. Then she started to giggle.

"What's so funny?"

"Wham, bam, thank you, ma'am."

"Sorry."

"Lover. Don't be ridiculous. Another marathon like last night and I wouldn't be able to walk. It was wonderful." She sat up, pushing her hair out of her eyes, breasts pointing upward in a kind of happy arrogance. "I'm hungry. Let's go to Moehring and eat croissants and drink chocolate with rum in it."

It was midmorning but the cafe was crowded. German cafes seem to be crowded at any hour of the day. We ordered hot chocolate with hunks of whipped cream and rum, croissants, butter and red currant jam. She ate greedily, grinning at me over the semicircular rolls. "What are your plans for the rest of the day, Herr Professor?"

"I'm catching the night train to West Germany."

"What?" She stared at me in disbelief.

"I've got a lead on von Bursian."

"You're kidding."

"May not amount to anything. But Cassierer is willing to finance a trip to look into it." I told her about the possibility of his sister being in the Kloster in Rothenburg.

"You're right. It's a breakthrough. Listen. I just had an inspiration. Why don't I drive you down?"

I started to protest, but she stopped me. "It makes sense. I've got a car. It's only about an eight-hour drive. We can go south through the Fulda Gap and Hof. We could leave right away if you like."

"It's dangerous, Kathy. Those clowns tried to waste me."

"Don't be silly. They're all running from the police. Nobody's going to do anything to us. Anyway," she reached over and ran a hand along my leg, grinning lewdly, "I have plans for you and your friend."

It took a couple of hours to pack and get under way. I stopped by my post office box and collected a Fulbright check, a bill from Cable Car Clothiers in San Francisco and a telegram from my ex-wife. "Arriving Frankfurt Saturday. How about lunch at the Panache at 13:00?"

It was almost noon when we wound our way through the control point at Drewitz Dreilinden and found ourselves on the original Hitler-built autobahn heading south. She drove within the hundred-kilometer-an-hour speed limit imposed by the East Germans, talking excitedly.

"Is that all you've got? A name and Kresche's notation? Maybe he checked it out, and she's not related to von Bursian."

"Then we'll have to think of something else to do in Rothenburg."

"You're right. It's too much of a coincidence. Also Kresche was obviously onto something, otherwise they wouldn't have killed him."

"Who says they killed him?" I was watching the slightly shabby East German countryside slip past.

"You did."

I had told O'Brien and Xerxes what Weber had said to his two neanderthals, but I had said nothing to the girl. She glanced at me, face tense.

"Yeah. I guess I did."

The featureless landscape slid past in a green blur. Ancient towns, shabby and unkempt as everywhere in eastern Europe, broke the monotony occasionally. On straight stretches, the median strip was paved over, leaving an expanse of concrete for several miles: emergency airfields for the Soviet air force. As we moved into the industrial area of the south, a haze of brown pollutants dimmed the sun.

"Jesus, it's a scandal," Kathy said.

"What?"

"They don't give a damn about fucking up the atmosphere."

"Costs too much to keep it clean. Now that the Soviets have doubled the price of oil, all they've got to burn is brown coal. Anyway, you know what Nehru said?"

"No. What?"

"Pollution is industrialization. Industrialization is progress. The more the better."

"Anyway, I know why the East Germans call West Berlin the 'sunny side.' It goddamn well is compared to this."

We crossed the border into West Germany at Hof without incident, and Kathy let the little car out in a burst of joyous speed. "Jesus, it's always a relief to get out of that goddamn prison of a country."

She drove with calculated recklessness, the eight-cylinder engine quickly pushing us up to a hundred and ten miles an hour, hurtling along the fast lane past a lot of people doing a sedate ninety or a hundred.

"Scared?" she asked, looking over at me.

"No. My knuckles are always white."

"You want to drive?"

"No." I hate driving. And she was good.

We pulled into Rothenburg just before dark. It's one of the best-preserved medieval cities in Germany, ancient wall intact, cobblestoned streets lined with fifteenth- and sixteenth-century houses and superb old early Gothic churches. I had booked us into the Goldener Hirsch, a quietly elegant hotel abutting the wall. The city was built on a hill surrounded by a deep gorge. Our rooms looked across the valley toward a sternly classic Romanesque church attached to a huge oblong building a couple of centuries younger.

"Teresianer Kloster," I said.

"Looks grim. When will you see her?"

"Tomorrow morning if I can get in." I took her arm. "Aperitif or digestif?"

"Both and, you gross pig," she said, laughing and

taking my arm. "Come on. I saw a bubble bath in that spa they call a bathroom." We climbed into the enormous tub together, entwining ourselves.

"Hey. He floats."

"I beg your pardon?"

"Little Alec. He floats." She bent forward, pushing aside the foam and took him in her mouth, stroking him gently, looking up at me, green eyes laughing. "You come and I'll kill you," she said.

A couple of hours later, feeling as if somebody had drawn most of the marrow from my bones, I took Kathy down to dinner in a small dining room overlooking the valley. We ate snails and boeuf bourguignon, downing most of a bottle of Barolo, closing up the place around eleven.

"Come on. Let's walk," she said, dragging me out into the narrow street. We turned right and reached the city wall a hundred yards farther along. A wooden staircase climbed up left of the gate to a covered wooden walkway running the length of the wall. She pulled me up the stairs onto the rickety passageway.

"This is where the population poured boiling oil on the Emperor's troops in the Thirty Years' War," she said, staring through one of the narrow apertures medieval archers had used.

I turned at the sound of footsteps behind us. Two men were mounting the staircase. Light from an open window threw one of their faces into relief for a split second.

"Weber?" Kathy asked.

"Yeah. We better move along."

"Didn't you bring that gun you bought?"

"Yeah. It's back at the hotel."

"Christ, you're brilliant, Dr. Thompson." She was moving swiftly down the wooden platform. "How the fuck do you get off this thing?"

"There must be stairways at intervals. Keep moving." The shadows behind us were gaining, Weber's big bulk in the lead. The wall ran along a narrow, deserted street. No lights shone in any of the windows. The wall took an abrupt turn, and fifteen or twenty yards ahead of us the shaky platform descended into a triangular park area shaped like the prow of a ship jutting out over the valley below. Ancient cannon stared with empty eyes from openings in the wall. A statue of some forgotten nobleman pointed to infinity and on the right another small jewel of a church stood guard amid ancient tombs.

I pulled Kathy along behind me past the church into a narrow cobblestoned street, with Weber and his companion less than twenty yards behind us and gaining fast. Rothenburg isn't very big, and we were moving toward the lights in the center of town when I spotted the *Gasthaus* up ahead on the left. Its lights were still on, and I turned abruptly into the archway, grabbing the door on the left. It opened into a classic old-fashioned German bar. Wooden booths and tables, low, beamed ceiling, heads of dead animals and bucolic pictures on the wall, and a woman who must have weighed two hundred pounds passing steins of beer around to men dressed in short leather pants.

Weber and a short dark man I didn't know came in as we slid into one of the booths, and took a table between us and the door. Across from us four men had turned to watch Kathy appreciatively. One, a little drunk, leaned over.

"Amis, huh?" Ami is a German diminutive, mildly insulting, for Americans. "You speak German?"

I nodded.

"Why don't you bloody Americans go home and quit putting atomic rockets in our country?" The man was red-faced and beefy, with the truculence of alcohol.

"Shut up, Otto. You're drunk," one of the others growled.

"Not so drunk I don't know what I'm talking

81

about." He turned back to me. "Well, American, what do you say?"

"Yeah. I'm sure you're right. We ought to go home. Only trouble is we're lost. Can't find our hotel. We keep walking in circles."

"No. No. I don't mean you personally should leave. I mean the American troops in Germany should go."

"Oh. Yeah. Well, you're probably right. Say, can we buy you a drink?" The red-faced man stared at me uncertainly, shifting his eyes to Kathy, looking her up and down, licking his lips.

"Sure. You come over here to our table," he said, pushing his chair aside and making room.

I signalled the waitress for another round of beer. "Where are you from, American?"

"Oklahoma."

"And your beautiful redhead?"

"Philadelphia."

"Philadelphia." One of the other men leaned across the table. "Philadelphia. My cousin Ralf lives in Philadelphia. On Morton Street. You know my cousin?"

"What's his last name?"

"Dahrendorf. He's a plumber. Emigrated after the war. Comes back every five years and buys a new Mercedes. He's a rich man in Philadelphia. You must know him."

"I think I do," Kathy said. "Is he a big man, gray hair and blue eyes, with a scar here?" She pointed to her neck.

"A scar? No, I don't think he has a scar. I mean, scars, yes. From the war. But on the neck. I don't know. What are you doing here in Germany?"

"Tourists."

"Why do you speak such good German?"

"Almost all Americans speak German."

"Is that a fact? I never met an Ami who spoke German. *Prost.*" He banged his big stoneware beer

82

stein against mine. "Here's to German-American friendship." He dropped a ham hand on Kathy's thigh and began to massage it.

"Listen, I've got a bottle of American whiskey in my room at our hotel. Why don't we all go over there? It's not far. Add some kick to the beer."

One of the Germans glanced at his watch. "Nah. I've got to get home. The old woman will hit me with a pot if I stay out all night again." I paid the bill and we moved outside into the street, the red-faced character clamped on Kathy's arm.

"Come on. We show the pretty redhead the town, no?" The German with the wife and another peeled off. The other two headed toward the center of town with us as Weber and his dark friend came out of the bar. They stood and watched us, making no move to follow.

"Jesus, this clown is an octopus. How long are we going to have to go on with this?" Almost as Kathy said it, the narrow alley opened up into a well-lit square.

"Come on. Where is your hotel? I am getting a big thirst. A very big thirst."

"It's down on the right. But first we have to find an *Apotheke* with night duty." In Germany certain drugstores were open all night for emergencies.

"An apotheke?" He stared at me stupidly. "Why? I thought you had a bottle?"

"I do. But my wife caught this disease in Africa earlier on the trip and she needs medicine."

"What kind of disease?" the big man asked, taking his arm from around Kathy's waist.

"Well, it's not leprosy but something like it. You know, you break out in sores all over, and your nose falls off if you don't get proper treatment? But she's all right as long as she gets her medicine."

The big man swayed under the street light. "Leprosy. Sepp, did you hear that? These fucking Amis have leprosy." They moved off rapidly across the wide square, not saying goodbye.

Kathy turned, trying to penetrate the darkness of the narrow street behind us. "You think they're back there?"

"No. Too many people around. Too much light. Our hotel is just around the corner."

At the desk, the clerk handed over a message along with my key. "A gentleman just left this for you, sir." It was in German.

"In the words of the great Mohammed Ali, 'You can run, but you can't hide.' "

"What does that mean?"

"It's a quotation, but not from Ali. Joe Louis said it about Billy Conn. Just before he knocked him out."

# Chapter 5

I SLIPPED OUT OF THE ROOM EARLY WHILE KATHY still slept and drove out of the city across an ancient stone bridge to the Teresianer Kloster. The church was an almost perfect specimen of Romanesque, its square towers of ancient brick in perfect proportion. The huge Renaissance Kloster attached to it, built in the late seventeenth century, was already encrusted with the degeneracy of early Baroque. The church and Kloster were surrounded by a twelve-foot stone wall, broken by a massive wooden gate which opened onto a courtyard. I parked in front of what looked like the main entrance and let the big brass knocker bounce off the plate beneath it.

A young woman opened the door. "Yes?"

"I'd like to see the mother superior. My name is Thompson. I called from Berlin."

"Wait, please."

She came back in about five minutes and motioned me to follow. We entered a long, high-ceilinged corridor gleaming with whitewash. The floor was stone, worn down by centuries of feet. Ancient doors of thick oak gave off it at irregular intervals. Our progress echoed off the walls and curved ceiling, building to a small crescendo.

The young nun opened one of the doors and motioned me inside. It was a relatively modern office with metal desks, an IBM Selectric III, and another nun, somewhat older, working a mimeograph machine which looked as if it had escaped from a museum.

"Sit down, please. Sister Clara will see you shortly." I could see our hotel across the valley rising above the walls of the town. It would have been a bitch to take in the days before artillery, the only attack lanes up steep hillsides open to enfilading archery from the walls and Kathy's boiling oil.

The inner door opened and a trim woman of about fifty, dressed in what looked at first glance like a normal gray suit, came out. "Mr. Thompson." She held out her hand. "Please come in." It was an immense room dominated by a refectory table which served as a desk. One wall was given over to a massive fireplace, books lined two others, and the fourth was made up of ceiling-to-floor glass doors giving onto a terrace the size of a basketball court.

"I am surprised to see you, Mr. Thompson, after our telephone conversation. What do you wish from our order?"

"First, I'd like to apologize, Sister. I lied to you on the phone. I am not looking for someone's relatives. I am an historian working on a book about the Nazi period. I have reason to believe that Margarethe von Benedickt is the sister of one of the men I'm researching. I would like to see her if possible."

"Why?"

"I am writing a study of young aristocratic Prussians who joined the SS. I'm trying to discover what motivated them to enter the service of a lower-middle-class Austrian arriviste, surrounded by equally unsavory characters, when they could have pursued an honorable career in the regular army."

86

"And you think Margarethe von Benedickt can help you? How?"

"I have only an official biography of her brother. I would like to know more about him and his contemporaries from someone who was close and is sympathetic. I am a researcher, Sister Clara, not a moralist. There must have been a reason these men acted as they did. I am not interested in repeating the monster theory of Nazism. I'm looking for rational reasons for what happened. I can only get a true picture from the subjective impressions of eye witnesses."

"Margarethe von Benedickt came to us two years ago when her husband died. She is childless and alone in the world, without friends or relatives. We have a limited number of apartments in the Kloster where devout members of the church can spend their declining years. She is a recluse. I am not sure she will consent to see you, but I will inquire. What was her brother's name?"

"Carl Ludwig Caesar Fabian von Bursian."

I waited for ten minutes in the cool solitude of the big room looking across the valley toward the medieval city on the hill, thinking of Kathy curled up under the down comforter, smelling of sleep and woman. Sister Clara returned with another nun in full habit. "Margarethe is willing to see you, Mr. Thompson. If you will go with Sister Ruth." She held out her hand. "Please do not stay too long. She is a fragile old lady with a weak heart."

Sister Ruth led me along the stone corridor and up a winding staircase to the second floor. The ceilings here were lower and the rooms on either side smaller. She stopped and knocked at one of the doors on the valley side.

"Come in."

Margarethe von Benedickt stood to greet me, an imposing figure, almost six feet tall, slim in a dark dress, her gray hair gathered in a loose bun. Pale blue eyes stared out of a strikingly handsome face, marred only by a jaw which jutted out sharply. The room was a simple white cell furnished with an iron cot, a comfortable chair, a lamp and a small desk.

"Good morning, Mr. Thompson." She dismissed the nun with a curt nod. "I understand you wish to speak to me about my brother?"

"Yes. I'm writing a book on the Prussian aristocracy's role in the SS. Some young men from good families chose to join the SS rather than the regular army. I'm trying to discover why."

"You are a journalist?"

"An academic."

"That explains it, then. In my experience academics always seek to complicate simple matters, whereas journalists make complex things simplistic. There is no mystery as to why my brother joined the SS. He and his friends wanted power and glory like all the stupid young Junker. It was clear by the time he left the cadet school that real power no longer lay with the old fogies in the army. The SS was the praetorian guard of the Nazi regime. It was there that names and careers could be made. Fabian's father, General von Bursian, was furious. He very nearly disowned him, accusing him of joining that 'canaille' Hitler."

"Was your brother political?"

"Political? No. Not really. He was a young idiot. Girls and horses, not necessarily in that order, were all he thought of. How could he get his Iron Cross with Swords and Oak Leaves without a war? They all wanted revenge, Mr. Thompson. Revenge on the French and British for their defeat in 1918. The rehabilitation of Germany. The poor fools. All they did was destroy their country and die in the attempt."

"How did your brother die, Mrs. von Benedickt?"

"In France. He had been seriously wounded. We hoped he would not have to go back to the front. But at the end they needed everybody. He became chief of staff for that criminal Sepp Dietrich during the Ardennes offensive."

"The Battle of the Bulge?"

"Yes. The one which almost threw the Allies back into the Channel." The old woman's eyes lit up for a moment and her mouth tightened. She passed a hand over her face quickly. "I'm sorry. Fabian was my favorite brother. When I talk of him the old memories, the old sadness, returns."

"Yes." I said, voice low. "I can understand the pain you must feel."

"You are too kind."

"Your name is von Benedickt. That name appears in the aryan file of your brother as a relative on your mother's side of the family. Did you change your name after the war?"

"No. I married my second cousin, Christian Kalau von Benedickt."

"Was he also in the SS?"

"You are impertinent."

"And you are a lying old fraud. Your brother didn't die in the Ardennes, and you know it. He and dozens of his fellow SS officers submerged with new identities. He's still alive somewhere in Germany using another identity. Where is he, Mrs. von Benedickt?"

I thought I'd killed her for a minute. She started to get up, gripping the heavy cane at her side like a weapon, and then sat back, face drained of color, one hand clawing at her chest as the angina started. Her mouth twisted into a savage grimace as she fought for air, eyes taking on the look of a predatory bird. "You won't find out, you insolent little man. He will kill you. You and that obscene old Jew who is tracking him like an animal." Her voice rose as the pain subsided and her strength came back. "Get out of our country. Leave us in peace. Stop persecuting us. We have had enough of your self-righteous Anglo-Saxon hypocrisy. The only crime Germany committed was to lose the war. Get out! Get out!" She called for the nun, voice rising to a screech.

Outside, in the warm sun, I turned to look at the dark old building, hunkered down in the shadow of the exquisitely proportioned church like a menacing vassal at the feet of its master.

Kathy was enraged when I got back to the hotel. "You son-of-a-bitch. You went without me. What did she say?"

"Nothing. She refused to see me. I couldn't get past the mother superior."

"Oh. I'm sorry, Alec. So the trip was for nothing. Cassierer will be pissed about wasting his money."

"He's got it to waste. Anyway," I grinned at her, "it wasn't all down the drain."

"Keep your filthy paws off me, you treacherous beast," she said, eluding my grasp. "Here I risk my life for you, and you cut me out of the most interesting part. Which reminds me, speaking of risking my life, what are we going to do about Weber?"

"I doubt if he's still hanging around. Too dangerous. He might think we told the police."

"Why didn't we?"

"What would we tell them? We don't have any proof of anything. They'd make us hang around for days, check with Berlin and do nothing. Waste of time."

"What do we do now?"

"Go back to Berlin. You want to spend a day in Goslar in the Harz? Used to be the capital of Germany back in the tenth century. Historian like you should have seen it." I realized how much I wanted to prolong the weekend.

She came into my arms, running her lips along my jawline. "Sure, lover. Why not?"

We almost missed breakfast and didn't get on the road until noon. She handed me the keys as we came out of the hotel. "I'm too blitzed to drive. Jesus, love, you wore me out. Be careful. It's a little bomb." She sank into the front seat and leaned back. "I'm going to sleep."

I wouldn't have noticed the little gizmo normally, but the Morgan's trunk is miniature and in moving the two small bags around looking for space I dislodged it from under the lock. It wasn't very big. About the size of a man's pocket watch with a foot-long wire taped to the car. I pried it open with a pocketknife and extracted the little round battery, dropping it through the open grill of a gutter alongside the car, reassembled the mechanism and put it back in place.

Kathy was asleep before we hit the autobahn, and I opened the little car up. It was a bastardized miniature rocket, looking about as it did when first designed in 1910, but with an eight-cylinder Chrysler engine under the hood which would take it up to a hundred and twenty like grease. It took me a while to spot the tail. But after about ten minutes it was clear that a maroon Mercedes 280SE was nailed to us. I dropped back a couple of times and let him pass. Then he'd move over into the slow lane and slip back behind us. His windows were of some kind of fogged sun-screen glass. He could see out, but I couldn't get a clear view inside. It had to be Weber.

I stayed in heavy traffic, always making sure there were a couple of cars in sight. Which wasn't hard. The autobahn was wall-to-wall cars until we were beyond Kassel, when it began to thin a little. German autobahns are racetracks. In the right lane you can survive driving between seventy and eighty. In the fast lane a hundred will get you run over by some clown sailing along at one-twenty, lights blinking imperiously to clear a track. Their accident rate per mile driven is four times what it is in the States, but the krauts keep saying it has nothing to do with speed. The only answer is that they love their souped-up cars more than living.

The median strip is usually a ditch, impossible to

navigate, but here and there a paved connection between the two divided highways has been built to assist during accidents and highway repairs. They're closed off to traffic by a chain. I watched them as we flashed past. The Morgan is a classic British sports car, about two-thirds as wide as a normal vehicle. At some of the crossings there was room to slip around the posts supporting the chain and move into the flow of traffic going in the opposite direction. The trick was to do it when nobody was tailgating you at a hundred and twenty miles an hour. I finally spotted one of the small paved strips in the distance when nothing was behind us except the maroon Mercedes. I moved over into the slow lane and watched him follow. Then, a couple of hundred meters from the crossing strip, I slipped the little sports car into the fast lane, decelerated into third, then second, and did a quick semi-bootlegger's turn onto the cement crossing, misjudging slightly and almost slamming into one of the posts. The little car spun and its engine died. Kathy came awake.

"What the fuck is going on?"

"Nothing. We're changing direction." I maneuvered the Morgan across the grass next to the left-hand post, almost tipping into the ditch in the process, let three cars flash past, and eased onto the highway in the opposite direction, gunning it to stay ahead of the flow.

"You're a total idiot, Alec. You want to get us killed? Or thrown in the slammer? What was that all about? The German police go ape when you try something like that."

"We were being followed. I had to shake them." We were coming to an exit. "I'm leaving the autobahn. Is there a map in the glove compartment? Be a doll. Get it out and plot our way to Goslar on back roads."

"You think it was Weber?"

"Who else?"

"Yeah. Of course. Who else?"

It was almost dark when we finally reached the little town, with its half-timbered houses and ancient churches, in the middle of the Harz mountains. Here modern Germany had been born in the years after Otto defeated the Hungarians on the plain of Lechfeld in 955. We found our hotel on one of the town's back streets, and while Kathy bathed I set out to explore the narrow winding alleys and streets of the town. I was careless. No question about it. I'd deactivated the bug and lost the tail. It didn't seem reasonable they would be able to pick us up so quickly.

The big Mercedes nosed along the street behind me and came abreast, crowding me against the wall. This time they weren't taking any chances. Three of them were on me before I could move, one with an automatic in my left ear.

"Make no sound. Do as you are told." Weber was in the driver's seat grinning when they threw me, handcuffed, into the back.

"We meet again, Dr. Thompson."

"Why didn't you just drive this truck over me?"

"Ah. That would have been crude. And anyway, somebody might have seen us. Have you got the keys, Georg?" One of them had been going through my pockets and had come up with the keys to the Morgan.

"Ja."

"Good. Bring it out to the mountain. Quickly. We want to get this over with."

We drove for about ten minutes on mountain roads before pulling onto a narrow gravel strip on the shoulder.

"Come on. Move your feet," Weber said, pulling me along by the handcuffs. "We don't have much time. If the girl thinks he's missing she'll bring on the dogs."

"Weber."

"Yes?"

"How'd you find me? I removed the bug. I shook off the tail on the autobahn. How'd you get here so quick?"

"Bug? Tail? What are you talking about? I asked the hotel where you had booked for tonight. They looked up your telephone call and gave me the name of the hotel."

I felt more than saw the punch coming. It missed the nerve at the base of my neck by a hair, landing mostly on the ridge of muscle I'd built up in twenty years of making neck bridges on a wrestling mat. It still felt like being hit by a log. I went down on my knees and face and lay still.

"Take the handcuffs off. Brush off his clothes, idiot. We don't want dirt all over him." I heard it all through a fog of pain as they picked me up and jammed me into the Morgan's cramped front seat. "Start the car. Jam his foot on the clutch."

I lay slumped over the steering wheel trying to penetrate the dark. The lights of the Mercedes threw a narrow beam ahead showing an abrupt right-hand curve. Beyond it was an abyss. The car was on a grade of nearly ten percent.

"Start the engine, Georg. Dieter, hold his foot against the clutch. Put it in third as I pull out the rock."

The big engine roared to life. Weber leaned over and pulled out the rock blocking one of the back wheels and the little car lurched forward, slipping out of the Mercedes's headlights into a pool of darkness. About fifteen feet from the edge I opened the door. As the front wheels went over, I flipped to my left, landing on the gravel shoulder, rolling myself over the edge, praying for enough vegetation to break the fall. A tree trunk stopped me about six feet down, slamming into my gut. Behind me the little car crashed down the mountainside for what seemed like minutes, flaming into a bright orange ball as the gas tank ignited.

"Let's get out of here," Weber said as the Mercedes purred to life.

I waited about five minutes before crawling back to the road. It took an hour to reach the main highway. Half a mile further along I found a gasthaus open and called a taxi. Kathy was on the phone when I walked into the room, face tight with tension.

"Jesus Christ, what happened to you?" she asked, hanging up. "I was just about to call the police. My God, Alec, you're a mess."

"I'm a careless wiseass."

"What happened?"

I told her.

"How did they know you were here?" She showed no interest in her lovely little car lying at the bottom of the mountain.

"Stupidity. I called the hotel here for a reservation. The hotel had a record of the call."

"Alec?"

"Yeah?"

"They won't screw up next time. They'll kill you."

"There's not going to be a next time."

"How are you going to stop them?"

"I'm dead. In that little car at the base of the mountain. At least for a while. It'll take them several days, maybe a week, before they find out I didn't buy the farm." I sat on the bed, wincing with pain. "I've got an idea I want to try out at the Document Center. It may work. If it does, I'll nail the Orpheus Circle."

"And if it doesn't?"

I grinned at her. She'd put on a blue knit dress, cut low, and pulled back her hair. Her green eyes, highlighted by black eyeshadow, leapt out of her face. "Then they'll have to catch me. Come on. Let's go eat."

"They may be watching the hotel."

"I doubt it. Somebody is going to find that car tomorrow. You'll be at the police station, or they'll

95

think you will, causing a row. It's a small town. They want to be out of here when the manure hits the fan."

We caught the bus to Hannover the following morning and a plane to Berlin, getting in around three in the afternoon. It was a typical Berlin summer day: slight drizzle turned everything into a late Turner painting. The pastel light played tricks with Kathy's eyes turning them from green to blue and back again, dulling the bright flame of her hair.

"Get Hugh to meet me at the gasthaus on Argentinische Allee. Don't tell him anything. He's going to be trouble. I've got to hustle him into letting me use the archive at night."

"Alec, it's dangerous. They'll find the car and no body. Weber and his thugs will know you got out. They'll be after you in a couple of days. Maybe less."

"A couple of days is all I need if my theory is right."

"Let me do it for you. Tell me what you want. I know the archive. You can hole up at my place."

I shook my head. "No. Weber's got a hook into somebody at the Document Center. They'd spot you." I took her in my arms. Germany is unlike most European countries, where public displays of affection are tolerated. Embrace in public in Germany and five people are likely to cite you the law prohibiting it. But in an airport it was allowed. "Anyway, I'm getting used to having a warm body around. Cold you wouldn't be so useful."

"Gross pig."

She made the call and an hour later Hugh LeRoy entered the gasthaus, an old traditional German bar converted into the inevitable Italian restaurant, with plastic crustaceans and wicker-covered wine bottles clashing with the stuffed boars' heads still on the walls. He was visibly surprised to see me.

"Hello, Alec. What the hell happened to you?" Bouncing down the mountain had stripped most of the skin off one side of my face, leaving it a vivid red.

"Ran into a door. What'll you have?"

"Beer."

The Italian waiter disappeared to draw the beer in a laborious ritual, half-filling the glass, letting the suds settle, adding beer, letting it settle, then topping it off. It was great beer. But you could die of thirst waiting for it.

"Why all the hocus-pocus?"

I told him what had happened, leaving out von Bursian's sister, letting him think Kathy and I had simply gone away for the weekend. He grinned.

"So you scored? You goddamn academic wimps. I don't see how you do it."

"Swave and debohnur, Hugh. Swave and debohnur. Listen, I've got a problem. I'm close to coming up with something. That's clear. Otherwise they wouldn't be after me. Somewhere in that archive, there's a key to the Orpheus Circle."

Hugh nodded. He lifted the bulbous beer glass with the *Berliner Kindl* coat of arms and drank about half of it. "Sure looks like it. What do you want me to do?"

"Weber thinks I'm dead. Or anyway, badly hurt. It will take him a couple of days to find out I wasn't in the car when it went over. But if I walk into the archive he'll know instantly."

Hugh frowned. "You think one of my people is on his payroll?"

I just looked at him.

"Yeah. Makes sense. We've got about forty clerks working for us. Wouldn't be hard to turn one. So what do you want?"

"I want to work at night."

He shook his head impatiently. "No. Out of the question, Alec. Totally against regulations. They'd hang my ass from the flagpole at high noon if I allowed it."

I ordered two more beers. "Look, Hugh. We're not dealing with some scholarly project anymore. Or even

97

with Cassierer's vengeance. These guys are out to kill me. They've got an organization capable of tracking me across West Germany and mobilizing hired killers. These aren't retired old SS veterans with Alzheimer's disease sitting around drinking schnapps and reminiscing about the Fuehrer. They're probably running some of the more important businesses in Germany. And they're sure as hell in the government."

"Yeah. I take your point. How much time do you think you'll need?"

"Two days maybe. Maximum of a week."

"Where are you holed up?"

"Kathy's offering me a bed."

"Among other things," he said, grinning and raising his beer. "Okay. It's against my better judgement, and it could cost me my pension. but if I don't let you in, you'll come in daylight and they'll knock you off. How do you want to work it?"

"You're closing at 4:30 now, aren't you? I'll be there at 5:00. Tell the guard to let me in. Your personnel will be gone by then. Also, Hugh, I need the computer."

"The computer?"

"Yeah. I've been working on an idea that might click if the computer can be programmed to do it."

"When do you want to start?"

"Tonight."

# Chapter 6

IT TURNED OUT TO BE RIDICULOUSLY SIMPLE ONCE I'D
mastered the Hahn system, a German knockoff of the
American Wang. It took me an hour to get through the
software instruction book Hugh had given me. It
wasn't all that complicated—although the German
writers, with their native genius for making the simple
complex, gave it a good shot. From then on it was scut
work. First I entered the two hundred and nineteen
names of the German participants attending the London Economic Council meeting where Passent had
seen von Bursian. I then told the computer to check
them one by one against the two million names in the
displaced persons files.

The machine took its time, emitting occasional electronic burps as I entered the instructions, flashing one
negative after another on the blinking screen. Then it
came to a halt. "Eberhard Koehler," the green writing
said. "Born Prague 1913." I checked through the file
quickly. Koehler had joined the German army in 1939
following the fall of Czechoslovakia. Invalided out in
1943 after the loss of a foot, he went to work for the
Siemens Company in Berlin. I checked the affiliations

on Cassierer's list. Eberhard Koehler was vice president in charge of Siemens Export. I printed out the information on the displaced persons file and hit the "enter" button again.

By three a.m. I had fifty printouts of men with names identical to those on Cassierer's list. Four looked promising. Another ten were possible, based on birthdates and personal data. I was down to the last fifteen names when I punched in Erwin von Kollwitz. Fritz, as I had begun to call the computer, went through his usual comic routine of electronic coughing and spitting before flashing the file on the screen.

"Erwin von Kollwitz. Born, Tallinin, January 13, 1918. Father, Klaus, electrical engineer. Race: German. Mother Ewa, born Sukowa, without profession. Race: German. Abitur, Stein Gymnasium, 1936. Army service, 1936-38. Reserve Lieutenant, Estonian 23rd (guards) Regiment, June 1937. Imprisoned Siberia, 1939-41. Private, Soviet Fourth Panzer Corps, 1942. Captured, May 1942, Leningrad front. August 1943, Second Lieutenant Vlasov Corps. Transferred to Wehrmacht, January 1944." His service jacket went on for a full page of citations for bravery, transfers and wounds before ending abruptly, as most did, early in 1945.

I leaned back and rubbed my eyes. Vlassov had been a brilliant Russian general captured during an offensive ordered, against all reason, by Stalin. Once in German hands, bitter at the stupidity of the Soviet high command and fearful of Stalin's paranoia, he had agreed to form a corps of Russian prisoners willing to fight against the Soviets. Clearly von Kollwitz had volunteered for this unit and later, proving his impeccable German origins, had been able to transfer into the German army.

I printed the file and stared at it for a couple of minutes, trying to call up von Kollwitz from the mists of time. The Germans had colonized the Baltic region beginning in the twelfth century, pushing back the primitive Wends and other Slavs, enslaving them, forcing Christianity on the populace with the sword. Then the Slavic wave had rolled back, washing around islands of Germans in the cities and fortresses, assimilating and absorbing each other. When the Second World War started all of Eastern Europe held pockets of Volksdeutsche, people who spoke German and were part of the greater German nation but still belonged to the artificial political entities left in the wake of the breakup of the great empires after World War One.

Estonia was one of those casualties of history. Von Kollwitz had been lucky. He had survived. Or had he? I turned to Cassierer's notes on the conference participants. By each name there was a one- or two-sentence biography. Von Kollwitz worked for something called SOFOL GMBH with headquarters in Frankfurt. A private investment company, according to the cryptic notations. An address and telephone number. I tapped another name into the computer and stood up and stretched while the machine worked. Fritz was installed in a corner of the main SS file room, an eerie, concrete hole, a paper graveyard twenty feet down in the earth. More to break the monotony than out of conviction I took the von Kollwitz printout and von Bursian's marriage file and walked up the two flights of stairs to the ground floor storeroom where the Displaced Persons files were kept. Row on row of metal stands packed with neatly tied and indexed manila folders arranged by country. I found Estonia at the end of one row and moved down to the K's. The von Kollwitz file gave off a faint puff of dust as I pulled it free. The first half dozen documents were in Estonian, a language akin to Finnish, with an ancient identity card dimly showing a youth of fifteen or so. Then the German file began with the classic trio of pictures. Full face, profile and at a slight angle. I have to admit it was

101

a shock. Oh, sure, my logic was impeccable, even elegant, but it was still a longshot. To have him staring out at me from the file was the kind of intellectual coup historians dream about. There wasn't any question. He'd used his SS photos. I compared the files. They were identical. I took the von Kollwitz folder over to one of the desks provided for researchers, flicked on the 150-watt bulb in the lamp above it and began going over the file with the small jeweler's glass I'd begun to carry years before when I first started in the archive.

The forgery was relatively clumsy. The paper did not quite match that in the rest of the file. Some of the biographic data in the later sections had been crudely altered, obviously to fit von Bursian's needs. The physical descriptions in the final pages were subtly different from those in the beginning, although von Kollwitz obviously shared von Bursian's blue eyes, blond hair and general physique.

I had him. And not only him. The rest of the Orpheus Circle would have used the same method to go under. It would take time and patience, but teams of researchers using computers could go through the Displaced Persons and SS files and match up those which had identical photographs. I xeroxed two copies of the von Kollwitz file, replaced it and went down into the silent maw of the building. There was a chill about the place even in midsummer. A morgue of dead paper. I filled out one of the gray envelopes from the archive and addressed one set of copies to the post office box I kept in Berlin. I took the other up to LeRoy's office and worked my way through the German telephone system for twenty minutes before finally coming up with the address of SOFOL GMBH in Frankfurt.

The letter took some time. I had a small file of crumpled paper in the front of LeRoy's ancient Lettra before I caught the tone I was looking for. I typed a clean copy and inserted it and the second set of xeroxes in another of the coarse gray envelopes, fumbling around in Hugh's drawer until I found some German stamps.

I realized my hands were trembling slightly. Hell, why shouldn't they? A hundred thousand dollars, tax free, was more money than I could save in forty years on an academic's salary.

Kathy moaned as I slid in beside her and moved close. Waking a woman up at six a.m. was a loser's game if ever there was one. But I couldn't sleep. I needed human contact. I ran my hand over her stomach as she turned away from me in protest, hips moving against me. I settled in next to her, slipping him gently between her legs until he came to rest against her. She moved again, awake now, and turned, half-exasperated, half-amused.

"Jesus, men are coarse, insensitive beasts." She turned toward me as she spoke, forcing me over on my back, running her lips down my cheek, along my neck, across my chest and stomach, taking him in her mouth. She moved up over me, opening herself and slipping him in. "Be still, coarse beast," she whispered. "Let me do it." Her big legs enveloped me, as she let herself down at full length, barely moving, her body swallowing him, beginning a long, slow rhythm, stopping just as my control was about to slip, beginning again, becoming increasingly insistent, driving her body against me until her breath suddenly expelled in a long moan. "Now, lover, now, now, now."

She lay on top of me, a mass of damp red hair a veil around my face, holding him inside her, finally pushing herself up on one elbow, grinning down at me. "Crude jerk. Waking me up for a quickie. What time is it?"

"Six-thirty."

"How did it go?"

"I found him."

103

"You're kidding?" She had sat up cross-legged in bed, pushing back a tangle of hair, tying it in a green elastic band. She stopped in mid-motion now, arms held high, breasts pointed upward. "How?"

"I programmed the computer to do all the work. It's complicated. I'll have to show you how I did it."

"Jesus. You're something else, lover. What are you going to do now?"

"Go to sleep," I said, feeling a massive lassitude flow over me. I was out before she finished kissing me, diving into a pool of near nightmares, running through the Document Center pursued by some nameless danger whose heels clicked like gunshots in the empty halls as I ran down endless off-white corridors. Whatever it was was gaining on me. I could feel it clawing at my shoulder.

"Wake up, Thompson."

I came out of the nightmare staring up at Paul O'Brien's preppie face, smelling his manly aftershave lotion. Beyond him the coarse bulk of Frank Xerxes loomed next to Kathy. I sat up mopping sweat off my face. "What the fuck is going on?"

Kathy came over and sat on the bed next to me. "They said they wanted to talk to you, Alec."

"How did they know I was here?"

"We've had a loose tail on you since you got back to Berlin," Xerxes said. "We've also had the apartment bugged. A couple of hours ago you came back from the archive and told Kathy you had found von Bursian."

"And?"

"We want the name. And we want the technique you used to find it."

I yawned. I'd slept for hours. It seemed like minutes. I sat up on the edge of the bed, wincing as my battered muscles protested. Kathy threw me my pants and I pulled them on.

"You got hit pretty bad in Nam, huh?" Xerxes said, staring at the scars.

104

"Forgot to duck."

"Come on. Quit stalling, Thompson," O'Brien said. "Who is von Bursian?"

"His real name is Strumpfbandguertel. Alois Harald Strumpfbandguertel. He works in Hintertuepfing-staedten as a garbage collector. Lives at Goethestrasse 13. Married, three children, twelve grandchildren. Sleeps with his neighbor's wife on Saturday afternoon when the guy goes bowling. Drinks too much. Cholesterol level 311. Incipient emphysema. Member of three associations. The Group of Disabled SS Men. The Order of the Iron Cross. And something called 'Veterans of Hand-to-Hand Combat.' To join that last one you have to be able to prove you killed somebody in combat with your bare hands. Got it all out of the file. You could look it up."

O'Brien had stopped writing halfway through and he now put down the pad and pencil to come over to stand in front of me. He was bigger than he looked and reasonably quick. He hit me open-handed across the face, twice, palm and backhand.

"Paul!" Xerxes' voice cut through the clanging inside my head.

"He's a comedian, Frank," O'Brien said.

"Apparently you don't understand the seriousness of this situation, Dr. Thompson," Xerxes said. "We're representatives of your government. We need the information you have come up with in that archive. It bears on the security of the United States. It's your duty as a citizen to assist us."

"Tell me about it." O'Brien had cut the inside of my lip. I was always surprised at how salty blood tasted.

"Why do you think the Document Center is kept away from newspapermen and the general public? I told you before. We'd close it completely if we could. As it is we've managed to keep it under control. But the goddamn place is an unexploded bomb. It has the record of every German who was ever even remotely

105

connected to the Nazi regime. A lot of them, forty years later, are important members of the German government, business community and intelligentsia. If this became public knowledge it would do irreparable damage to this German regime and to society as a whole, giving ammunition to nutty fringe groups on the left and aid to the Soviet Union in splitting Germany off from its allies. And right now the last thing we want is to see one of our major allies being beaten up on for what is ancient history. It's time to forgive and forget, Thompson. The one thing we don't want is a series of dramatic trials of war criminals. The Germans are sick of hearing about it. So is everybody else. It's time to let it die."

"Von Bursian killed about forty thousand Jews. Forced them to dig their own graves and shot them."

"He was in the army," O'Brien said. "German soldiers were being shot by Russian partisans. It wasn't as black and white as the propaganda says it was."

"Cassierer hired me to find him. I took his money. He wants the man punished."

Xerxes lit a Gauloise from the butt of the last one, stubbing out the stained remnant in a coffee cup beside the bed. Kathy didn't smoke and refused to put out ashtrays. "Look, Thompson, I shouldn't tell you this, but I guess you deserve some information. Cassierer isn't some harmless old banker following his hobby. He was head of Mossad, Israeli intelligence, during the whole Eichmann incident and for a couple of years afterward. He retired, officially, but nobody who has been in intelligence ever gets out of it completely. Mossad has used him repeatedly on delicate assignments over the past decade. They're using him now.

"The Israelis aren't interested in war criminals. Take this Mengele thing. You think that skeleton is Mengele? That's a joke. The Israelis have known for years that Mengele has been living in luxury at a series of safe houses in Paraguay, tucked away in the German community there. He had his face lifted in Switzerland in 1957. Nobody could possibly recognize him. He travels on phony passports. When things heated up, they found some old bastard who had drowned and turned him into the Angel of Death."

"So why don't they knock him off?"

Xerxes lit another cigarette. "Look. What do the Israelis want? To keep the holocaust before the public eye. Not let anybody forget that six million Jews died in those camps. You knock off Mengele, and all the publicity dies. There are not too many documented monsters still among the living. He's worth his weight in gold to their propagandists.

"Also, there's another reason. Stroessner, the Paraguayan president, has backed Israel in the UN for years. He's also had a good thing going, bringing in Israeli goods for transshipment to the rest of Latin America. Taking a cut, of course.

"It was the same with Barbie. Everybody knew where he was. The last thing the French wanted was Barbie on trial. And we sure as hell weren't interested in washing our dirty linen. He'll spill his guts about a lot of important Frenchmen once that trial starts. If it ever does."

"So what does the old man want? Why is he looking for von Bursian?"

"Leverage. Influence. The Germans make the best tank in the world. The Leopard. The Arabs want to buy it, especially the Saudis. With information that some of the top German bureaucrats and businessmen are ex-Nazis, the Israelis can blackmail them into stopping such arms sales. But it's more subtle than that. The Israelis need capital. International support. The country's broke. A lot of these ex-SS men are probably in business. If Cassierer gets his hands on the Orpheus Circle, you'll see a surge of German investments in Israel. And a lot less sympathy in the government for improving relations with the Arabs. Oil won't carry quite the weight it does now."

"Sounds sensible. How come we don't help the Israelis out? Sounds like a nice, civilized way to get revenge."

"Don't be stupid, Thompson," O'Brien said. "The Germans are our major allies in Europe. The only ones who are half-assed reliable. We want to keep them that way."

"So we get the information on who's a Nazi and use it ourselves. Some permanent undersecretary in the foreign ministry turns out to have been an officer in the SS when he was twenty. If it comes out, he's ruined. We take him out for a drink, show him what we've got and he's in our pocket. With luck we might even land a few bankers which would help out with the dollar when it gets in trouble again. Is that what you're saying?"

Xerxes shook loose another cigarette, lighting it from the butt of the one he was smoking. "Crudely put, yeah. There is all that. However, none of this concerns you. We want the name. And how you got it."

I stood up and pulled on a faded blue tennis shirt, the little lizard pulling loose from being washed too often. "I haven't got the name. Not yet. What I've got is a system for finding him. Eliminating all the other possibilities. It can probably be used to nail most of the others if you put a couple of dozen trained researchers and some computer wizards on it."

Xerxes took a long drag on the foul-smelling French cigarette, spitting out loose shreds of tobacco. "On the tape you told Kathy you had him."

"I do. All I need is one more session in the archive, and he's mine."

"He's lying, Frank. Let's take him in and stretch him."

108

"By tomorrow morning you can give us the name? And the system?"

"Yeah."

"Okay. You've got twenty-four hours," Xerxes said.

"Don't try anything funny, Thompson," O'Brien said. "We've got two guys who will be on you twenty-four hours a day."

Kathy closed the door behind them and leaned against it. "I'm sorry, Alec."

"Yeah. Let's find the bug." There were four scattered around the apartment. Small modern ones with solid state technology and a range of a couple of hundred yards. One in a lamp by the bed. One in the phone. Another in a light fixture and the last one high up on the shower curtain. I looked at Kathy. She shrugged.

"Maybe they think we take baths together. Talk in the tub."

"Maybe. Let's eat. I'm starving." I took her to the Borbone, an Italian place in the Windscheidstrasse somebody had told me was the best in Berlin. The service was superb. Two or three Sicilian waiters kept hovering over us, their hands fluttering close to Kathy, never quite landing.

"Ever been to Italy?"

She grinned. "Once. It took three weeks for the bruises to go away. They pinch. Jesus. I'd go down the street and fourteen hands would come out of nowhere. If I ever go back, I'm going to dye my hair."

"They're all salivating. The waiters."

"Saliva's cheap. Alec, you've got the name, haven't you?"

"Sort of. I mean, I've got him nailed. It'll just take a couple of hours to get it all together."

"Why not just give it to them? Let them finish it off?"

109

The snails were superb, swimming in butter redolent of garlic. He'd given us a Corvo, a Sicilian generic, the best of which was as dry as manzanilla, and you could drink it all day. It was a pale, golden green which almost matched her eyes. "I will. Eventually. I just don't like being pushed."

"Did he hurt you?"

"Who?"

"Paul. Don't you remember? He hit you."

"Oh. Yeah. I guess he did. No, he didn't hurt me."

We got a little tight, knocking off another bottle of wine with the scampi pescatore, cooked in a sharp sauce and eaten with flat bread flavored with garlic, freshly baked in the house. "Good stuff, huh?"

"Yeah. Say, where'd you get the money to pay for this?"

"Cassierer's last honorarium."

"Oh. . .You think I told them, don't you?"

"Told who what?"

"Don't act dumb. Xerxes and O'Brien. About your finding von Bursian."

"Did you?"

One of the Italians came over and bowed. His hair was greased down until it looked painted. "Signorina Chapin? Telephone."

She came back after a couple of minutes, leaned over and kissed me gently, on the mouth. "Listen, lover. I've got to run. Something urgent. I'll tell you about it when you get back from the archive."

I sipped the last of the wine, remembering that if you drank too much of it, it turned bitter on your tongue. Nobody but Xerxes and his two myrmidons outside could know that we were in the restaurant. I spent ten minutes on the phone at the end of the bar booking a flight to Frankfurt on the first Pan Am plane the next morning, which left at six a.m.; arranging for a rented car in Frankfurt, hoping that my one credit card still had enough on it to cover the cost and getting a room in a cheap gasthaus on the outskirts of town where I'd once spent a couple of weeks while researching the book on the SS.

I killed the afternoon leading my watchdogs on a walk through the zoo, watching the filthy pandas defecate in their water dish and meeting the unwinking yellow-eyed stare of the snow leopard, a graceful cat who seemed to be sizing me up as he would a tasty rodent in his native Bhutan.

Leaving the zoo I went through the aquarium and grabbed a taxi, slipped the tail and headed for the main post office. The gray envelope was there along with the *American Historical Review*, a rejected article from the *Journal of International Relations*, and a letter from the Dean informing me I had been elected Chairman of the Equal Opportunity Committee. I put the gray envelope back and threw the rest away.

The guards at the archive let me in at five p.m., carrying a sack of sandwiches and a couple of cans of *Berliner Kindl*. I went through my papers first, making sure I'd left no tracks. Somebody had been there before me. My notes had been examined and put back together in a slightly different order. It didn't matter. Nobody was going to be able to make any sense out of them in the shape they were in. I settled in to run computer comparisons on SS men born in 1915 and displaced persons with similar birthdates. I ran through the SS files quickly, looking for anybody with a Von in front of his name who came from Prussia. After a couple of hours, I had a hundred names. Half of them had survived the war, which eliminated them as possibilities. All the members of the Orpheus Circle would arrange a phony death in action in order to submerge, using a dead displaced person's identity. I then had the computer isolate all the male displaced persons who were born in 1915 from among the two million files. Von Bursian had transferred the physical description information verbatim from the SS folder into the DP file of von Kollwitz. It was exact, down to the last comma. I figured they might all have used the same procedure. The walls had been caving in on them. Time was running out. So they took short cuts. Who was going to check? Computers hadn't even been conceived of, much less invented.

I entered in the computer, one after the other, the physical characteristics of the dozen or so SS names I had left and asked it to match them with the DP files. While it worked I drank a beer and wolfed down the sandwiches, listening to the machine belt out its little electronic song. It took a while. As I finished the second beer, the machine became quiet. Two names blinked at me from the small screen. Bernd, Freiherr von Kuester, and Christian, Freihrer von Erlangen. Opposite them were the names of their mirror images in the DP files.

I moved down the empty halls of the cellar corridor to the SS marriage files and found their envelopes. Slim embodiments of Prussian nobility. High foreheads. Good chins. Noble visages. Both had impressive military jackets, having participated in every major campaign from Poland to the North African desert and Russia. Always Russia. I took the folders up to the ground floor and found among the DP files those of Guenter Boelling and Eberhard Koehler, flipping immediately to the pictures.

It was almost too easy. I could probably find them all, working alone, in a couple of weeks, once I got used to the computer. I had slipped the two files back into the metal racks, turned off the lights and started back toward the stairwell when I heard the glass break. A clean ping which echoed through the empty building, no sound of shards landing on the floor. Somebody had taped a window and broken it. I moved toward the sound and stopped.

There were nine of them, lithe figures in black, stocking masks over their faces. They spread out, four heading for the cellar, three moving in the direction of the party files and two coming straight at me carrying satchels. I stepped back into the shadow, immobilized, as they raced past and into the big file room. The main security alarm, wired to an electronic system, was just inside Hugh LeRoy's office. I moved along the corridor and slipped through the door. The alarm box, of classic German construction, was made of gauge steel and locked. The system, Hugh had once told me, was wired to sound if any entry was breached. I moved over to a window, picked up a chair and swung it in a short arc, smacking into wood and glass, feeling the cool evening breeze hit me in the face through the shattered window.

It sounded like an explosion, but the alarm didn't go off. Down the hall I heard a door ripped open. "*Links, Hans. Ich nehme die Rechte.*" he kicked open the door like a good American cop and came in fast behind it, the Uzi swinging back and forth the way they told you to in the books. It wasn't very subtle. I hit him with a chair leg which had broken off when I smashed the window and pushed him to one side.

"*Hans,*" I whispered, "*hier.*" His buddy came out of the room across the way, gun at port arms. I drove the chair leg into his gut and brought a knee up against his jaw as it bent him over. I was out of practice. Anxious, maybe. I could feel the bone go as he dropped limp. I turned him over on his side, so he wouldn't choke on his own blood if I'd ripped something loose in his throat, and moved down the hall to the DP file room. The canisters were in the middle of the floor. Filled with a sort of napalm. When they blew the whole room would be covered with a fine film which would burn everything to a cinder when it ignited. The fuses were set for fifteen minutes. I reset the safety pins dangling to one side and moved back into the corridor. The electronic alarm system was shorted out. In fifteen minutes the whole place would go up in smoke. I headed for Hugh's office. It would take the German fire department a half hour to get here but they might save something. As I moved against the wall I banged into one of the portable fire extinguishers littering the walls of the buildings. Next to it was a box with a red lever. I smashed the glass and pulled it up. The old-fashioned mechanical fire alarm let go with a piercing scream. "Hahn, Ree! Hahn, Ree!" like a French police car run amok. I dropped flat and waited. They erupted out of the main party archive in seconds, followed by the four in the cellar.

*"Raus! Raus! Schnell! Verdammt mal, schnell! Was ist passiert?"*

I gave them ten seconds, then began to run. The three canisters in the main party files were easy. Nobody had bothered to hide anything. They just stood there among the wooden file cabinets. The cellar was a different proposition. I wasn't sure what they wanted. The regular SS files extended for hundreds of yards. It took seven minutes to locate three canisters and defuse them. In the room with the marriage archives there had to be at least two more. I was down to the last minute when I found the first one. If the second blew while I was in the room, I'd go up like a torch with the files or die from lack of oxygen. I sprinted for the door and spotted it off to one side, standing on a file cabinet in full view. I grabbed the slick aluminum and skidded into the corridor. There wasn't anything else to do. I bowled it the length of the long, cement-lined tunnel, listening as it smashed its way along and stopped against the far wall. It blew just as I started up the steps, and I could feel the heat on my back like a furnace. With luck the iron doors would protect the files from too much damage.

The main gate was closed, the two guards peacefully asleep, obviously drugged. I climbed it quickly, listening for the sound of the German fire department over the howling alarm. The voice came out of the shadows. *"Hans, schnell. Wo ist Peter? Wir muessen weg."*

I ran toward the sound, then cut right as I reached the edge of the woods and dove for cover.

*"Hans, Hans. Bist du verrueckt? Komm hier. Wo bist du?"*

He was alone, obviously left behind to wait for the two missing men. I would have left him alone normally. He was stumbling around in the dark, panic coming through like a sour odor. But I needed to be sure. As he came opposite me I stood up and caught him in a choke hold, gripping his right wrist and twisting back until the little machine pistol dropped. My luck ran out about then. He was good. And young. And strong. He went into a nice little routine, lifting his left foot and bringing it down on my instep, slamming an elbow into my gut, followed by a quick probe for my eyes with the fingers of his free hand. They practice this stuff until they can do it in their sleep and his thumb missed my eye socket by about a quarter of an inch. I jammed the back of his knees and pitched him forward on his face, burying a fist in the back of his neck as he landed, hoping I hadn't killed him. There was no identification on the uniform, but in an inside pocket I found his wallet. I took it and headed into the woods. Behind me, I could hear the vacillating tones of the German fire trucks turning into Wasserkaefersteig.

# Chapter 7

THE KURFUERSTENDAMM WAS ABLAZE WITH LIGHT when I came out of the U-Bahn station at Wittenbergplatz. I tossed the wallet into one of the little orange trash baskets adorning every second light pole in Berlin and turned up toward the Kurfuerstenstrasse, away from the river of humanity pulullating along the main boulevard. The papers I'd found identified Michael Eser as a sergeant in the SEK, the *Sonder Einsatz Kommando*, the Berlin equivalent of West Germany's *Bundesgrenzschutz Gruppe Neun*, the same elite unit of border police which had freed prisoners from a hijacked airliner at Mogadiscio with such brutal efficiency. They had been hunting down terrorists with lethal silence over the past decade. Small, self-contained, highly secret, trained in all the latest techniques of close combat, armed with sophisticated high-technology weapons, they, along with the British SAS, the Israelis and the American Delta Force, were the most effective small action shock unit in the world. I crossed the Uraniastrasse past the Cafe Einstein into a two-block long stretch which was usually lined with

116

young prostitutes in high-heeled boots, net stockings and hot pants. Kathy's apartment was on my left.

Rust-flecked cars, mostly filled with Middle Eastern guest workers, cruised the streets, their occupants halting briefly to bargain with the girls. I stopped next to a tall child of about sixteen who glanced at me through a mask of makeup.

"You want to play?"

"How much?"

"Fifty marks. French, seventy-five. Anything you want that doesn't hurt for a hundred."

"What about all night?"

She glanced at her watch. It was almost midnight. "I'm tired, *Liebling*. Can't we just make it a quickie?"

"I'd like to take my time."

"Okay. Sure. Two hundred."

"Can we go to your place?"

She looked up and down the street, searching the cars, looking for her pimp. "I don't take the ragheads there, but you look okay. Sure."

She put her arm through mine, rubbing a slim hip against me. "It's just around the corner." She turned into a dead-end street and stopped at a five-story apartment house, leading me into the hallway smelling of stale sauerkraut and lysol. "There's no elevator, and I'm on the fifth floor. Christ, it's a drag, coming home after a hard night and having to walk up these steps. The bastard won't let me keep enough for a decent apartment. I'm saving my money, then I'm telling him to fuck off. What's your name, lover?"

"Georg."

"Hey, that's a nice name." She walked ahead of me, gyrating her hips, long muscular legs rippling under the net stockings. The apartment had one room with a miniature bath and a kitchen built into the wall, concealed by folding shutters.

"You want something? A drink maybe?"

"A beer if you've got it."

She hesitated, standing in front of me, hands on her hips. "You're, ah, forgetting something, aren't you, love?"

"I'm sorry?"

She held out her hand. "The money, love." Her tone had hardened and her whole body had suddenly become wary.

"Oh, sure." I counted out two hundred marks and passed them over. There wasn't a hell of a lot left, although I'd lifted almost a hundred from the young border policeman's wallet before throwing it away.

She disappeared around the corner, stashing the money, and came back. "You want a hit?"

"Hit?"

"God, you're green. Where are you from anyway? You're not German." She gave my clothes a quick once over. "My God, you're an Ami. Jesus, if I'd known that I would never have brought you up here."

"Why not?"

"Amis are bad news. Nothing but trouble. Would you believe it? One of the soldiers fell in love with me last year." She laughed, opening the miniature refrigerator and taking out a can of beer. "Can you believe it? Me? A whore? He wanted to marry me. Take me back to America. *Das Land der unbegrenzten Moeglichkeiten.* I told my pimp, and he wanted me to do it. He figured we could get a free trip to the States out of it and dump the kid once we got there. You're not going to fall in love with me, are you?"

"No."

"You want the hit? I'll throw it in for free," she said, opening a drawer and laying out the paraphernalia on the counter. "I need it, love. It'll make me better." She lit a candle and poured the white powder into a large blackened spoon, added a little water, and heated the mixture carefully, deftly sucking it all up with the needle, chattering as she worked.

"It keeps me going, you know. These goddamn Turks and Pakistanis. They all want to screw you in the ass. I keep asking them, why don't they get boys, for Christ's sake, if they like it that way so much. God knows there are enough boys around. But they're clean, the Moslems, I will say that. Everybody thinks they're dirty, but it's the Germans who stink, not the Arabs." She stripped off the hot pants and pulled down the net stockings, looking for an undamaged vein on her inner thigh, inserting the needle. She saw my glance and giggled.

"It's because of the Turks. Their women all shave themselves, and they pay more if you're shaved. It itches like hell." She sat down and leaned back in the chair. "Jesus, it feels good. I mean, I know it can't, not yet. But it does. You know, like thinking about a good fuck, it's almost better than doing it. Am I keeping you waiting, love? I won't be long. Just let it sink in a little."

"Look. All I want is to stay here 'til morning. You don't have to do anything. I just need a place to sleep. I'll take the chair. You go to bed."

She had pulled off her halter top and stood nude in front of me now, a strikingly handsome child with long slim legs, a flat stomach and the small breasts of a young girl. In the dim light of the apartment I could see the bruises around her nipples and on her arms and thighs.

"Hey, what's going on? You don't want to fuck? You think I'm ugly. Or maybe I've got something? Listen, mister, I go to the doctor every week. And I get shots all the time. Not just this shit. Penicillin. I'm so full of the stuff, a clap or syphilis bug doesn't have a chance. You think I'm too old. Is that it? Listen, I just turned seventeen. I've only been doing this for a year. I lost my apprenticeship at Siemens." She giggled. "I was screwing the foreman, see, hoping I'd get a better spot, and a manager caught us in the locker room. He was screwing me on top of the lunch table. It was pretty funny, him with his big fat ass and his pants down around his feet. He was a nice guy, though. He tried to make them keep me but he was lucky not to get fired too. Getting kicked out wasn't so bad, but they told my family and my father threw my ass out of the house. So what was I supposed to do? Starve? That's when I moved in with Lech."

"Lech?"

"Yeah. He's a Polack. At least he says he is. He's a rough bastard. That I can tell you. He's the one who gave me these." She indicated the bruises. "He shouldn't do that. Customers don't like it when you're all beat up. You're running from the cops, aren't you?"

"What makes you say that?"

"Oh, come on. A room in a hotel costs fifty marks. You gave me two hundred. Somebody's after you. Anyway, I can tell. I can smell it. You're always kind of looking over your shoulder. Even sitting here."

"You mind if I stay?"

She shrugged. "You paid your money. You might as well enjoy yourself." She came over and straddled my knees, running her hand between my legs, stroking me. "See, he's getting it on."

I lifted her up. "Look. Thanks a lot. But I'm really tired. I'd just like to sleep."

She stood beside me, the provacative thrust of her body gone, slumping. "Jesus, you must be queer or something. Nobody's ever turned me down before."

"Yeah. I didn't want to say it. You know? I'm queer."

She nodded, grinning a little. "Okay. You can sleep in bed with me if you like."

"No, thanks."

He must have been very quiet when he came in. I'd slept lightly, half-dozing, waking with the early northern light, then dropping off into a deep half-coma around four. He slapped me across the face, open-handed, and I came up out of the chair in a crouch, focusing on him a split second too late. The punch caught me on the jaw. A right which he pulled or it would have taken my head off.

"Lech! Cut it out. He's nothing but a *Tunte*. He needed a room. The cops are after him." She was out of bed, wearing a cotton nightgown, looking about twelve, grappling with the pimp, a big Slavic-looking type in a black leather jacket, pink pants and pointed yellow shoes. His hair hung down to his shoulders like a sixties hippie, but he had the face of a three-time loser working on his fourth fall. He slapped the girl, backhanded, knocking her across the room. "I thought I told you no all-night stands, you little bitch. You, get up. How much have you got? Hand it over."

"I'm broke."

"Broke. Like shit you are. Hand it over, or I'll beat it out of you."

He grabbed me by the shirt and pulled me up against him. Garlic, sweat and male perfume mixed with his own stale animal odor. I brought my right knee up into his groin, closing a hand over his mouth to stifle the scream as he went down on his knees. I moved back and kicked him in the jaw as the girl got up, wiping blood off her mouth. The wad of bills was in his hip pocket. I peeled off three hundred marks and handed the rest to her.

"There must be four thousand there. Why don't you get the hell out? Get dressed and leave. He won't come around for a few minutes."

She stared at the money and threw it on the table, dropping to the floor, taking the pimp's head in her arms, cradling him like a baby.

I walked down the Kurfuerstenstrasse toward the main railroad station. Sweepers in orange uniforms moved slowly behind the sanitation department trucks, brooms made of bundles of long twigs flicking under the parked cars, turning the streets into neat, unsullied rivers of gray filling up with the kind of people who get up at five a.m. Waiters in cafes. Bus drivers. Maids. Factory workers on the early shift. Men who opened the doors in office buildings. Cops.

I took the S-Bahn, the city's elevated train system. Nobody was on the car but me. It was almost six when I got off at the Wannsee station and started walking toward the border crossing point at Drewitz Dreilinden. They'd be waiting at the airport, having checked the flight list, and have realized by now that I wasn't going to show. The machine would go into action any minute now, closing all routes out of the city. I had an hour, maybe two. There were already four or five people standing along the road with signs. Hannover. Hamburg. Saarbruecken. I unfolded the poster I'd stripped off the station wall and wrote "Frankfurt" on the back. Underneath I pencilled in "Will pay for gas." Fifteen minutes later a two-CV Citroen, a car the Germans call "the duck" because of its ungainly shape, pulled over. A young beard leaned out.

"You're willing to pay for the gas?"

"Yes."

"Get in. It won't cost you much. This thing runs on air and spit."

We went through the East German border crossing without incident, paying the five marks for a transit visa and heading into the strangely different country-side of the East. "What's an American doing hitch-hiking?"

"I'm on vacation. My money started giving out."

"Where's your luggage?" He was in his mid-twenties, wire-rimmed glasses, T-shirt with Yale stencilled on the front and Harvard on the back, and Levis. Classic German student type.

"I left it in Frankfurt. Just came up for the day to see the wall."

"What work do you do?"

"I sell cars."

"What kind?"

"Used."

"You speak good German."

"A lot of Americans do."

"Really? I thought nobody spoke anything but English."

"No. Spanish. Vietnamese. We've got a lot of immigrants."

"So you're really German. You must be a Jew. A lot of German Jews went to America. That's why you speak German."

I stared out the window, trying again to figure out what it was that made the countryside different from its mirror image in West Germany. The colors seemed somehow dimmer, the green less rich, the trees more scraggly. It was all in my head, of course. What was different were the houses and villages, scabrous from lack of plaster, unpainted and unkempt.

"No. I'm not Jewish."

"What do you think of Germany?"

"It's very prosperous. In the West, anyway."

"Yes. The East has had a tough time. They paid for all of us. The Russians have looted over here for forty years. We're trying to help them now. With loans and gifts. Did you know that?"

"Yes." The kid wasn't going to shut up. Still, the first law of hitch-hiking was to let the driver talk. It was his nickel.

"Tell me. Why is America so imperialistic? Why do you keep trying to dominate other countries?"

"Like?"

"Nicaragua. Chile. I mean, I know, of course. It's money. Your big business controls their regimes and loots them. But why do your people permit it?"

"You think we're trying to dominate Germany?"

"Of course. You need us to fight the next war for you. But you know that. Your plans call for the war to be fought on German soil. That's why you put the rockets here. You want to fight the Russians on our land and not on yours."

"You think the Russians would go for that? I mean, if we laid down rockets on them from Europe, you think they wouldn't attack the United States?"

He looked impatient, as if dealing with a particularly dense young child. "You read your own propaganda. You Americans are naive. You don't understand world politics. Your government can wrap you around its little finger. Make you believe anything."

I had given up arguing with European intellectuals a decade earlier, particularly Germans. They lived in a world of stereotypes, misinformation and prejudices, all wrapped around Marxist concepts poured into them in their schools and universities.

"You're a Marxist?"

"Of course. Isn't everybody? His view of society provides the analytical insights necessary to arrive at a correct view of the sociopolitical world. Without his guidelines, you become lost in a sea of capitalist propaganda and consumerist advertising."

I stifled a yawn. Years ago I'd gone to the British museum and stood next to the desk the bearded old eccentric had sat at while ripping a thousand-year-old social system to shreds. It was his cathedral.

"If you get tired, I'll be glad to help with the driving. I've got a German driver's license."

"No, thanks. I hate this miserable piece of junk, but I love to drive. All Germans love to drive." He sat straight in his seat, hands at ten and two, accelerator flat on the floor, pushing the bouncing little box along at a hundred and ten klicks an hour, ten over the GDR speed limit. "When I get a job, I'm going to buy a new Audi Quattro. It'll do two hundred."

I worked it out in my head. A hundred and thirty miles an hour.

"Were you in Vietnam?"

"No."

"Oh." He sounded disappointed. "I've never met anybody who was. I've always wondered how anybody could participate in that criminal war."

"They got drafted. Or they thought they were saving South Vietnam from oppressive communist tyranny." I was exhausted. If the clown would shut up I could sleep.

"Communist tyranny! You Americans are such simplistic people. They were fighting for their freedom."

"Yeah. I read somewhere about a million of them got into boats and left after the North Vietnamese took over."

"The capitalist classes, of course. The regime was taking their money and dividing it among the poor. The same thing happened in Cuba. The rapacious, unproductive classes were driven out."

"What are you studying?"

"Chemical engineering. I'm in a program with Hoechst." Hoechst was the biggest chemical concern in Germany. "I might eventually go to America. They have a big factory complex in," he hesitated, "South Carolina? Does that sound right?"

"Yeah. A lot of Germans are investing in the United States. Especially in the South. No unions."

"Yes. It's criminal. Good German capital fleeing abroad when it should be here building our own industry." He wore down after a while, and I dropped off to sleep, coming awake as we approached the border, the ubiquitous wall enclosing us again, following the road to the control points. "Impressive."

"What?"

"The Wall. Must cost a lot of money to maintain. What is it? Eight hundred miles long from the Baltic to the Adriatic. Lights, guns, dogs, guards."

"You know why it was built, of course?"

"Tell me about it." We'd gone through the final checkpoint now, entering the neat, well-manicured landscape of West Germany, moving into the outskirts of the industrial city of Braunschweig.

"Western propaganda. People in the East were bombarded day after day by consumerist advertising portraying some sort of paradise in the West. Three hundred thousand East Germans were leaving every month. They had to do something."

"Yeah. I heard a joke about it. Erich Honecker, the maximum leader, fell in love with a pretty girl, but she wouldn't have anything to do with him. He bought her furs, jewelry, everything, but the answer was still no. Finally he asked what he had to do to win her favors."

"I know the joke," he said, staring at me with intense hostility. "'Take the wall down, Erich,' she said and he replied, 'You little devil. You just want to be alone with me.' Very funny. You sound like a reactionary."

"No, I was just thinking of the difference. In the East they build walls to keep people in. In the United States we're having to build walls to keep people out."

He pulled the car over and reached across me to open the door. "Get out."

"I owe you for the gas."

"Get out, you reactionary fascist pig."

I walked a couple of hundred yards to a bus stop and caught one headed for the center of the city. A couple of kilometers further along I saw the little Citroen pulled over surrounded by three West German police cars, the young beard spread-eagled against the vehicle, face white with fear.

At the Bahnhof I caught the first train south, getting off in Kassel. I bought a cheap suit, a clean shirt, tie and some shaving gear at a big, sleazy department store. Armed with a little blue canvas travelling bag, I'd ceased to be an American and blended into the plastic-clad German lower middle class. I caught a milk train to Bad Godesberg, a suburb of the federal capital in Bonn, and walked from the railroad station across the picture-book town down to the Rhine. The river here is wide and deep, a great trench of water draining west central Europe from Switzerland to the North Sea. A bicycle path follows the shore for fifteen kilometers to Bonn. I walked along it to the Hotel Dreesen, an antique hostelry which had been one of Hitler's favorites. The owner and namesake had served with him in the Great War.

It was here in 1934 that he spent the early evening hours before boarding a plane for Munich to begin the Night of the Long Knives ending in the murder of SA chief Ernst Roehm, former Chancellor Schleicher and dozens of other enemies and former friends. And it was to the Dreesen that British Prime Minister Neville Chamberlain came in 1938 to offer Czechoslovakia as a sacrifice to "peace in our time."

The old hotel had fallen on hard times, catering in shabby splendor to travelling salesmen, the overflow from the American Embassy guesthouse up the road, and a few Nazi nostalgics. In the afternoon its faded public rooms fill with retirees from the town, drinking tea and playing bridge.

I had no trouble getting a room. Nobody asked for my identity documents. I dialed the number of the SOFOL GMBH in Frankfurt. It took twenty minutes to get through three layers of snotty secretaries to his private office.

"My name is Alec Thompson. I'd like to speak to Herr von Kollwitz. He received my letter from Berlin today."

"What is the purpose of your call, Herr Thompson?"

"Personal."

"You are a friend of Director von Kollwitz?"

"No."

"Then I'm afraid I will have to take your name and call you back."

"That won't be possible. You check with him. Tell

127

him it's about von Bursian. I'll call back in five minutes."

I had a third-floor corner room with a view of the Rhine and the Siebengebirge rising from its opposite shore, dark blue, almost black mountains, harboring the Teutonic ghosts of Wagner and Nietzsche. Down below, two waiters from an Italian restaurant up the road were smoking cigarettes in the sun, waiting for the evening rush. Across the way, in front of a large bay window three floors down, a girl of about fourteen banged away at a grand piano playing what might once have been a Bach étude. She had the touch of a blacksmith.

The second time around the secretary put me through.

"Herr von Kollwitz?"

"Yes."

"My name is Thompson. You got my letter?"

"Yes. What is it that you want?"

"I think we should get together. Talk a little."

"Why?"

"It is in both our interests."

"You don't intend to pass this information you have on to the Israelis?"

"Not if we can reach a satisfactory agreement."

He waited so long I thought the connection was broken.

"You know Weber, of course."

"Yes."

"He will pick you up. Give me an address."

There was a map of the region in a plastic cover on the table in front of me. "Bad Nauheim. In the Bahnhof. Give me an hour to get there."

"Very well."

# Chapter 8

It wasn't far. The inter-city train got me there in twenty minutes. Weber was waiting on the platform, taking up space. He grinned when he saw me, sticking out a big paw. "We meet again, Herr Thompson."

"Yeah."

He led me through the station to the big Mercedes standing in front of a no parking sign. "Where are we going?"

"Bad Durkheim. The director spends his summers there." He glanced across at me. "You know, Herr Thompson, I have not yet decided about you."

"Decided what?"

"Whether you are a very smart and very brave man or a cretin."

"Yeah. Well, when you find out let me know. Meantime, why don't you shut up and drive?"

It took a couple of hours on back roads. Bad Durkheim lay in the middle of one of those forests you come across occasionally in Germany. Massive tree trunks, black with age, the sky obliterated by the lowering dark green canopy, the feeling of some unknown spiritual menace as you walk through the ca-

129

thedral-like silence. There's a name for it. The *Urwald*. The primeval forest. Somewhere near here in 9 A.D. the Roman consul Publius Quintilius Varus and the second legion were surrounded and decimated by hordes of painted Teutons suddenly erupting from the menacing silence. We emerged from the forest into the formal gardens of the hotel, a four-story structure dating from before the First World War. The Kurpark was German elegance at its most understated. Weber parked the Mercedes and led me into a large marble-floored lobby covered with Persian rugs. Mahogany panelling and lush beige drapes alternated along the walls with windows overlooking the gardens.

"This way."

The elevator was the only thing about the hotel that had changed since it was built. It moved on a silent cushion to the fourth floor where Weber opened the door to a private suite with an odd-looking triangular key. He led me into a large living room overlooking the gardens and motioned me toward a chair. "Wait."

The sun was dying among the trees in the distance, casting a faint yellowish glow over the gardens, converting green to deep purple. A few aging couples strolled the paths, stopping occasionally to chat, moving on in slow motion against a background dappled like a Monet painting of the late period.

"Dr. Thompson?"

"Herr von Bursian?"

He bowed slightly, a tall man, still slim, with a big head and a mass of blond hair going gray at the temples. His picture did not do him justice. He was strikingly handsome in the manner of German actors of the thirties. A less fleshy Curt Juergens.

"You don't have a drink? Weber is atrocious. What would you like? Sherry perhaps? I have a superb manzanilla from my vineyard near Jerez."

"Sure."

130

He poured the pale, greenish-yellow wine and raised his glass. "Your health, Dr. Thompson."

"Yours."

He laughed. "I assumed you must have a sense of humor. Most intelligent people do, though, I must admit, some of the academics I have known are exceptions."

"To the humor or the intelligence?"

"Perhaps both, Dr. Thompson. But you are clearly a rather exceptional member of the breed. I'm afraid in your case I have made the mistake of the aging. I tend to underestimate younger adversaries. A dangerous complacency."

I sipped the wine which was so dry it curled the edges of my tongue. "Nice wine."

"It is said to combine the fierceness of the southern Spanish sun with the harshness of the soil, distilling some of the essence of the Iberian soul."

"Yeah."

"You will pardon my discursiveness, Dr. Thompson, but before we get down to business, I have to know a little about you. You have suggested in your letter a payment of one hundred thousand dollars, a modest sum, as you point out, by my standards. You guarantee that it will be the one and only payment. You will forgive me for being sceptical. The history of such, ah, affairs is that the *demandeur* returns again and again to the source."

"Only if he's stupid."

"And you are not."

"No." I finished the wine. "I figure if you get irritated you'll kill me and take your chances."

"Why not immediately and get it over with?"

"I've got proof of who you are stashed away. You kill me, it goes to Cassierer. You know who he is, don't you? The old Israeli who's been on your tail?"

He nodded. For a man in his early sixties he had a

superb jawline. Probably worked out every day and watched his weight. "Go on."

"I figure it's in your interest to pay me the first time. It's not a lot of money, and if it takes me off your back for good, you've gotten off cheap. If not," I shrugged. "You haven't lost much. You can find somebody a little more efficient than Weber to knock me off."

"An excellent analysis of my options, Dr. Thompson." He glanced at his watch. "Forgive me. You must be hungry. I suggest we take a ten-minute walk through the forest to an old Gasthaus just over the hill there. I've arranged for it to stay open late tonight. We can talk there without being interrupted. Also the food is much better than in the hotel."

It was almost dark outside. We walked out of the hotel grounds onto a small path running through the forest. "The gasthaus is an old hunting lodge which belonged to the local duke. Quite colorful. Its original owner used it for trysts with local farm girls. As you probably know, in the middle ages the nobility had certain rights over their peasants."

"*Droit de seigneur*," I said, controlling the urge to look over my shoulder. Weber seemed to have disappeared.

"Yes. In any event this duke, von Gehardus was his name, I believe, carried this right to impressive extremes. He was rightly known as the 'father of his people' until one day he chose the wrong girl."

"What happened? She give him the clap?"

The laugh was unexpected. It boomed through the trees, ricocheting amid the emptiness. "Very good, Thompson. I knew it would be a rewarding evening. No. Not the clap. But as he prepared to mount this particular filly, her peasant lover buried an ax in his skull. The duke's son then slaughtered some two hundred of his comrades and impaled them along this road."

"There's new research to the effect that this so-called privilege was looked upon as a fairly wearing duty by the nobles. The peasant girls all lined up eagerly to participate."

"Revisionist historians should be abolished, Dr. Thompson. They take all the fun out of life. Myths are much more satisfying than reality. Here we are."

He was right. The gasthaus was charming, an old rectangular log building with green shutters and a steeply pitched, shingled wooden roof with dormer windows. A stream ran alongside it, past an old unused mill, the wheel turning uselessly, unattached to the heavy stone.

The owner was waiting for us by the stream. He bowed to von Bursian without obsequiousness. "*Herzlich willkommen, Herr von Kollwitz.* Would you perhaps like to start with a trout tonight?"

Von Bursian turned to me questioningly.

"Sure."

We watched as he unhooked a circular net on a long pole and leaned over the stone wall, staring into the dark stream, reaching in and deftly pulling out a fish. "Excellent specimen," he said, dropping it into a bucket at his side and repeating the process.

"With a little butter, Herr von Kollwitz. Nothing more."

"Yes. And as a main course that venison steak you do so well with the cherries."

Von Bursian led the way into the deserted inn to a table by an ancient fireplace which took up most of one wall. "It's much more *gemuetlich* in winter with a roaring fire and filled with people. But then one can't have everything, can one, Dr. Thompson?"

"You seem to be doing a pretty fair job."

"It was not always so, I can assure you. For the first five years after the war, when I was finishing my studies, I worked in construction. As a laborer. Ex-Waffen SS officers had few usable skills, as you can imagine." He looked down at his hands, the skillful

133

care unable to conceal the scarred and muscled remnants of hard work.

"Tell me, Dr. Thompson, what is it exactly that you propose?"

"Cassierer hired me to find the members of the Orpheus Circle. I've figured out a way to do it. So far I've got you and two others. Von Kuester and von Erlangen. In a couple of weeks I can probably dig out most of the rest."

"Von Kuester is dead. Prostate cancer three years ago."

I shrugged. "There must be plenty more who aren't."

"How did you do it?" He lit a pipe and leaned back to listen as I explained the process. He obviously knew a lot about computers.

"You're right. It's relatively simple once you've worked out the process. Of course very few people would combine your unique knowledge of the Nazi era, intimacy with the Berlin Document Center files and a working knowledge of computers."

"I had some luck."

"And, as Cassierer said, some rapport with the people you were looking for. Do you feel no particular pangs of conscience at selling out, Dr. Thompson? You are, after all, betraying a trust Cassierer has placed in you. And you are allowing a Nazi monster to escape punishment. Also, your own government is clearly interested in the information. Are you not, in a way, a traitor?"

The gasthaus owner had brought a tray with twelve glasses of white wine in thimble-sized glasses ranged in two rows. I looked at von Bursian. "Take your choice, Thompson. He has one of the finest collections of German wines in the country. Try each one and take your pick."

I sampled the wine, nibbling a chunk of black bread

between sips. They ranged from the heavy sweetness of a Beerenauslese to a wine almost as dry as the sherry he had served me earlier. I picked a medium dry which reminded me vaguely of a Puligny Montrachet.

"Excellent choice," von Bursian said. "A Mosel which will go well with the trout. If you will permit me to order the red for the venison? I know the cellar here quite well. We'll have the Château Malescot St. Exupéry, Hans. The '81." He turned back to me. "It's a young wine, full of tannin, but it will not allow the venison to dominate it. Well, Thompson, why?"

"I don't feel any particular loyalty to our CIA. Their interest in you is political, not moral. They won't punish you. They'll let you swing in the wind and use the information they've got to blackmail you and other high-ranking German functionaries into doing their bidding. All things being equal, I don't have any problem with that. But they aren't offering me money. You will. As for Cassierer." I shrugged. "He's analyzed my character and decided he knows where I'm coming from. If he made a mistake, that's his problem. We've got an expression in America. An honest man is one who stays bought. But you've got to pay a fair price. Cassierer knew his previous researcher was killed, I assume by Weber and his boys, and he neglected to pass on this little piece of news to me."

"So you have rationalized your treachery?"

I shrugged.

"How do I know you won't treat me the same way?"

"You don't. Like I say, you can always kill me."

The owner brought the trout, skinned and boned, filmed in clarified butter. It had the consistency of mousse, the delicate flavor sealed in by the quick heat, pointed up by the slightly sour country butter.

"Superb, no?"

"Yeah."

"You realize, of course, Dr. Thompson, that I do not consider myself a criminal?"

"Most of your countrymen wouldn't either. Just a victim of circumstances."

"When I joined the Waffen SS in the nineteen thirties it was an elite combat unit, one where you could make a name. I left one of the most prestigious military units in the German army to join, the Ninth Regiment of Potsdam. You've heard of it, no doubt?"

I nodded. "The present German president, von Weizsaecker, was in it. And a lot of other upper-class Germans who are important in your government and business classes today."

"Yes. We of the Ninth are accused of being a club."

"Do they know you? I mean, do they know that von Kollwitz is von Bursian?"

"A few do. Men who knew me in the regiment. Old comrades. You must understand. Nobody regards having been in the Waffen SS as a disgrace. It was a combat organization, nothing more. After all, both von Weizsaecker and the former chancellor, Helmut Schmidt, served six years in the German army during the war, mostly at the front, and nobody ciriticizes them. We in the Waffen SS had nothing to do with the Allgemeine SS atrocities in the camps."

"What about Einsatztruppe B?"

Von Bursian put down his wine glass and met my eyes. He suddenly looked very tired. "Yes. There is that. I will try to explain. It was the winter of Stalingrad. Already things were going badly. We had not been able to take either Leningrad or Moscow. The Russians, after falling back for thousands of miles and losing millions of men and most of their materiel, had not surrendered. On the contrary, resistance was beginning to stiffen. We had spread our forces too thinly, at Hitler's insistence. Deep in the Caucasus an entire army wandered through the endless steppes in a pointless campaign ordered by the Fuehrer. Before Moscow, masses of troops were mired down in a modern form of trench warfare. We had reached our limits. And still the orders came to attack. Our nerves were frayed. In the rear resistance was mounting. You cannot perhaps conceive of what it was like, Dr. Thompson. Suddenly, a dozen or so bearded, ragged spectres would emerge from the forest, wild-eyed savages, firing primitive submachine guns or perhaps hunting rifles and shotguns. Then they would disappear into the endless woods." He paused, light blue eyes staring into the past.

"Sometimes they would capture a straggler and take him into the forest. We would find them occasionally, some still alive, tortured, castrated, tongues nailed to tables. You understand me, Thompson?"

"Yeah. The Vietnamese did the same thing."

"And did you take prisoners?"

"Not many."

"Exactly."

"The Einsatztruppe didn't kill resistance fighters. They shot harmless Jewish civilians. Women and children."

"I do not defend myself, Thompson. I seek only understanding. It was wrong to do what we did. I was badly wounded, ordered to the unit to recuperate. I had a vague idea of what was going on. You must believe me. We were all sickened by the senseless slaughter. I was not an anti-Semite. On the contrary. I was horrified at the Nazis offending one of the most effective and patriotic portions of our population. Anyone who had read German history knew the role Bleichroeder played in furthering Bismarck's plans to unite Germany. One of my father's friends was a banker, an officer in the First World War, Iron Cross First Class. I knew him well. He gave us children candy when we came to the bank. He was the only Jew I ever knew as a child."

The owner brought the venison, cut it into strips, and served it with sour cherries and potatoes in a heavy cream sauce. Von Bursian lifted the red wine and examined it against the light. "Not the very best Bordeaux, of course. The French would never sell their best. They drink that themselves. Quite rightly. But extremely good. To a successful completion of our affair, Dr. Thompson." He touched my glass with his, careful to hold it by the stem so the crystal rang with a clear ping.

He was right. The wine was superb. I can live without venison, but the gasthaus owner knew his business. He had cooked it so that it retained its juices while losing some of the heavy gamy flavor.

"There is, of course, another problem, Dr. Thompson."

"Yeah. What?"

"You are capable of discovering others among the Orpheus Circle. How do I know that you won't attempt to, shall we say, sell them this information as well?"

"You don't."

He leaned back, warming the wine with his big hands. "Very well, Thompson. I will pay you one hundred thousand dollars for your silence about me. It will take several days to accumulate that amount of cash. How do you wish it paid?"

I gave him the number of a German bank account I'd opened that day in Bad Godesberg. "Pay it into that account. When do you think you can do it?"

"Today is Friday. Perhaps by Tuesday. Wednesday at the latest." He hesitated. "I think I should tell you that you are in considerable danger."

"Who from? Aside from the usual suspects."

"In order to stop you, I alerted a friend in the *Bundesnachrichtendienst*. An old comrade."

"Orpheus Circle?"

"Yes. He arranged for the SEK attack on the document center. He has also ordered one of his elimination teams to kill you."

"Call him off."

"It's not as simple as that. He used official cutouts to pass along his orders so that they could not be traced back to him. Needless to say, after the abortive attack on the center the Americans are furious. A big investigation is under way to find out who authorized it. They will sooner or later find out about the order to the team and annul it. In the meantime, you are at extreme risk."

"Thanks."

"Our self-interests coincide, Thompson. Otherwise I would cheerfully see you dead."

"Yeah. I guess I feel the same way about you."

He laughed and lifted the wine glass to toast me. "What will you do?"

"Run."

# Chapter 9

Next morning Weber dropped me at the Frankfurt-am-Main railroad station. I caught a taxi to the restaurant my former wife had picked. It was in a private house on a tree-lined street in the suburbs. To get in you had to punch a button and wait for a myrmidon to come out and open the iron gate. I was led through a couple of glass doors thick enough to be bulletproof, past a small bar, all white plastic and glass, into one of the three small dining rooms.

Facing the entrance beyond the bar was a full-sized painting of the place's inspiration, Cyrano de Bergerac, rapier at the ready, long nose pointed insolently up as he contemplated his next victim.

"Dr. Thompson?"

"Yes."

"This way, sir."

His English was impeccable. Everything about the place was impeccable. Glistening crystal, each glass obviously polished individually, linen so white it hurt to look at it. The maître d'hotel turned out in a morning coat and striped pants like a court lackey or a funeral director. Four German businessmen were at a table in the corner and two Arabs leaned toward each other at another. Marianne was alone in the second room, bent over a folder, blond hair tumbling about her face. She's a classic WASP. Translucent skin, high cheekbones, blue eyes set wide apart around an aquiline nose.

"Hi."

"Alec! God, how good to see you." She stood up and kissed me, her slim body pressed against me, arms around my neck. It had been a long time. I'd almost forgotten the effect she had on me. She leaned back, grinning. "Well, at least he hasn't forgotten me. How are you? You look like the wrath of God."

"Okay. And you?"

"Busy as a one-armed paperhanger with the hives." It had been one of my favorite expressions, one she had hated. "I'm trying to get some of our European affiliates to adopt our techniques. It's like pulling teeth without anesthetic. They're worse male chauvinist pigs than Americans. At home, once you get their hands out from under your skirt, you can usually manage to talk seriously. Over here anybody who doesn't look like the ass end of a cow is clearly a dumb bimbo."

"I'm sure you got their attention."

She laid a hand on mine. "Still pissed?"

"No."

"I miss you. You know that?"

"Sure. I miss you, too."

"It's not exactly what I expected."

"What?"

"You know. Success. Power. The whole schmear. Also, I seem to run into clones of the same male."

"What are the symptoms?"

"Oh, intellectual arrogance, unphysical aggressiveness, compulsively verbal, the need to be mothered."

141

"Well, at least it's different."

She laughed. "Yeah. You won't believe it but I miss that goddamn stony Indian silence of yours sometimes. And your body. Your goddamn body. I'm tired of soft men with no edges."

"Bad love affair?"

"No. That is, a series of unsatisfactory 'relationships.' Christ, I hate that word. What about you?"

I shrugged. "Nothing permanent."

"Still working on Nazis?"

"Yeah. And you?"

"We're into fashion at the moment. You know. What makes a woman buy a short skirt one year and a long one the next? We're finally digging into their psyches, getting away from all the superficiality, really trying to relate fashion to inner problems. The Europeans think we're nuts."

The waiter hovered over us in low-keyed obsequiousness. "This is a great restaurant, Alec. For God's sake, have something besides steak."

I closed the menu. "You order for me." She looked up, the flicker of annoyance I knew so well crossing her face.

"A steak au poivre, rare, for Dr. Thompson. I'll have the trout amandine. And a bottle of Sancerre. You don't mind drinking white, do you?"

I grinned. "Why don't we cut that polite horseshit, Marianne? You want something. What?" She fiddled with the silver, lifting her lovely blue eyes finally and locking on me.

"What I said earlier is true. I miss you, you son-of-a-bitch. I miss the cynicism, the toughness, the humor, the sensuality, the softness. I even miss the goddamned stubborness. I want to give it another try."

"I don't think you'd be able to hack Santa Cruz."

"You know I'm not talking about going to Santa Cruz. You could get a job in New York. You've had two books published. You could get something paying twice as much as that grubby college. In journalism or editing."

The waiter came with the wine and started to pour into my glass. I motioned him across to Marianne, and he stopped after a couple of drops and moved to her glass. She sipped it impatiently and nodded to him. "Will you cut the crap?"

"You're paying, aren't you? You'd better be. I'm broke."

"Nothing much changes, huh?"

"No."

"Well?"

"Well, what?"

"What about New York?"

"Look. We've been over it all before. It won't work. In theory, I don't mind being kept. In fact, I can't handle it. You're a twentieth-century woman. Competent, logical, a straight-line thinker. You see life in terms of concrete goals and you go for them. Anything, or anybody, who gets in your way, you eliminate. It's great. I admire you. I lust after you. You're right. I'm probably one of the few men who can handle you. But only because you can't dominate me. If I moved in with you we'd last a month."

The waiter served the food with understated elegance, carefully positioning the Gascon crest at the top of each plate in the best French style. The steak was excellent. Across from me Marianne ate with her usual intensity, occasionally glancing at her watch. "You in a hurry?"

She grinned at me over a forkful of trout, eyes merry. "My plane isn't until six." We skipped the coffee and she slipped her arm through mine as we left the restaurant, leaning her body against me. "Christ, I miss you. We have to do this more often." The iron gate clicked behind me as they moved in. O'Brien and two others, big men, walking on their toes.

"Shit."

"What's the matter?"

"Dr. Thompson, I'm afraid you'll have to come with us."

Marianne looked from me to him, pale in the late afternoon sun. "What the hell is going on? Who are these thugs?"

"Friends. I'm going to have to take a raincheck, love. See you on your next trip to Europe." I followed O'Brien and the other two to a big BMW double-parked in front of the restaurant. Marianne stared after me, fists on her hips.

"You took your time, asshole," O'Brien said. "Give us any more trouble, and this time we break some bones."

They drove through back streets to a small gate on the military side of the Frankfurt airport. We came out onto a circular parking area for small planes. An Air Force C-12 in the new camouflage configuration was parked at the end. An hour later the little plane circled over the center of Berlin, preparing for a landing at Templehof Airport, the former main terminal in the city, now an almost-deserted U.S. military airport. It is a huge building, one of the few major projects planned by Hitler and Speer which was actually built. Its massive, lowering sprawl sits empty now except for a few offices used by the U.S. Air Force, the whole thing maintained in a state of readiness in case the Russians close off the land routes and we need it to replay the airlift that saved the city in 1948-49.

"Jesus Christ, what the fuck is going on?" O'Brien was staring down at masses of people milling about the terminal in front of tents and stands.

"Air Force Open House, sir," one of the thugs said. "They open the airport every year so the Berliners can come and visit. Bring in a couple of C-141s for them to look at. Good public relations."

O'Brien made his way up to the pilot's cabin, and then came back to stand in front of me. "Look. We can't get close to the terminal, and I can't get hold of anybody to authorize a car. The whole fucking base is out there serving hamburgers. You got a choice. We put you in irons." He held out a pair of handcuffs. "Or you give me your word you won't make trouble."

"Sure. You got my word." I was beginning to think a new age of chivalry had begun. Either that or the United States was being secretly infected with British public-schoolboy morality.

"We'll walk through the crowd and pick up my car at the main gate."

The plane parked a couple of hundred yards out from the milling throngs of Berliners crowded around hamburger and hotdog stands, riding on the carnival machines and drinking beer. The two thugs walked beside me, occasionally bouncing against my shoulders to let me know they were there. O'Brien brought up the rear, right hand ostentatiously in the pocket of his fashionably aged beige Burberry. We were elbowing our way through the crowd toward an exit when I saw Scottie and two of his friends with mugs of beer leaning against one of the C-141s. He saw me at the same time, took in the situation and slid over to cut us off. The thugs were moving people out of the way now, muscling through the jammed masses.

Scottie planted himself in front of the one on the left, grinning a drunken grin, not moving as the muscle boy put his shoulder in to him. "Hey, man. Take it easy. You in a hurry? Get yourself a beer."

"Move it, soldier. Now." The beer shot up out of the glass as if somebody had jolted Scottie's arm and splashed into the muscle's face. A knee came out of somewhere and caught the other one in the groin. I looked back only once to see O'Brien sprawled on the ground, clawing at his pocket, then the crowd closed behind me.

The massive terminal forms a semicircle, overlooking the parking area for the planes and the runways beyond. Entryways were roped off and Air Force MPs were scattered around the area. Dead ahead a VIP lounge at ground level received a steady stream of visitors showing pink invitation cards. I moved in line and slipped past the MP who turned to shout after me. "Sir. Your invitation, please."

It looked like a dead end for a minute until I spotted the door at the back where a stream of waiters was marching through. The MP had left the entrance and was moving toward me as I went through the door into a long windowless corridor which conformed to the semicircular shape of the building. I stopped and waited for the MP to come through the door, driving a knee into his crotch and bringing it up into his jaw as he jacknifed forward. I let him down just as another bunch of waiters with trays of hors d'oeuvres came around the circle.

*"Was ist los?"*

*"Krank. Ich hohle einen Arzt."* I headed down the corridor at a run looking over my shoulder to see the waiters and food pile up behind me. I tried a couple of doors before one on the right opened onto a circular metal staircase going down into semi-darkenss. At the bottom, illuminated by dim single bulbs at intervals of fifty feet, an ancient narrow-gauge rail line headed off to nowhere. I started to run, the sound of my feet hitting the cobblestoned paving and rattling off the walls. Two hundred yards farther down another iron staircase loomed up on the right. At the top a steel door was clamped shut by a rusted metal bar. I stood back and kicked it twice before it loosened. The door gave off onto a dark tunnel, moving upward toward the light.

I came out into an immense empty room, blinking in the bright light. To my left a huge American flag covered one end of the huge hall, reminding me of the scene in *Patton*. The walls were lined with deserted airline counters for Pan Am, British Airways and Air

France. In the center a massive baggage claim area with its circular baggage runways was empty. To the right, opposite the flag, a wall of doors up one floor led out to the main parking lot of the airport. I raced up the stairs and hit one of the horizontal bars, feeling the door give. As I came out into the parking area the alarm sirens began to scream their distinctive "hee haw" and gates leading from the parking lot into the streets of the city slammed shut. Blue-uniformed Air Force MPs in neat black berets erupted from guard-rooms and headed for emergency posts. I walked across the parking lot to an arcade of post exchange stores and moved along it until I came to an open door leading into what a sign proclaimed to be the base Officers' Club.

"Please, sir. The reception is in the Richthofen room at the top of the stairs. Sorry for the inconvenience. The emergency will be over shortly." He was an earnest young sergeant with thick glasses, looking nervous, directing a mixed group of Germans and Americans up a staircase. I joined them. Ahead of me two Germans discussed a ceremony they had just attended.

"Of course the eagle had a swastika in its claw, Guenter. Don't be ridiculous. This place was built by the Nazis. You think they'd put up an eagle without a swastika?"

"The Americans mean well, Helmut. You can't really blame them. How can they know such things? They just wanted to make a kindly gesture. Return our eagle."

"They are barbarians, Guenter. Barbarians."

"More like children, I would say. Good-hearted, powerful, dangerous children."

I followed the two men into a room packed with German dignitaries, a covey of Air Force colonels and a four-star general who looked as if he might have been in the Second World War. He was staring a little

147

grimly at the photographs depicting the history of the airport. On the back wall hung a huge portrait of Baron von Richthofen, white scarf blowing in the wind, leather flying suit in studied disarray, one foot on the wing of a Fokker triplane. Galland, Germany's most famous Second World War ace, stood in an insolent pose by his ME 109. Nowotny, with over two hundred kills, leaned out of his jet to shake hands with a mechanic. Ten Allied kills were painted on the cockpit of his squat, cigar-shaped jet, the first one to fly in combat.

The four-star motioned to a fleshy colonel with bombardier's wings who scuttled across the crowded room, sweat popping out on his face.

"Sir?"

"What the fuck is this all about?"

"What, sir?"

"This fucking Nazi museum. Who put up all this German horseshit?"

"Sir, we thought it would be nice to have a little history of the airport, sir. For the locals."

"Redwine, you're a fucking moron. This airport was built by Hitler and Speer. It's a goddamn monument to Nazism. What the fuck are you doing celebrating Nazi history?"

"The Germans like it, sir. Shows we're sensitive to their history, sir."

"And that goddamn vulture out front. Is that part of the sensitivity?"

"Sir?"

"The fucking eagle you've got mounted out there. It's the same one that used to be on top of the airport building, isn't it? The one with the big fucking swastika in its claw. I remember seeing the goddamned bird when I flew in here in 1945."

"Yes, sir. But we had the swastika cut off, sir."

"You dumb shit. Where the hell were you during Bitburg?"

148

I slid away as the colonel's face began to crumple in terror as the four-star continued to chew on him in a voice of low, controlled fury. Two of the German guests had bowed formally to the general and were heading for the stairs. I fell in behind them. The sergeant directed us through a bar with a huge television screen showing a fifties western. A young Henry Fonda's head was three feet across. He looked a lot like his daughter. At the door an officer motioned to the guards to open it for us. A large black Mercedes coughed to life and glided up to pick up the two Germans.

I walked up to Mehringdamm and took a taxi.

"Yes, sir?"

"The Meineckehof." I needed time to think. The Meineckehof was a sauna and bathhouse on Hardenbergstrasse, a warren of swimming pools, hot and cold tubs, showers, sun baths and massage rooms. Dozens of Germans strolled around bareassed, worshipping the water god.

I paid fifteen marks, picked up a towel and some soap, and changed in one of the blue-tiled locker rooms. As I walked out, an ancient male moved past me slowly, eyes rheumy, legs bowed, huge belly hanging down over his upper thighs in flaccid folds. Clinging to his arm was an equally ancient lady, paps dry and flat against a bloated stomach, face a mask of lines. Both bareassed.

The sauna was almost empty. An obvious hangover victim, head in his hands, skin the color of silly putty, sat staring at the floor. On the top bench a leggy blonde lay flat, dark pubic mound proclaiming the artificiality of her hair color. She turned on her stomach as I came in, eyes meeting mine for a moment before the heat closed around me.

I followed the ritual. Fifteen minutes in the wood-paneled room with a temperature at the boiling point of water, dry heat, searing your skin, digging into your bones. About seven minutes into it, the girl sat up. She had nice breasts, small, round, uptilted. *"Aufguss?"*

Aufguss means you pour dippers of water onto the hot stones in the sauna, sending up a blast of steam. It doesn't increase the heat, but it parboils anybody within range. The drunk and I nodded, and the girl moved down to the stove, carefully dipping the big wooden spoon into a brass-bound wooden bucket and spreading the pine-scented water on the rocks.

The drunk gave in first, fleeing the heat and diving into the ice-cold tub, wallowing like a walrus, then moving on to the warm pool. I followed him a minute later, feeling the shock of the cold water slam into me as I submerged.

I spent three hours in the sauna and pools, moving the options around in my head. They were not enticing. I had a little over seven hundred marks left. The spooks had neglected to lift either my wallet or my passport. There was only one problem. I couldn't get out of the city. This time they would have sealed it like a bottle. There wasn't going to be any way out. The airport was simple to close. Every passenger had to identify himself as he passed through the control. Trains were easier. I could pay somebody to buy me a ticket. There were no western passport controls. But Xerxes was sure to have every station covered. The highway was still the best bet. The German cops hardly looked at you as you went through the controls at Drewitz Dreilinden. But again, every police booth would have somebody in it looking for me.

I swam fifty laps, driving through the water, wiping the problem out of my mind, feeling my muscles respond, stretching it the last ten, sucking in the air, driving harder and harder until my hand slammed into the pool edge. It was getting dark when I came out. The summer sun reflected yellow and orange off the limestone and plastic of the central city. I walked

150

down Hardenbergstrasse past the Amerika Haus to the underpass under the city's elevated railway tracks. The poster was plastered on a kiosk.

"Wallenstein—a theatrical production in two parts at the National Theater." A famous East German actor was playing the brooding general immortalized by Schiller at the newly repaired theater in the center of the Eastern sector of the city. There were two ways to go East, you took the S-Bahn, the subway connecting the two sectors, and passed through a set of East German controls at Friedrichstrasse or you walked across at Checkpoint Charlie.

They would not be expecting me to go East. Not initially anyway. I would obviously be trying to get back to western Europe where it would be possible to go under in any big city and disappear. Nobody asked for identity documents anymore. The borders were porous. Once out of the Berlin rat-trap, they would have real trouble laying hands on me again. I caught the U-Bahn at Breitscheidplatz and got off at Checkpoint Charlie, the main crossing point for the three occupying powers and all foreigners wishing to enter East Berlin. The procedure was simple. You presented yourself at the border, exchanged twenty-five West German marks at the legal rate of one to one for East German marks, gave up any western literature, newspapers or magazines and you were in the East. The visa was valid for twenty-four hours. If you wanted to stay longer you could get it extended at a tourist office on the Alexanderplatz. The East Germans desperately wanted Western currency. For dollars or West marks, doors opened. Wide.

I strolled down Friedrichstrasse to the three Allied control booths in the center of the street. It was nearing eleven o'clock. The crowds of curious tourists had thinned. The Checkpoint Museum, a collection of devices people had used to escape from the East over

151

the years, was closed. Two couples occupied the platform overlooking the wall into the East. There was no obvious watch on the border. I could step across and be in East Berlin. There was only one problem. The visas ran from midnight to midnight. I was going to have to wait another hour before crossing.

Four blocks from the Checkpoint at the corner of Anhalterstrasse and Stresemannstrasse was one of the city's famous cafes, the Stresemann, named after a Weimar Republic chancellor. Across from it the bombed-out remnants of the Anhalter Bahnhof, the facade of the main building, stood in an empty field. It was in this railroad station that Hitler had greeted his famous guests, Mussolini, Molotov and the groveling leaders of his satellites coming to pay tribute.

The cafe was packed with young German yuppies, self-consciously outfitted in designer jeans, leather jackets and a variety of oddball getups just this side of punk. It was a late-night crowd, young males making a final pitch, the women trying to figure out whether it was worth it, conversations worn out over the course of the evening, leaving people staring off into space waiting for time to pass. I ordered an Asbach Uralt, warming the raw German brandy in my hands. Even in July it gets chilly on the North German plain when the sun goes down.

The cop car pulled up on the pavement in front of the cafe, and four green-uniformed city police got out, stretching, bored. They fanned out across the intersection, stopping pedestrians, politely asking for identity documents, moving on, methodically sweeping the area. I called the waiter and paid for the brandy as they came through the door. The john was in the back across from the kitchen. I headed back and veered left through the swinging doors, almost banging into a waiter.

"Hey, you're in the wrong place. The john's across the hall."

152

"Where's the back door?"

"Cops?" he was a long-haired, dark-skinned youth with a heavy accent.

"Yeah. I haven't got any documents."

"Through the kitchen to the right. It opens into an alley."

Nobody looked up as I threaded my way through the stoves and found the back door, moving into a narrow passageway lined with garbage cans. Another waiter was leaning against the wall with a girl glued to him, right hand up her short leather skirt working rhythmically as she moaned and chewed on his neck. He winked at me as I slipped past them toward the street. The cop car was still parked on the curb. I turned left and headed back to the Checkpoint.

Going across is easy. You follow a fenced-in path to a series of low prefab buildings where you buy a visa and change the required West marks. If you're lucky that's it. You come out through another fence onto Friedrichstrasse and you're in the German Democratic Republic, more familiarly known as East Germany. If you're not lucky, or your name is on a list of people forbidden to enter, you can be held for five or six hours, be strip-searched and, for women, occasionally be subjected to a gynecological exam to make sure you're not smuggling something. I was lucky. It was late. The guard was ready to go off his shift.

"What is the purpose of your visit?"

"Tourism."

"You have a hotel?"

"The Metropol." It was new and glitzy, built for the East Germans by the Swedes. To get a room you had to pay in hard currency.

"You are very late coming over."

"My plane came in late."

"Where is your luggage?"

"The airline managed to lose it in Frankfurt. They said they would deliver it to the hotel when they find it."

153

He stamped the passport and passed it across. "Have a nice visit to the GDR." Behind me a Syrian diplomat and his West German girlfriend began the process. Across the way, in the military-diplomatic lane, an American army bus had pulled up. One of the East German guards circled the bus, checking the so-called flash cards the military held up with their pictures. It was the only control exercised. Pro forma. Neither the Russians nor the three western allies recognized the right of the Germans, East or West, to check them.

I'd spent a lot of time in East Germany, grubbing away in the archives in Berlin, Merseburg and Potsdam, where many records had been moved during the Second World War. You got used to it quickly. The grimness, the lack of light, the fine film of soft coal dust which lay on everything like skin, the pallid, overweight people with bad teeth, plastic clothes, and a mask of anxiety.

I walked up Friedrichstrasse to Unter den Linden, the main boulevard of the city. A block further on, the Metropol, a glass and bronze box, squatted in Teutonic solidity. The desk clerk took my passport, glanced at it, and handed it back. "I'm sorry, sir. You do not have a reservation."

"But I booked it at your tourist agency in West Berlin."

"We have no record of that, sir. And we have no rooms. I regret." His English was good but a little off-key.

I took the passport and inserted a fifty-mark bill in it, passing it back. He looked down at it for a moment, then glanced in either direction without seeming to.

"I believe we might be able to find you something, sir," he said. The passport disappeared and a key took its place. "The bar is open downstairs, sir."

"Thanks." The Metropol basement bar was a hangout for the foreign colony of East Berlin. Western businessmen. Diplomats. Students from third world countries with hard currency. Among its attractions were some of the handsomest Polish and Hungarian hookers in the trade. I went upstairs to my small antiseptic room, knocked back a brandy from the miniature refrigerator and fell asleep, dreaming of O'Brien. At least I think it was O'Brien. He had blond hair, wore a preppy suit and had no face.

# Chapter 10

I WAS IN A CAVE. AT THE END OF IT A SPECK OF LIGHT kept moving away as I ran toward it. But as it grew smaller it also became more intense until I had to turn my head. I came awake with the phone ringing beside the bed, an insistent high-pitched electronic beep, and the morning sun in my eyes.

"Alec?"

"Hello, Kathy. How'd you find me?"

"I'm psychic. How about a coffee?"

"Sure. But not in the hotel. There's a cafe on Unter den Linden. Across from the Soviet Embassy. I'll meet you there in half an hour."

It wasn't far. I turned left after leaving the hotel and walked past the U.S. Embassy to Unter den Linden. The cafe, modern and plastic with a few tables on the sidewalks, walled in by flower boxes on stilts, could have been in the West. Across the way the great beige bulk of the Soviet Embassy occupied most of one side of the broad avenue. A white bust of Lenin dominated the courtyard, and phalanxes of Zil limousines were lined up at an angle in front, guarded by a dozen VOPOs—*Volkspolizei*, the People's Police. The ubiquitous control mechanism of the regime. In the distance the Brandenburg Gate, framing the victory column with its massive golden Valkyrie, was outlined against the summer sky.

"Hello, Alec."

"Hi."

"I ordered mocca." Mocca was the East German code word for real coffee as opposed to the ersatz dishwater which was usually served.

"Who sent you? O'Brien?"

She stared down into the muddy brown coffee.

"Xerxes?"

"Look, Alec, I'm working for them, okay?"

"On contract? Or are you an agent?"

"Sort of a freelance. I started doing it a couple of years ago for kicks. Little things. Nothing dangerous. Then Paul asked me to keep an eye on you. He said what you're doing is damaging to U.S. security. I agree. Raking up all this Nazi business doesn't serve any purpose. All it does is make the Germans unhappy and weaken the alliance. That's exactly what the Soviets want. You know that".

"So this was all an act?"

She looked puzzled. "Oh. You mean us? Yeah, well, sort of." She grinned. "God, men are dolts." She reached over and covered my hand with hers. "I wouldn't have slept with you if I didn't like you. But it wasn't any big deal."

"You'd better go back to West Berlin."

"Why?"

"It's dangerous over here. They must have somebody in Xerxes' organization. They'll pick you up."

"They're not interested in me, Alec. You're the one they want."

"Why me?"

"That archive is full of names of ex-Nazis. Some of them are sure to be on this side of the wall. They might even be pretty high up." The guy with the brown plastic windbreaker at the next table had moved his chair, pushing a plastic bag on the table so that it pointed directly at us. The tip of a small radio antenna peeped through the opening. I paid the bill and took Kathy by the arm.

"Where are we going?"

"On a tour of the city. Don't look back." The brown plastic windbreaker had followed us out of the cafe and was looking in a bookstore window behind us. Ahead, in an identical blue windbreaker, another man moved with apparent aimlessness.

"Oh, shit. That's what Paul was afraid of. They've already made you."

"Yeah."

"What does that mean?"

"They made me by following you across the border. Those two guys were in place when I came up. There was nobody behind me. I doubt if they know who I am."

"Jesus, I'm sorry, Alec. Maybe I can distract them. We'll split. One will follow me. You can shake the other. I'll meet you in the West."

"It's too late."

Two uniformed VOPOs had stopped in front of us. "Your documents, please."

We handed over our passports. They ignored Kathy's, carefully writing down the information in mine, saluting and handing it back.

"Alec, let's get the hell out."

"They've got my name and description. In five minutes it will be on tap at every border post. I'm not going anywhere."

"What will they do?"

"Depends on what they know. They've obviously got somebody on the inside in West Berlin. But he may only know that you do some freelance jobs for the spooks now and then. They may not do anything but

158

follow us around for a while, see what we're do-ing."

"You don't believe that."

"I think you'd better get back. Have they got a way of getting you out if you're burned?"

"No."

"They didn't give you a parachute? The name of somebody in the Embassy to contact if things went sour?"

She shook her head.

"Let's tour the city." We had been walking down the Unter den Linden toward the center of the city. "On our right is the famous equestrian statue of Frederick the Great, once consigned to an empty field, now again enthroned as an enlightened despot and great hero of Prussia. They put it back up last year. On the left, Humboldt University and the tomb of the unknown soldier."

Suddenly out of a side street behind us martial music erupted, followed by a column of East German soldiers in parade uniforms.

"What in God's name is that?" Kathy asked.

"The Rosa Luxemburg Regiment. They guard the tomb of the unknown soldier." We stopped at the base of Frederick the Great's statue and let them pass, impressive troops, all just under six feet, impeccable in hand-tailored parade uniforms, following a band playing with professional skill.

"What are they doing?"

"Every Wednesday there is a changing of the guard ceremony." The troop, five hundred strong, had marched in normal step past the Arsenal and wheeled, in perfect formation, coming back in our direction. As they drew even with the elegant little tomb a sabre-bearing officer shouted *Im Stechschritt, Marsch!* As one, the five hundred men began to goosestep, their jackbooted feet lifting in unison and coming down on

159

the street with the same jangling menace I'd seen in old German newsreels from the thirties.

"I don't believe it," Kathy said. "They've got to be kidding."

"Why? Or maybe a better question is 'why not.' The goosestep was introduced into the Prussian army in the seventeenth century. The Poles, Russians, Chileans and god knows who else still use it. Why not the Germans?"

"Because it calls up an image of Hitler's Thousand Year Reich, you clown. That's why."

"Shall we go to the Pergamon and see all the loot nineteenth-century German archaeologists collected in the Middle East?"

"You're pissed." I could feel her body against me, a muscled firmness. She moved like a cat, not bouncing but flowing.

"No. I'm trying to figure out where the holes are."

"Holes?"

"The bureaucratic mind works with relentless conservatism. Xerxes and O'Brien are trying to shut off my options. Box me in. Force me back into their cage. So they close all the obvious exits, neglecting East Berlin. Obviously nobody on the run would risk coming over here. Once they realized I'd done it, they sent you over, knowing the East Krauts would make you, maybe even making sure they would, and that closes another exit. Forces me back to the West. There's only one problem. If the STASI knows Xerxes wants me, they're going to want to know why."

"You don't think they already know?"

"No. If they did we wouldn't be walking the streets."

We had turned left off the Unter den Linden and circled behind the Arsenal to the Museum Island, a collection of ornate buildings devoted to the booty collected by Germans fanning across the ancient world, playing catch up thievery with the British and French.

"They're still with us. The two guys in the windbreakers. Jesus, they're not very subtle."

"Why should they be? We're not going anywhere."

"Why don't they pick us up?"

"Probably figure we've got a rendezvous with some East German agent. Anyway, that's not the way the game is played. Picking up the other side's agents is a little silly. They just send over more, ones you don't know. Once you've got somebody isolated, you begin to work on him, trying to turn him. Filter phony information back through him. Make the opposition think all its agents are turned. Or some, at least. Sow doubt."

"How do you know all this?"

"Read it in a Le Carré novel." I'd bought tickets to the museum, and we entered the immense room housing the temple of Pergamon. A century ago German archaeologists had dismantled the central temple of a ruined Greek city and brought it back to Berlin piece by piece, reconstructing it faithfully in a specially built museum.

"It's immensely impressive," Kathy said. "And I've seen it at least six times. What are we doing?"

"Killing time."

"Why?"

A busload of U.S. army troops in uniform and a gaggle of civilians poured through the door into the big room. Fifty or so of them, chattering excitedly. "Look, Kathy. Nobody over here is going to do anything to me. I've got something they want. I can probably parlay it into a ticket out. You, on the other hand, are trade goods."

"Trade goods?"

"They probably know you're an amateur, so you can't do much for them. You don't know anything useful. But you could be embarrassing for your own people. They'll probably snatch you and try to make a deal for one of their agents. Xerxes will have to cough up somebody for you."

"So you don't think I can get out?"

"Not the way you came in."

"How?"

"On that army bus."

"No way. They check everybody."

"Fall in with the group." We dropped in at the tail end of the bus group, following them into a room filled with a Roman building stolen from the ancient city of Miletus and on into a long hall mounted with the remnants of Babylon's Ishtar Gate. Ahead of us a tall blonde with hair cut like Kathy's looked up at the endless unicorns marching in eyeless blindness along blue brick walls more than four thousand years old.

"Crowd up against her from the front. Just enough to irritate her. Step on her foot maybe."

Kathy walked around in front of the blonde and stepped back, bumping into her, jamming a foot down on her instep.

"Oh, Christ, I'm so sorry. Did I hurt you?"

The girl bent over to rub her instep. "No. Just broken," she said, grinning up at Kathy. The purse was easy to get into. A little metal catch turned, and I'd slipped the wallet out and into my pocket. She moved away, looking at ancient Babylon.

"You did that like a pro."

"Picking pockets is one of the world's least skilled professions. That and shoplifting."

"What good is it going to do me? She's going to get on the bus and discover her papers are gone and they'll catch me."

I pulled her off to one side, letting the tour group wander past to the Egyptian room. "She won't get back on the bus. And tell those assholes you work for that they either lay off or I'll pass on what I know to the STASI."

"You wouldn't."

"Why not? Turning in a few dozen ex-SS criminals is hardly an act of treason." The army group had turned and started back, young soldiers with crew-cuts, overweight young women and a few, like the young woman whose purse I'd picked, Department of Defense civilians or teachers in the army school system. "Join them, Kathy. Get on the bus. I'll take care of her."

I moved over next to the tall blonde who was laboriously deciphering a German inscription in the Babylonian gate. "It was built in 2500 B.C."

She looked up with the hooded wariness of young women everywhere. Horn-rimmed glasses and no makeup enhanced a look of scholarly plainness. "I saw you trying to figure out how old it was."

"You speak German?"

"Yeah. I'm with the State Department."

"A diplomat?"

"Yeah. I'm stationed at the embassy here. Are you with the tour?"

"I'm a teacher in Wiesbaden. History, political science. We're up for a couple of days. I'd better get back with the tour." The group had moved off toward another wing.

"They're skipping the Arabic stuff upstairs. It's the most interesting part of the museum except for the Roman and Greek ruins. Come on, I'll show it to you. Don't worry about the tour. They'll be here another hour." Kathy's red head disappeared around the corner.

"Well." She looked doubtfully at the disappearing tour group as I took her arm. "I guess it's okay. They treat us like children anyway. And it's a relief to get away from that pompous guide."

"Yeah. It's not the best way to see the city. How long are you going to be in town? I could pick you up and bring you over as a guest and show you some more interesting stuff. My name is Jim Clark."

"Mary Pancoast," she said, holding out her hand. She wasn't so much homely as a little ungainly despite the trim athlete's body she didn't seem to know what to do with. It was clear she wasn't used to men trying to pick her up. She was both scared and intrigued.

"What do you do in the embassy?"

"Political officer. I write reports on what's going on here. You know. The usual stuff. Go to a lot of cocktail parties. Pretty dull, really."

"It sounds romantic."

"Yeah. I guess. This is the Arabic section. The krauts really did a good job of vacuuming up loot all over the Middle East." We moved slowly through rooms full of mosaics, tapestries and sarcophagi, chattering aimlessly. She reminded me of my earnest young graduate students, eagerly soaking up knowledge, extending their horizons, open to any new experience.

"If you like I'll take you to a diplomtic reception. The British national day is on Sunday. They call it the Queen's birthday, but she had that a month or so ago. They celebrate it in the summer so they'll have good weather. They're famous for their strawberries and whipped cream."

"You know, it would be great if you could come down and lecture to one of our classes. All this stuff would be fascinating. The kids are bored stiff."

"Sure." I slipped my arm through hers, letting it brush up against her breast, feeling her quiver almost imperceptibly.

She glanced at her watch. "My God. I'm going to miss the bus." She started to run for the stairs. I followed her through the Ishtar Gate, the Roman and Greek ruins, and down the long passage from the street to the museum. "Oh, Christ, they're gone. They can't be. Now what am I going to do?"

"Hey. Relax. They've got another couple of hours to tour before they go back to the West. We'll pick them up at the Checkpoint at two o'clock. Have lunch with me. I'll drive you back to West Berlin if anything fouls up."

"You really think it will be okay? I mean, they should have counted the people on the bus and be missing one."

"Did you have friends on the bus?"

"No. I came up with a girlfriend but she didn't want to see the East."

"They lose people all the time. You just do what they told you. Go back to the Checkpoint if you get separated."

"Well, if you're sure."

At the restaurant I ordered her a double Polish vodka, ignoring the protests, and a bottle of semi-sweet Meissner wine. The waiters hovered over us in blue tails, serving with the baroque flourish the hotel schools in the East had obviously copied from twenties movies. She wasn't used to drinking. But the waiter kept refilling her glass as she emptied it, and the meal dragged on.

"Maybe we should get the check," she said, glancing nervously at her watch. "It's awfully late."

"Look. Why don't you forget the bus. I'll drive you back over in my car. I've got diplomatic plates. All you have to do is show your passport. That way we can have a leisurely lunch and forget about the time."

"You think? Is that okay?" She was a little tight, the firm line of her lips had loosened, eyes a little unfocussed.

"Sure. We'll call the army transportation people in a few minutes and tell them. No problem. They've got a radio to the bus."

165

"Really? You think it will be all right?"

I paid the check and took her by the arm. "We can call from my room. I'm living in the hotel while they redo my apartment."

She giggled, leaning against me in the elevator. I slipped an arm around her and tipped her face up. Her mouth opened and glued on mine, suddenly frantic, tongue moving across my lips. "I'll call the bus office," I said, disengaging to let us in the room. She disappeared into the bathroom, and I picked up the phone, pretending to dial.

She came out about five minutes later, nude. Like a lot of big women, she looked better without clothes. Suddenly the awkwardness was gone. She was trembling slightly, arms across her breasts. And she was spectacular, big athlete's body suddenly freed. "It's what you wanted, isn't it?" She looked scared.

I crossed the room and took her in my arms, kissing her gently. "You're beautiful."

"No, I'm not. But sometimes I feel like I am. You know what I mean?"

"Yeah."

"Take me to bed." I almost threw my back out again picking her up. "Hurry."

She was all over me, her tongue enthusiastically exploring my mouth, body wiggling erotically. A little desparate. I stroked her, calming her mouth and body, holding her gently, running my hands over her. "God, that's nice. I feel like going to sleep in your arms. Is that awful?"

"If you do more than think about it, it will be."

"Hey, where'd you learn to do that?"

"It's part of our diplomatic training."

She giggled. "I'll bet." She moaned, lips parting and pulling back as I stroked, feeling her harden and moisten between my fingers. I moved away and ran my lips down the side of her neck, over her breasts and stomach, parting her legs, opening her up. Her body

166

arched beneath the caress. "Oh, my God. Nobody's ever done that before."

She pulled me up and over her, running her hand down between us, guiding him in. Her big, muscular legs tightened around me. "Don't move. Let me do it."

She woke me later, pushing my shoulder, smiling down at me, blond hair a tangled mass around her face. "Typical male. Get what you want and roll over and go to sleep. Somebody is knocking at the door."

I got up, pulled on a pair of pants and opened the door. The goon hit me in the gut and caught me as I fell forward. He had a shaven head and wore one of the same windbreakers Kathy and I had seen earlier on our two escorts. His was beige. He spun me around and twisted my arm up behind my back. Very professional. "No noise, please. We are the police." His English sounded like some forties German emigré playing a Nazi. Helmut Dantine, maybe.

The other two followed us in. Mary Pancoast covered herself in bed, eyes big. "Jim, what's going on?"

One of our two companions, obviously the leader, answered her. "Please do not be concerned, Miss Pancoast. We are police. We would like to talk to Dr. Thompson for a few minutes. Alone, if you don't mind. I suggest you get dressed. Perhaps in the bathroom."

She stood up, wrapping the sheet around her and disappeared. The leader, a tall slim man in his forties dressed in a brown leather sports jacket, black turtleneck and light brown corduroys, motioned to the thug to let me go. "Wait outside."

"Cigarette?" He held out a pack of Marlboros.

"No, thanks."

"But of course. How stupid of me. You don't smoke." He sounded like a bad English play, down to the accent, which was perfect but somehow missed the intonation.

"My name is Lorenz Tumerius, Dr. Thompson. I'm an officer in the Staatsicherheitsdienst. The STASI. If you like I'll show you my credentials."

"Thanks."

He smiled. "First, what do you propose we do with the young lady? That was very clever of you, incidentally. Putting Miss Chapin on the army bus with her documents. We were taken completely by surprise. But how do we arrange things with this young woman now?"

"You could take her down to the border and push her across."

"Yes. We considered that. But it's a bit crude, no?"

"Take her to the embassy. It's just around the corner. She can tell them she lost her passport and bus pass. They must have ways of getting people out who've lost their papers."

She stood by the doorway to the john looking pale. "You stole my papers to get somebody out of East Berlin. Then you seduced me to keep me from causing trouble."

I stood up and moved toward her. "Don't come near me, you son-of-a-bitch. And don't worry about my getting back. I'll find the embassy on my own." She ripped open the door and walked past the guards who, looking at the guy in the leather coat, let her go.

"Unfortunately our walls are very thin in the GDR, Dr. Thompson. She clearly heard what we were saying. However, it solves our little problem."

"Part of it, anyway."

"Yes. Part of it. The rest is a bit more complicated, and I must admit to being somewhat puzzled. Perhaps you can clarify some things for me. If you would be so kind, that is."

"Sure. What do you want to know?"

"Why is Xerxes after you?"

"What makes you think he is?"

Tumerius looked pained. "Please, Dr. Thompson.

They have an informant in our border headquarters. We have doubled him. He reported to me immediately when he received an urgent inquiry as to whether you had crossed into the East. They wanted to know with the utmost rapidity. Naturally I alerted our people in the West. I now have bits and pieces of the story, but not all. Unfortunately, our network was decimated by a defector recently and has not been completely re-established. You see, I am being quite frank with you." He glanced at his watch. "It's late. You've had a strenuous afternoon. Perhaps we could continue this conversation over dinner?"

"Sure." I wasn't hungry, but a restaurant was better than a cell. Also, the chances of slipping the leash were greater. He read my mind.

"I would recommend that you not attempt to elude us, Dr. Thompson. There really is no place to go except over the wall, and that is extremely dangerous. Also, I have no desire to harm you. You have certain information I need. And you clearly have problems with which I can be helpful. I suspect we can come to an agreement with relative ease."

"Yeah. The perfect deal, as my old man used to say."

"And what is that?"

"One where everybody gets what he wants."

"Precisely. You do not seem infected with the usual shabby bourgeois attitudes toward nation, loyalty, and patriotism which sometimes reduce us to distasteful methods. I'm sure we'll reach an understanding."

"One way or another."

Tumerius's Volvo stationwagon drew up as we left the hotel. We got in, and it turned right toward Friedrichstrasse. "I'm taking you to one of my favorite places, Dr. Thompson. It's quiet, elegant and traditional." Up front the driver cursed under his breath.

"What is it, Georg?"

"The old man is coming through." Up ahead, four

policemen had closed off the intersection of Friedrich-strasse, one of the main arteries of the town. Traffic piled up behind us and across the way. Friedrich-strasse had suddenly emptied of cars.

"What's going on?"

"Honecker, the party chairman, is going home. He always takes a different route for security reasons. A few minutes before he leaves his office, the police spread out and shut off the side streets. It won't be long." Tumerius lit a cigarette and leaned back against the upholstery of the car. "Don't look so surprised. Your people do the same thing for your president."

"Nobody closes off any streets. There would be a revolution if they tried."

The cops up ahead suddenly came to attention as police outriders on small, 500-cc BMW motorcycles roared past, followed by two Volvos. Sandwiched between them and two following Volvos was a long gray Citroen with curtained windows.

"That's him."

"Where does he live?"

"In a party enclave outside of town."

The restaurant, like a lot of other things in East Germany, was preserved in amber, as if time had stopped somewhere back in the twenties. It stood on a corner in an old building next to the Brecht Theater. The Ganymed. Waiters in dinner jackets, red plush walls, a scarred old grand piano in front of an ancient mahogany bar that seemed to be waiting for Marlene Dietrich to come and sit on it, decked out in garterbelt and straw hat. Little lamps with tassels decorated each table.

The waiters snapped to attention when Tumerius walked in, leather jacket draped over his shoulders cape style. The maitre d'hotel showed us to a table in the corner away from the window. "It's not the West, of course, but the food isn't bad. I recommend the Mexico steak. It's a specialty of the house."

I wasn't hungry. I wondered if the girl would tell the embassy people what had happened. Probably not. She was too humiliated.

Tumerius read my mind. "I doubt if she will say anything. First, she would have to explain what happened and that is too shabby. Then, she would not realize who I am or what was going on. She would not feel that you were in any danger. She will simply get a new document and cross the wall back to her normal dull existence and attempt to forget her little adventure in the East." He ordered two Mexico steaks and a bottle of Egri Bikavar, a Hungarian red wine that translates as "bull's blood" and looks and tastes like its name.

"Now, Dr. Thompson. Perhaps we can talk seriously."

"Sure."

"Why does Xerxes want you?"

I told him the story, or most of it, leaving out von Bursian and a lot of details.

"You mean you can locate all the members of the Orpheus Circle? Identify them positively?"

"Maybe not all, but ninety per cent of them."

"Suppose I asked you to write down for me just how you would do this, Dr. Thompson. In detail, step by step. Could you do that?"

"What choice do I have?"

The waiter came with the steaks, slabs of over-cooked beef smothered in canned tomatoes. He poured the wine with a careful flourish and waited for Tumerius to savor it. It reminded me of one of the Brecht plays being put on at the theater next door.

"Several. You can, to begin with, give me false instructions. It will take me some time to realize this. Then, after some serious discussion, you can give me another set of instructions which are not obviously flawed but which for reasons of detail do not work."

"What good would any of this do you? You'd have

171

to have access to the archive to use anything I could give you."

Tumerius chewed on his steak which seemed to have been born of a water buffalo bred to a truck tire. He wiped his mouth and grinned across at me, lifting his glass of red wine in a toast. "You are quick, Dr. Thompson."

"How?"

"Obviously the archive has been of some interest to us for years. We have managed to seed three clerks among the forty personnel there. Unfortunately, none of them have your talents, Dr. Thompson. They are total illiterates when it comes to computers, and, in fact, their knowledge of the archive itself, while extensive, is nowhere near as useful as yours. We have known for some time the general outline of old Cassierer's search. Needless to say, we too have an interest in the outcome."

"Yeah. Might be embarrassing."

"You mean if you were to come up with a leading East German personality who had been an SS man during the war? Yes, Dr. Thompson. It would be highly embarrassing. It might even be dangerous if your people discovered such an individual, kept his identity secret and began to blackmail him."

"You could do the same thing. I mean, most of them are going to be in the West. You get the names and start to squeeze. Be worth a lot to you."

Tumerius, who wore his slightly greasy black hair long over his ears in a kind of Prince Valiant hairdo, grinned. His teeth were irregular and yellowed by tobacco.

"As I said before, Dr. Thompson, you are quick."

I fiddled with the remnants of the steak, surrounded by tomato sauce congealed in cold grease. "Maybe we can make a deal. I'll work the archive for you, find any names I can over the weekend and you get me on a plane to Paris."

"There are no planes to Paris from East Berlin, Dr. Thompson."

"Then get me a ticket to Prague. I'll find my way from there." He took his time thinking it over. I wasn't going anywhere. He let me sweat a little.

"You have, how do you say, a deal, Dr. Thompson. I hope you will be sensible and not cause any difficulties for us once we are in West Berlin."

"Like what? Turning myself in to the CIA?"

173

# Chapter 11

HE PICKED ME UP EARLY IN A LIGHT BLUE VOLVO stationwagon with Outer Mongolian diplomatic license plates. "You don't look very Outer Mongolian."

"Nobody checks us when we cross into West Berlin, Dr. Thompson. Except occasionally a West German customs guard looking for smuggled cigarettes."

"Where are we crossing?"

"Bornholmerstrasse." This is one of seven crossing points through the wall open to diplomats and West Berliners. Everybody else had to cross at Checkpoint Charlie or Friedrichstrasse on the S-Bahn. He'd picked it because it was a quiet crossing in a suburb out near the French Embassy. Almost nobody used it. We moved through the saluting East German guards without stopping, threading the concrete barriers and coming out onto an ancient iron bridge flanked by a disused S-Bahn station with an excellent view of the killing ground between the two walls. He was right. In the West a couple of bored German customs guards watched us go through with hardly a glance. A block further along a gray Volkswagen Golf fell in behind us.

"More Outer Mongolians?"

"What else? I don't think you are going to try to escape, Dr. Thompson, but you are clearly a devious man. I do not take chances. They have orders to shoot you if you do anything other than what you are told."

"It would save time if we swung by my apartment and picked up my notes."

Tumerius glanced over at me. "You don't think Xerxes has cleaned out your apartment?"

"Most of the stuff is meaningless to anybody except me." In fact I'd put all the data into the computer under a code nobody was likely to crack anytime soon. But I wanted something else out of the apartment.

"Very well. It's the last place they would expect you to turn up." He stopped half a block away and motioned one of his goons to go with me. The landlady was still asleep as I let myself in followed by the STASI goon in the brown windbreaker. I changed clothes quickly, stuffed my research notes on the SS into a plastic folder and slipped an invitation to the Queen's birthday reception into my coat pocket. The British cultural attache had done his doctorate on Nazi medical experiments on prison camp inmates. We'd had lunch together a couple of times and he'd put me on the invitation list. Somebody who knew what he was doing had gone through my notes and taken anything dealing with the Orpheus Circle, leaving everything else neatly collated. Kathy was earning her pay.

On the way out I handed the goon my notes and slipped into the library as he stood in the hall. From the bookcase on the left, behind the first edition of Heine's collected works, volume twelve, I extracted the forty-five I'd bought at Scottie's, slipped it into my waistband just as the STASI barrelled through the door. I indicated a book lying on a side table and held it up, sticking it in my pocket. He motioned me toward the door with his head, growling at me to get moving.

"Well?" Tumerius asked.

"You were right. Xerxes cleaned me out."

"Meaning?"

"It'll take a little longer. I'll have to start from scratch. But it's easy now. The system works. All it takes is patience."

Tumerius parked three blocks from the archive, the Volkswagen tight behind us. "We'll walk from here. The guard is very nervous. Nobody comes to the place on Saturday, but naturally he's concerned. One of my people will be there."

At the gate an aging German auxiliary guard in a caricature of a U.S. army uniform opened the gate and hustled us through. "Quickly, please. If they find out I've let anybody in, it will cost me my pension." He had the paunch and red, veined face of a drinker. An aura of cheap Steinhager surrounded him. A slim, gray-haired man in an expensive tweed jacket met us at the door. "I think you know Ludwig."

We shook hands. Normally he was dressed in the white coat the archivists wore to protect themselves from the dust.

"Where do you wish to begin, Dr. Thompson?"

"With the computer."

He led us into the cellar to the room with the SS marriage files. "We're least likely to be bothered down here. Even if somebody were to come. What is your system? I've been trying to work out how you found them."

"You need a name. Somebody you suspect. You enter it in the computer along with all his vital statistics, birthdate, father and mother's name, et cetera. Then you compare this, using the computer, to the SS files, isolating anybody approximately the same age with the same physical characteristics. Then you compare the SS files to the Displaced Persons file."

Tumerius frowned. "That could take days."

"More like weeks."

"You didn't tell me this, Dr. Thompson."

"You didn't ask."

He handed me a name. Lothar von Schoenborn. "Run it through."

I turned on the computer and watched the software explode onto the screen.

"Lothar von Schoenborn, born December 12, 1920, Prague. Father Klaus, mother Helga, born Thierry, Abitur, Goethe Gymnasium, June 1938. Joined NS-DAP August 1938. Commissioned Untersturmfuehrer, January 1939." Schoenborn, scion of an ancient Austro-Hungarian family, participated in virtually every campaign the German army fought between 1939 and 1944, dying in a tank defending the hedgerows behind the Normandy beachhead in July 1944.

"You think he went under?"

Tumerius stared at the screen. "No. He died in his tank, like some archaic knight out of a fairy tale. I just wanted to see how the machine works. You can call up any SS file with it?"

"SS, Nazi party, members of special groups like actors and writers. About a third of the SS files are missing, of course. So it's not foolproof."

Tumerius looked over at the archive clerk, and gave him a curt order, dismissing him. He then handed me a name. I looked at the slip of paper and at him. "You've got to be kidding."

"Enter the name." Tumerius was clearly tense. I ran Michael Walkowski through the SS file, coming up with nothing, then through the Displaced Persons listing. The computer did its little electronic dance and the display laid out Walkowski on the screen. "Born Krakow, Poland, March 15, 1919. Father Jerzy, mother Ingrid Schmidt. Realschule, 1933. Apprentice watchmaker 1934. Member, Communist Party of Poland 1935. Convicted of conspiracy against the state 1936, sentenced to five years. Released 1938. Military service, 10th Polish Hussars 1939. Captured October 1939 by Soviet unit near Bialystok. Released to German government March 1940 as ethnic German. Entered German army June 1940." His service jacket showed a military career replete with petty disciplinary infractions, insubordination and alienation. It ended with his transfer to the Russian front in December 1944.

"Can you find his double?"

"You mean you think some SS man took his identity?"

"Let's just say there are anomalies. He was born in Poland, yet he can barely speak the language. He is a peasant. But he has the manners and bearing of an educated man. He is lower-class, but there is about him a sense of security and a native insolence that I have only seen among the German aristocracy. He has no family that we can check on."

"What did he do to you?"

Tumerius grinned, crooked teeth showing through.

"Whatever it was, we will make him regret it, no, Dr. Thompson? What is your next step?"

"Enter the data on Walkowski and ask the computer to compare it to all the SS files extant."

"How many are there?"

"A million or so. Like I say, about a third are missing."

"But that will take forever."

I shook my head. "An hour at the outside. The machine scans and rejects. It will focus on one piece of data first. Say the birthdate. Once it isolates everybody born on the same day as Walkowski, it will move on to eye color, weight, height, physical characteristics."

178

"Suppose he didn't pick somebody with his birthdate? What if he went into the files on a random basis?"

"He could have." Tumerius was good. He was zeroing in on some of the weaknesses of the system. They wouldn't matter if you had time. But we didn't. "I'm betting he did it quickly, took shortcuts, the way the others did. They didn't have all that much time. The SS files were originally catalogued by *Jahrgang* which would have made it easier for him." Jahrgang is a German expression meaning the year of your birth, an important statistic in the country's culture. People in Germany are always asking what your Jahrgang is. Which accounted for the filing system.

"So the easiest thing for him to do would be to pick somebody exactly his age and with the same physical characteristics. Yes. I see your point." He glanced at his watch. "Let's start."

The Hahn was good. Half an hour later it had displayed more than a hundred names. Tumerius stared over my shoulder at the screen, visibly impressed. "My God, we've got to have one of these things. It would simplify our task immensely. We would have virtually total control of the whole population with a network like this. Nobody could move without our knowing it." He shook his head regretfully. "But it will never happen. There's no way we could get the purchase order through the bureaucracy."

"Why buy them? Just steal the technology. Your guys are good. They could copy this stuff. Hell, I hear at Leipzig your computer people displayed the world's largest microchip."

He stared at me, frowning. "Really? Where did you read that?" Then he got it. His right hand lashed out, backhanded, taking me across the face. I came out of the chair staring into a vicious little Czech Zbropvka Strakonice automatic.

"Very funny, Dr. Thompson. But I think we will cure you of your sense of humor fairly quickly." He put the gun away. "What do we do now?"

"We need Walkowski's file from the displaced persons archive. With that we can compare him to each of these hundred SS files. They used the SS pictures to falsify the DP files, so you'll recognize him instantly, if he's in there."

Tumerius snapped his fingers and the dapper archivist appeared at the door. "Tell him what you need."

I watched the man leave. "How much do you trust that guy?"

Tumerius stared at me. "What do you mean?"

"Is he one of yours or a freelance?"

"Be more clear, Dr. Thompson. What are you suggesting? I pay him extremely well. He is compromised. He cannot betray me."

"He could if he had enough trade goods. Did you see his eyes when he understood Walkowski was your man? You realize what he could get if he could hand the Bundesnachrichtendienst a Nazi East German politburo member? Not to mention you. They'd give him a medal and a fat pension."

Tumerius motioned me out of the low-ceilinged room, once again pulling out the nasty-looking little gun. We went up the stairs fast to the displaced persons file room. The dapper little man was bent over the xerox machine making copies, the oddly shaped paper forcing him to run them through individually. Tumerius fumbled in his jacket and freed a short thick cylinder which he screwed onto the barrel of the little automatic.

"Well, Ludwig. Perhaps you'd like to explain."

The archivist spun away from the xerox, hand going to the knot of his expensive French tie with the little gold crown at the bottom of it. "I thought you would like copies, Herr Tumerius."

The little gun spat three times. He wasn't a particularly good shot. The first one caught Ludwig high in the chest, the second in the stomach. The third blew away part of his head.

"Finish making the copy, Dr. Thompson. Then replace the file." I stepped over the body and worked the machine quickly.

"You are not particularly disturbed by death, Dr. Thompson."

"I've been there before."

"Ah, yes. Of course. The heroic soldier. Are you finished? Let us go quickly." Back in the cellar, I showed him how to find the SS files. It was simple. They were arranged alphabetically in two huge rooms.

"Very well. Begin." He stood behind me.

I ran through each file on the computer first, rejecting the ones which were unlikely. Men who'd lost an arm, a leg or an eye. The clearly lower or lower-middle class. Those who were unsuccessful soldiers. We wound up with thirty and moved back into the stacks of dusty orange files. Walkowski turned up in the fourteenth folder. Slim, arrogant, self-possessed.

"Harald, Freiherr von Stettin. Born Wurzburg, December 12, 1920. Schottengymnasium Vienna, 1938. Officer candidate school 1939. Commissioned 9th regiment, June 1939." His military career took off almost immediately. Iron Cross in Poland. Iron Cross with Diamonds in France. Battle after battle in North Africa and Russia. The final entry listed him as missing in action near Koenigsberg in early 1945.

Tumerius stared at the picture for something like thirty seconds, stained and twisted teeth appearing finally in a snarl. I shot him as he shifted the little Czech automatic into his left hand and reached for the file. The forty-five spun him around and slammed him against a set of files, smearing blood across the ancient folders as he crumpled to the floor. The explosion ricocheted off the walls, building on its own echo before gradually dying away. I put the file back and

181

picked up the little gun, unscrewing the silencer and dropping it in my pocket. He was hard to roll over without getting blood on my clothes but I needed the car keys. They were in his coat pocket along with Walkowski's xeroxed file. I slipped the bloodstained xeroxes into von Stettin's folder and turned back to the machine.

It still displayed the SS files, and I quickly cancelled out the whole program, going back through the codes and wiping out all trace of anything I'd done. When they found the bodies they'd bring a team within hours, wringing the computer dry. I'd almost left when, as an afterthought, I called up and erased both the Walkowski DP entry and von Stettin from the master files. I moved down the rows of file folders to N, inserting the Walkowski-Stettin file between Nannen and Nannenberg. The two men had effectively disappeared from the Berlin Document Center, irretrievably lost among two million files. I had some trade goods.

The guard opened the gate, looking over my shoulder. "Where is he? It is time for him to go. It is almost noon. I told him my relief was due at noon."

"He'll be out in a minute."

The two goons got out of the Volkswagen as I approached. "He needs help carrying out some stuff. He wants you in there to help."

The two stared at me uncertainly, used to obeying, uncomfortable outside their own turf, where they were minor gods. "I'll go, Georg," the younger one said. "You watch him." The big one nodded as his comrade disappeared up the road.

I showed him the forty-five, slipping it out of my waistband, letting it lie in my palm. "You want to take a little walk in the woods?" There were enough dead bodies lying around. I hit him hard enough to drive him to his knees but not enough to kill him, taking another of the little Czech automatics out of his side pocket and throwing it through the trees. Back at the cars I ripped loose the ignition wires under the dashboard on the Volkswagen, and pulled out in the Volvo just as the younger goon came racing down the road from the direction of the archive and his buddy staggered out of the woods, blood running down his face. Behind them the red-faced guard had yanked his sidearm loose and was gesticulating wildly.

I drove the Volvo through the quiet side streets to the Schlachtensee, one of the myriad small lakes seeded through the city, and stopped in a parking lot under the trees. The area was deserted. Everybody was walking with German determination along the path around the lake or preparing to picnic on one of the open meadows. I took a screwdriver out of the Volvo's neat little tool kit, selected a Mercedes virtually hidden under the trees and relieved it of its license plates, replacing the Volvo's red East German CD plates with the white and black Berlin ones.

It took half an hour to cross the city into the British sector and work my way through the military guards, flashing the invitation to the Queen's Birthday celebration, embossed with the royal coat of arms, before I wound up at the headquarters building, another of the heavy stone piles built by Hitler and Speer for the greater glory of the Thousand Year Reich. A hundred or so chauffeurs were milling around limousines drawn up at the entrance. I showed my invitation—my ancient blazer shiny at the elbows drawing raised eyebrows from the master sergeant decked out in the finery of the Royal Artillery regiment—walked up some stairs and came out at the top of an imposing set of steps overlooking a spectacle out of the lost glory of Empire.

A large tent rimmed a lawn area the size of a football field covered with a milling crowd of men in dazzling uniforms and women in colorful summer dresses, wearing wide-brimmed hats. And waiters. Endless waiters with trays of food and drinks. Here and there a uniformed flunky passed among the guests with a bottle of champagne, refilling glasses.

"If you could wait a moment, sir. The prince is about to give his address." In front of me a figure in a black uniform and plumed headdress stood in front of a microphone, holding a glass of champagne. He took off the funny-looking hat and held it off to one side, not looking, and a colonel stepped forward to take it from the extended hand. He had a good voice, a little high-pitched but under control. Only there was something wrong with the public address sytem which distorted his upper-class accent making his final phrase come out: "Gosh sruf slee quinn!" Somebody handed me a glass of champagne and as he raised his glass I lifted mine, spotting Xerxes in the crowd below. It was cheap German champagne.

"You may join the others now, sir," the NCO at my side said. The Prince of Wales had moved down the steps and was circulating among the guests, his handsome vacuous young wife at his side in a hat the size of a small umbrella. More waiters appeared now with great bowls of whipped cream and strawberries, a tradition at the celebration. Xerxes was talking to a tall slender Brit in a chalk-stripped double-breasted suit and regimental tie.

"Yeah. The bastards are trying to cut our pensions. Instead of the high three, they're talking about the high five. I might just go ahead and retire." He poured a full glass of champagne down and held it out to the Guards sergeant standing permanently at his elbow, spotting me as he turned. I have to give it to him. He was good. He didn't miss a beat.

"Oh, hello, Thompson. You know Colonel Crawford, don't you?" We'd never seen each other. The Brit shook hands and drifted off.

"What the fuck are you doing here?"

"Looking for you."

"Yeah. Well, if you want to talk, I can probably get our hosts to let us have an office somewhere in the building."

"Someplace nice and quiet?"

He looked at me. "You mean you'd rather talk here?"

"If you don't mind."

O'Brien had seen us and was moving through the crowd, trailed by a handsome blonde looking scared. He turned and said something to her. She stopped dead, staring at us, and walked away.

"Yeah, I see your point. Okay. Let's go over under the tent. I sweat a lot out here in the sun." By the time we got to the tent there were four of them around me, athletic young men with expensive suits, fashionable haircuts, conservative ties and immobile faces.

"Okay. Let's hear it," Xerxes said.

"Get rid of the Sumerian cavalry." I nodded at the tight throng around us.

O'Brien was talking to the tall Brit, nodding toward us. They were disagreeing about something.

I grinned at Xerxes. "That MI-5 guy is not happy about your messing up his Queen's birthday party. You try to take me, and your boys are going to wind up in the whipped cream and strawberries."

The tall Brit shook his head violently and turned on his heel, leaving O'Brien standing alone on the lawn.

"Shit." Xerxes motioned the four young spooks away. They separated like the Blue Angels, peeling off in different directions but not moving far, keeping us at the apex of a rough circle. O'Brien joined us.

"Okay. You wanted to talk. Talk."

"I've got a lock on the Orpheus Circle. Within forty-eight hours, maximum a week, I can deliver ninety percent of them."

"In return for what?"

"Safe passage to western Europe. And a clean slate. No retaliation. Eventual permission to return to Berlin to work in the archive."

"Why the fuck should we go for that?" O'Brien asked. "We've got you, buddy. You're going nowhere. You'll give us the names and everything else you've got or spend one hell of a long time in the slammer. That's the deal we're offering."

Xerxes took out a cigar and clipped the end with a small silver guillotine, carefully removing the band, which said Partagas, Havana. O'Brien flicked open a gold Cartier lighter and held it for him. "Well, Thompson?"

"What are you going to do? Drill my teeth? Use cattle prods on my balls? Pour water down my nose? Put a rat under a brass bowl on my stomach and build a fire on top of it the way the Chinese do?" I shook my head. "Not even here in Berlin, where we rule by right of conquest, proconsuls among the yahoos. You've got no real leverage."

"We could have you killed." Xerxes stared down at the neat quarter-inch of ash which had formed on the cigar.

"For what? You want the Orpheus Circle. Junior here might kill somebody for kicks, but not you." I shook my head. "It's a good deal all around. You get what you want and I get out from under."

"How much is he paying you?"

"Who?"

"This guy you're blackmailing."

"You're guessing."

"Yeah. I'm guessing. But it's the only thing that makes sense. You wouldn't be risking your ass if there wasn't some money in it. How much?"

I grinned. "Look, I offered you a deal. You want it or not?"

"No deal, Thompson. You give us what we want and we'll try to get you off with manslaughter."

It was warm on the lawn, but I was a little cold. "What does that mean?"

"Couple of bodies at the Document Center with your initials on them. At least one eye witness. Fingerprints. I figure you'll be lucky to get off with life."

# Chapter 12

THE EXITS WERE COVERED AND TWO OF THE YOUTH-
ful spooks had been assigned to me. They followed at
about five paces, boxing me in the crowd, occasionally
brushing up against me to let me know they were
there, herding me toward an exit. The MI-5 colonel
and O'Brien were watching the scene from halfway up
the steps. I circled the exits, spotting the British
security people by their heavy policemen's shoes and
cheap, ill-fitting suits. Only in America did plain-
clothes cops sport a spurious Ivy League elegance.

The crowd was beginning to thin when I spotted
Kathy. She'd been at one of the tables behind a gilded
rope where the prince and his princess had joined the
glittering military brass and top diplomats for a seated
lunch while the proletariat milled about the lawn and
stood in line for smoked salmon, caviar and roast beef
sandwiches.

"My God. What are you doing here?" Her glance
flashed around the crowd, immediately spotting the
thugs at every exit and my two chaperones.

"Eating strawberries and whipped cream."

"Be serious."

"I tried to make a deal with Xerxes. He doesn't think I have anything to trade."

"Alec, they'll kill you." She took me by the arm and led me through a dense mass of ladies, temporarily losing the tails against the unmoving female bulk. "You don't know what you've gotten into. It's not just the CIA. Everybody is in it now. The Germans are enraged. Xerxes is being chewed out by Washington for letting the whole thing get out of hand. The French and the British are pissed. Nobody wants a big Nazi scandal right now. Even the Israelis are backing away. Cassierer has been told to cool it."

"Why?"

"The West Germans have finally agreed to sell them that tank. What's it called?"

"The Leopard."

"Anyway, they've also agreed not to sell it to the Saudis. And, there's something about a loan. Anyway, the bottom line is Cassierer is going to have to give up on the Orpheus Circle. The Germans say they will handle it quietly. But without a major national scandal. They can't afford another Bitburg."

"Cassierer won't go along."

"He doesn't have any choice."

"And the CIA?"

"Paul says the wimps at State found out what was going on. They were horrified that we were going to try to get blackmail material on our friendly Germans. Also, we've been sucking up to the East Krauts lately and nobody wants trouble right now, what with a new detente with the Soviets building. Paul says State went right up to the President and got the whole thing called off."

"So nobody's interested in finding old Nazis?" I started to laugh, remembering von Bursian.

"No. But they know you've figured out a way to do it, and they're going to stop you. One way or another."

She looked different. The wide-brimmed light green

189

hat reflected her eyes, and the summery dress soft-
ened the muscularity of her body. A low décolleté
lifted her breasts, freckles muted by a film of makeup.

"What are you looking at?"

"The butterfly out of its chrysalis. An upper-class
young woman *bien dans sa peau*. You'd better go
home and marry some Yalie stockbroker and quit
playing cops and robbers. I'll see you around."

Her hand clamped on my arm as I turned to leave.
"Where are you going? Every exit is blocked. How
are you going to get out?"

"See that big beefy British cop over there? I'm
going to ask him for the time. When he looks at his
watch, I'll stick a knee in his groin and start running."

"How far do you think you'll get?"

"About a hundred yards. You got any better ideas?"

Her eyes swept the rapidly emptying lawn. "Yes.
Quick. Follow me." She moved across the grass with
long awkward strides, ankles not too sure of themselves in the high heels as they sank into the soft lawn.
The sign said "Ladies," and I hesitated.

"Come on, you idiot. Hurry." We moved down the
long corridor of a tent toward the main building,
passing a stream of women, several of whom stopped
dead and stared as we headed toward the john.
"Quick, damn it." She brushed past two startled mid-
dle-aged ladies into the powder room, a row of stalls
off to the right. On the left, a leggy blonde, skirt up
around her waist, was examining a run in her stocking .

"Shit, Brenda. They were brand new," she said to a
companion in nasal aristocratic British accents, looking up and meeting my eyes, giggling in disbelief as we
swept through toward the rear exit. She had superb
legs.

"Run, Alec. Through there. It comes out into the
parking lot. If you make it I'll meet you at the Stabi in
an hour. In the cafeteria." She turned back to the john.

I had a couple of hundred yards on them before somebody gave an order to go through the ladies' room. The Volvo was at the far end of the parking lot. I slipped it in behind a cavalcade of VIP limousines moving out in the left-hand lane past the normal traffic and swung around them, tires screaming, once we were through the gate. The Volvo was underpowered but nobody was in a hurry. Horns blasted and various vulgar gestures were made, but I was ahead of the flow when the British military police sirens began to bleep behind me. I disappeared into the back streets, avoiding main arteries, and crossed the city in the direction of its main library and archive, the Staatsbibliothek, repository of books and manuscripts dating back centuries.

I parked across the street in the empty Philharmonic Hall lot in the space reserved for the first cellist and walked across the street into the immense library. Both the Philharmonic and the Staatsbibliothek had been built at the same time as the Beaubourg in Paris when the modernist school had carried reductionist architecture to its ultimate logical absurdity and entered a phase of degeneracy comparable to late Baroque. At the Beaubourg, unable to make a facade more monotonous and featureless, they had reversed course and hit upon the supreme witticism of putting the plumbing facilities on the outside. In Berlin they had reached out for the mindless complexity of geometric shapes, creating, on the outside, buildings of consummate stupidity and ugliness.

Inside the Staatsbiliothek, however, some final spasm of Bauhaus genius had produced a magnificent inner space, a modern cathedral of stone and steel, full of books and a kind of chilly Teutonic warmth reflecting the Prussian sense of order, discipline and controlled emotion.

I liked the place.

German libraries are basically prisons for books.

They parole one once in a while, but only after a procedure designed to discourage all but the most fanatical of readers. The stacks are closed. If you want a book, you can't just browse through, look over the titles, pull a book down and check it out. You need to know what you want before you get there, preferably from having read a review by some pompous expert telling you what to think. You fill out a form, hand it in and, if you're lucky, in a couple of hours they'll find the book and deliver it to you, after filling out another form. When you bring it back, you can't just fling it in a bin. You'll have to get in line again, fill out another form, have the book examined for flaws and finally get turned loose.

Aside from this, it's a great research library. Full of German esoterica from all ages. I moved through the control point and up the immense sweeping steps to the small cafeteria and waited. She arrived just before closing time, dressed in jeans and a blue sports shirt with some little animal just above her left nipple, looking as if he were about to sink his teeth into the protruberance below.

"I'm sorry it took so long. I had to shake O'Brien's goons."

"They squeeze you?"

"They tried."

"You're out?"

She nodded. "I'd had enough anyway. After I found out that Paul had sent me over to the East knowing I'd be spotted and probably picked up."

"It's their job. Get sentimental and you fuck up."

"I guess so. What do you plan to do?"

"Lay low for a few days. Get some documentation. Slide out some way when things die down. Maybe on the train. They'll have to let up on the surveillance in a few days."

"Have you got money?"

I grinned. "There's a name for guys who take money from girls."

"How much do you need?"

"Couple of thousand should do it. I'll pay you back when I get to West Germany."

"You've got to get out of Europe, Alec. Back to the States. The British and French are looking for you, too."

"I wonder who's in those files. Somebody right at the top?"

"Maybe. They're as tight as I've ever seen them. The pressure is really on."

"Can you get into the archive?"

"What?"

"I'll give you the system. See what you can come up with."

She covered my hand with hers. "Jesus. That's the first sign of trust you've ever shown, Alec. You know what?"

"What?"

"You're like an animal. A paranoid animal. You're always waiting for something to happen. You never quit looking."

"Yeah. Well, like one of our famous statemen once said, 'Even paranoids have real enemies.' Right now I see half a dozen cops coming through the main door. You ever see any cops in here before?"

She turned. "Never."

"Let's go." They had fanned out across the main floor, heading for the various sections of the immense library. Outside, four others lounged against the iron railings. Another had stationed himself at the ramp leading to the underground garage.

"Is there a back door?"

"Probably. But they'll have somebody there by now."

We came out through the turnstile into the massive

main hall. In about a minute the cops would surge back into it from the special study sections leading off to the left. The main exit was blocked. Kathy grabbed my arm and pointed to a poster on a notice board. A Grosz drawing of a World War I German officer, thick-necked, crew-cut and monocled, dominated an announcement of a meeting of the Leo Loewe Institute, an organization of emigres to the United States set up to study the history of the German Jews.

"Hans Lieblich is lecturing."

"Fascinating. I'd love to hear him. Some other time."

"Alec. He's lecturing here. In the Otto Braun Saal. Right now. Look." At the end of the massive main hall, through heavy glass doors, a mass of people were making their way up to the library's auditorium. We moved quickly down the cavernous building. On the left a bored-looking, pimply-faced cop was checking the identity documents of a German about my age. "Christ, he's got your picture." Kathy said.

"Copy of my passport photograph. I had it replaced at the consulate here a couple of years ago. When I shaved off my beard."

We were at the glass doors now. A young woman in a powder blue uniform and a Robin Hood hat barred our way. "Your invitations, please."

I fumbled in my coat, pretending to look. 'Must have left them at the hotel," I said, smiling at her ingratiatingly.

"I'm very sorry, sir. I cannot allow you to enter without an invitation."

Kathy was scanning the crowd milling past. "Dr. Stein," she called to a stooped ancient moving toward the steps. He turned, directing a pair of startling blue eyes in a seamed face toward us and broke into a grin.

"My dear, what are you doing here?" he asked, moving over to the door.

"Trying to get into the lecture. We forgot our invitations. This is Dr. Thompson from Santa Cruz. You remember. He did the book on the SS."

"Of course. Excellent work. I found your character-ization of the reorganization of 1937 a trifle sparse, but an excellent work nonetheless. Come in. Come in. What is this nonsense about invitations?" He waved away the young woman's protests and led us into the stream moving up the stairs to the auditorium. "And what are you working on these days, my dear? I read your dissertation with great interest. The old guard is dying out, you know. We expect great things of you."

"I'm out of brothels and into comparative women. Pre-1914 Germany versus the Nazi era. Who treated them worse."

The old man laughed. "We must have tea. I'm at the Kempinsky. Come by tomorrow around four. Bring your young man along. That bit on 1937 needs expand-ing. I must go now. I see one of Weizsaecker's myrmi-dons looking for me. Ironic, isn't it? A group of rejected German Jews coming home to Berlin. To be greeted by whom? A man who spent six years in Hitler's armies and whose father was one of the bas-tard's closest collaborators. Still, he is the President of Germany, and he makes very pretty speeches about guilt and reconciliation. And he gives us a great deal of money. One cannot ask for more. Until tomorrow, then." He moved off in the clutches of a young Ger-man in an expensively tailored pin-striped suit and spotted tie, so slim he hardly cast a shadow.

"You studied with him, didn't you? He must be ninety years old."

"Eighty-nine. We had an informal seminar a couple of times a week at his house in Princeton. The select few. No credit. Just talk. God, he's magnificent."

"Yeah. *Pour le Mérite*. The German equivalent of the Congressional Medal of Honor before 1918. One of the three Jews who got it in World War I. Wounded and captured at Verdun when he was twenty."

"How'd you know that?"

"There was a debate among the Nazis in 1934 about how to handle Jews who had been wounded and decorated for heroism in World War I. He was one of the examples cited. People like von Seeckt tried to protect him. Goering finally solved it by saying, 'I decide who is a Jew,' and simply declaring certain people were aryans, exempting them from persecution. Milch, the Luftwaffe general, was an old friend of Goering's from the First World War. He was half-Jewish. Nobody ever touched him. Remember, 'A foolish consistency is the hobgoblin of little minds.'"

"How about 'Little minds are the hobgoblins of a foolish consistency'?"

We moved up a wide staircase into the auditorium. In the library's main hall a covey of cops had gathered near the control booth. Nobody seemed to be paying any attention to the scholarly meeting.

"Don't worry," Kathy said. "No German policeman is going to come into a gathering of Jewish emigres hosted by President von Weizsaecker, and begin checking documents. We're okay for a while."

The speeches went on for hours. The Germans' *Sitzfleisch,* their capacity to absorb punishment in the form of boredom, is exceeded only by their ability to deliver it. Ancient emigres, men of distinction in pre-war Germany, thrown out of their professions, homes and country, stood up to castigate the Nazis, evoking the horrors of the holocaust in heartrending detail. Seeded through the speeches was a reluctant gratitude to the present German government and its president for their attempts at atonement.

Weizsaecker is a distinguished, graying German aristocrat. His father, the senior career diplomat in the German foreign office throughout the Hitler era, had arranged to transfer himself as ambassador to the Vatican in 1943 in the hope of escaping punishment when he knew the war was lost.

"I wonder what he would say if somebody had the tactlessness to ask him why he spent a year preparing the defense of his father at the Nuremberg war crimes trials," I whispered to Kathy. "Or how he explains his six years as a recklessly brave officer in the Nazi armies, fighting right up to the end."

"Don't be stupid, Alec. He was just following orders."

A German sitting to my right shushed us indignantly as Weizsaecker led into the most moving portion of his speech, a call for mutual reconciliation, an end to recrimination, a forgiveness and coming together to start a new era beginning on this day when Germany's former citizens were welcomed home again. About a third of the audience seemed on the verge of tears. Another third looked as if it wanted to vomit.

Weizsaecker sat down and Professor Hans Lieblich, eminent historian of the sexual mores of the French nineteenth-century bourgeoisie, noted wit, biographer of Wallenstein and expert on all forms of chocolate desserts, took the podium. Small, graying, slightly paunchy, in a suit clearly in need of pressing and a size too big, glasses drifting down his nose, he looked like an intense owl as he stared at the audience and began his speech in a gentle, penetrating voice, speaking German with the merest trace of an American accent.

"Mr. President. Ladies and gentlemen. I wish to preface my remarks on the history of the Jews in Germany by noting that I wholeheartedly supported accepting the invitation of the city of Berlin to hold this meeting here. I am a Berliner. Or I was until I was forced into exile at the age of fifteen. For many years I refused to return to Germany, having determined never to forgive the nation of my birth for what it did to my people. Over the years, urged by my many friends in the German academic community to at least make a visit, I weakened, and, some twenty years ago, returned. I must tell you it was a wrenching emotional experience. One cannot escape one's youth. There was much that attracted me in this new Germany. Its evident devotion to democracy. The lessening of authoritarian structures. A more easygoing way of life. The high level of popular culture. The discipline and lack of individual violence which I, as a former German, have occasionally missed in my new country. The profound, if sometimes turgid, scholarly competence of my colleagues.

"There was also much that disturbed me. I found an almost eager willingness to admit guilt in the abstract, but virtually no sense of personal responsibility for the actions of the Hitler era. It was, always, 'the others' who did the evil things. A younger generation, encouraged by some of their elders, sought to trivialize the holocaust by comparing it to the slaughter of the American Indians, the Vietnam war, and even, as one classicist argued at some length, the Athenian massacre of the Potideans. This desire to escape from such harrowing guilt is an all too human emotion. I understand it. I do not, however, accept it. For the seeds of the holocaust grew out of a German historical tradition rich in intellectual and practical anti-semitism, a tradition only weakly contested when not abetted by the German ruling elites—governmental, aristocratic, military, academic, journalistic and, above all, and least forgiveably, by the intelligentsia to which so many Jews belonged.

"Many have described the German-Jewish relationship as one of love-hate. I would agree with one slight alteration of the intent of the phrase. The Jews loved the Germans, and the Germans hated the Jews."

Lieblich stopped and peered across the audience, his blue eyes resting on the German government personalities seeded among the members of the Institute in the first rows of the auditorium. "Jesus, he's going to stick it to them," Kathy said.

"The icepick is already in to the hilt, perfumed and

monogrammed. It looks as if he's planning to use an ax from here on out."

Lieblich turned back to his text. "There are those here among my colleagues at the Leo Loewe Institute who do not agree with what I am saying. Or perhaps I should say, do not agree that it must once again be said. Again, I disagree. I think it is essential that, between the Jews and the Germans, there exist a total frankness and understanding. To paper over the past with anodyne phrases serves the interest of no one. I will not do it."

Lieblich continued his brilliant analysis of the history of the Jews in Germany in his gentle, monotonous voice for another twenty minutes, ending with a denial of the Jews' responsibility for their own destruction. "There is still another postulate with which I must take issue. There are those who say that the German Jews were responsible for their own fate. That they should have left when Hitler came to power rather than waiting for him to destroy them. Again, I must disagree. First, there was no place to go. Nobody wanted us. Not even the United States, the most generous haven, would take us all. Israel was impossible. The British and French would allow no more than minimal numbers of Jews to settle. Other European nations repeatedly pushed escapees back across the border into Germany. Ironically, Fascist Spain was the most humane, accepting virtually any Jew who could reach its borders. One must also never forget that, in the beginning, Hitler seemed simply an aberration in the German psyche. A passing phenomenon. An odd little man with a funny moustache and a strange accent who had reached power by a fluke. The anti-Semitism which he preached was after all not that much different from Karl Lueger's in pre-1914 Vienna, and the Jews survived and prospered then. Why not stay and wait it out, exercising that instinct for survival which had stood us in good stead since the

Roman massacre at Masada. No, ladies and gentlemen, there are no easy ways out. For any of us." He closed his manuscript and walked off the stage to polite, restrained applause.

"Nobody wanted to hear it," Kathy said.

"The Germans are tired of being beat on. Most of those in the auditorium are too young to have done anything in the Nazi period. They've had enough hand-wringing. They want to get on with living. For them, this is history, Kathy. Lieblich would be better off letting it lie, coughing up some bland phrases everybody wants to hear about human brotherhood, forgiveness and all that crap. Come on. Let's get out of here."

Weizsaecker had shaken Lieblich's hand and said goodbye to the leaders of the Loewe Institute and, his covey of aristocratic young aides closing around him, headed for the door. We fell in behind him in a crush of courtiers, moving through the door past two young policemen whose eyes scanned the crowd with indifference.

"Where's your car?"

"At the bottom of a ravine in the Harz mountains. Seems like about a century ago, doesn't it?"

"We'll get a taxi at Potsdamer Platz."

"Where to?"

"There's a little hotel I know in Luebars. It's to hell and gone out in the boonies. I'll hole up there until things cool off and I can slip through the net."

"Alec, they're going to find you. Why don't you give up? They can't really do anything to you."

"There are two dead East Germans at the Berlin Document Center. With my name on them. They can nail me for life if they want to. And I have a feeling they may want to."

# Chapter 13

LUEBARS IS A VILLAGE IN THE MIDST OF FARMLAND, an island of rural tranquility in the city's northern corner. The Wall dividing Berlin cuts through its fields like a concrete serpent, its towers and barbed wire rising out of the bucolic terrain in obscene ugliness.

"I'm afraid I must ask you to pay in advance, sir, since you have no luggage."

"It looks like a whorehouse out of Hansel and Gretel," Kathy said, giggling at the gasthaus motif of the place.

"Yeah. Well, the food is just as bad as the decor. But I can hole up here for a couple of days. They can't keep the squeeze on much longer than that. The city's too big. They'll have to relax. Then I'll go."

"How will you do it?"

"Dye my hair. Let my beard grow. Put on a phony moustache. Buy some Turkish worker's identity card at the railroad station and slip through on the train." You could buy anything from a pound of heroin to a twelve-year-old boy at the railroad station. It was the club of the two hundred thousand Turks, Pakistanis,

Tamils and Algerians who lived in, but were not of, the city.

"You'll need some money."

"I'll have it by then."

She turned and stared at me. "So Xerxes was right. You sold out Cassierer. You found one of the SS men and blackmailed him."

"Let's just say I made him pay a little rent on his past sins."

"That's obscene."

"Look. Maybe you'd better go back to your nice, simple, moral WASP world, full of warmth and love and charity, and leave me to mine. These supercilious upper-class representatives of American virtue you've been working for sent you over to East Berlin without a parachute. They'll crush me without a trace if they can get their manicured hands on me. Face it, Kathy. There aren't any good guys or bad guys. Just balls and ego looking for an edge. Your Manichean world is a batch of shit."

"And yours is a grubby, treacherous, murderous jungle." She leaned against the hotel door, hugging her breasts, and shivered.

"And you're licking the scabs like some neurotic saint, trying to get a taste of the real world and rid yourself of some of the poor-little-rich-girl guilt all that money and security have given you. But, goodness, no dirt under the fingernails, please."

"Just who the hell are you to patronize me? Just being born a stupid peasant doesn't make you my moral superior."

"You're looking for kicks. A little safe danger with your Ivy League lover in a three-button suit playing spy. I'll bet in college you punched every obligatory ticket. Brilliant young Jew, worshipping the schicksa ice goddess. Sensitive black, grateful and aggressive. Safely dangerous."

Her hand came out of nowhere and caught me

across the face with an explosive crack, twisting my head around. She was big, and she hit me with everything she had. I reacted reflexively, stabbing a short right hand into her stomach, pulling it at the last second, too late. She doubled up, and I caught her just before she fell, lifting her onto the bed.

"Jesus. I'm sorry, Kathy."

"You play rough," she said when she could breathe, face pale with the effort to speak.

"You caught me by surprise. It was instinctive."

"That was mean and nasty. What you said."

"You've got to get out of here. Somebody's liable to knock you off by mistake when they come for me."

"Is that why you said it? To make me leave?"

"No. You pissed me off. I'm a little weary of being broke, approaching middle age with no prospects and grub street stretching out into the distance, surrounded by rich preppies whose only claim to fame is having ancestors who ripped off fortunes at a time when industrial thievery was legal. I can't afford radical chic and fashionably leftist posturing. von Bursian is my ticket to a piece of the good life."

"It's a pretty awful ticket, Alec. I mean, he's an ex-Nazi war ciminal who killed a lot of Jews. And he tried to kill you. You ought to turn him in. Him and all the others. Doesn't it bother you? Saving him for money?"

"Look. The world is divided into winners and losers. You can't be neutral. Either you're getting kicked or you're kicking. For most of a decade I've been kidding myself that this little academic cocoon I'm in is out of the rat race. That I was very cleverly hiding out in one of the few safe, comfortable cracks. In fact all I've been doing is opting out, cringing away from combat, hunkering down in the archives and letting the dust settle on me."

"You don't like it?"

"Yeah. I like it. But I like the cutting edge, too. I

need the jolt it gives you to go up against somebody like Xerxes or von Bursian and put him to the wall. I've been conning myself that all I wanted was a nice quiet life."

"You know something? You look different. You're almost oriental. Your face has changed. It's," she hesitated. "It's all corners and planes. What's happening to you?"

"Returning to my Indian ancestors, maybe."

"Very funny. Look. It isn't going to work, you know."

"What?"

"Your plan for getting out of the city."

"Why not?"

"That STASI officer you killed. The East Germans are going to be watching for you, too. You get on that train through East Germany, and they'll have your picture and a description. They're sure to spot you."

"No."

"Why not?"

"I don't think he let his people know he had me. He was out to get somebody. Not Walkowski, who was just one of a series of suspects he'd collected. He was probably after one of the top intelligence people. Some sort of vendetta. And if not him, he wanted some leverage over anybody else he could find among the Orpheus Circle who might have worked his way up to the top. It was his ticket to promotions and power."

"You really all think alike, don't you? Cassierer. Von Bursian. The STASI officer. Xerxes. You. I'm beginning to think women ought to take over the world."

"Yeah. Well, take a look at a few of the sisterhood who have reached the heights if you want to see some real sharks. And they have the added advantage of their sex."

"Advantage? What does that mean?"

"Anybody ever turn you down when you wanted to

204

go to bed with them? Or for that matter any other woman who isn't deformed. You can walk out on the street and have a man in bed within fifteen minutes in any city in the world. A man, and I don't give a shit how charming or handsome he is, is going to have to work his ass off to get laid. That's power, baby."

"You're disgusting. There's a lot more to life than sex. My generation doesn't blackmail men with sex. If you like a man and he wants to screw," she shrugged, "you screw."

"You want to screw?"

She stared at me, rage turning slowly to comprehension. "Nobody is going to do anything to me, Alec. I just found out that Xerxes chopped Paul up in little pieces for sending me across to find you. My father is a big wheel in the Republican Party in Oklahoma. If anything happens to me, Xerxes's head will roll, and he knows it." She sat up, grimacing and holding her stomach. "Jesus, you hit hard. A lot harder than my brothers."

"I reacted."

"I know. You said it already. Hey."

"What?"

"I've got an idea."

"Yeah?"

"Why don't we go to bed? I'm cold."

Her red hair fanned out on the pillow next to me as she melted into the crevices of my body. "Just hold me. Please." She lay glued to me, breathing lightly, shivering occasionally until the down comforter had turned the bed into a furnace.

She moved away, grinning up at me. "Men really do have it tough, don't they?"

"Tell me about it."

"You really can't hide anything. He comes to attention like a Prussian sentry, ready for action. No way you're going to be cool and sensitive, pretending indifference."

"Like you?"

"Yeah." Her hand ran down my stomach, finger-nails digging ever so lightly into my skin, taking him in a gentle grip. "Does he like that?"

"Yeah."

"He's a fairly uncritical animal, huh? Easy to please."

She pushed me away and sat up, tying her hair in a pony tail with a small, colored elastic band, breasts rising as she did. "No touching," she said fending off my hand. "Lie still. Let us do it." She crouched over me, running her mouth across my chest, stopping to extract a hair from between her teeth, giggling as she moved down my chest and took him in her mouth.

"Careful, baby. No teeth."

"You come and I'll kill you," she said, looking up as I stroked the back of her neck. "He likes it."

"Yeah."

"Now you."

She moved above me, muscular legs covered with the finest film of downy red fuzz and twitched as I touched her, ever so gently. "Just kiss her. Gently. She can't take any more." I ran my lips over her, feeling the moisture as she opened to the caress, barely touching her.

"Love, love, love," she murmured, suddenly pull-ing away and letting her body down on mine, inserting him, extending herself full length, gripping him tightly. "Be still. Let her do it." We lay there, hardly moving, as she tightened and loosened her grip, lying extended against me, breathing in little gasps as she came over and over again. "Kiss my breasts," she said, pulling up and kneeling over me now, driving him in in long slow strokes, revolving her hips. I bit the nipples of her breasts lightly, running my hands over her back, down her hips.

"More, lover. More, more. Now, now, now. Oh, please, now."

After a couple of minutes she propped herself up on one elbow and stared at me in the semi-darkness. "You know something?"

"What?"

"I can't figure out the attraction. I mean, one crude male is pretty much like another."

"Good sex."

"Yeah. Well, there is that. But there's something else."

"*Nostalgie de la boue.*"

"God, you're gross."

"I'm the first real peasant you've ever known. Virile, earthy, uncomplicated. Sort of an intellectual truck driver."

"How do Indians make love?"

"In trees."

"Huh?"

"They climb trees. He hangs from a limb and she crawls down over him. Well, it gets kind of complicated. Sort of natural selection. I mean if you can't climb a tree, you can't climb a girl."

"I suppose you learned all this arcane lore from your ancient crone of a grandmother, sitting at her feet in the tepee."

"Well, actually there's this ceremony, see? Like in that movie where they hang the guy from sticks stuck through his chest?"

"Tell me about it."

I reached over and pulled her toward me. "*Tristesse coital?*"

"No." She burrowed into my shoulder, into the niche she seemed to have found there, a perfect fit. "I'm scared. I'm afraid they're going to kill you, and for some stupid reason I don't want them to."

"Nobody's going to kill me, baby. Go to sleep."

I slipped out of bed the next morning, careful not to awaken her. She lay wrapped in the comforter, gripping it to her, legs entwined in it, red hair a tangle on the pillow, one foot protruding into the icy atmosphere of the room. Berlin could be cold, even in June. The breakfast area was empty except for a bulky figure with his back to me in a corner. I started for the buffet when a familiar voice cut through the stillness.

"Herr Thompson."

"Hello, Weber."

"Perhaps you would care to join me?"

I picked up a yoghurt cup and an apple and sat down facing him with my back to the wall. He confronted a plate heaped with ham, cheese, rolls, butter, honey and an unappetizing white mess vaguely resembling sour milk which the Germans maintained was good for the digestion. They call it *quark*.

"You are surprised?"

"How'd you find me?"

"The police, Herr Thompson. We have very good contacts in the police. They have a signal out on you."

"Yeah. Well, if you found me, then Xerxes's men will, too. I think maybe I'd better be getting the hell out of here."

Weber put a meaty hand on my arm. "Be calm, Herr Thompson. Your CIA will not find you here for some time. We have, how do you say, friends who have shortened their circuits. You have about five hours of grace. By then, I'll be able to get you tucked out of sight."

"Why?"

"Herr von Bursian keeps his word, Herr Thompson. He will pay you the money you asked. And if you betray him he will kill you." He stuffed a piece of bread loaded with cheese in his mouth and washed it down with half a cup of black coffee. "The food is lousy in this place."

"Why try to get me out of Berlin? Why not just let them have me?"

"And have you talk to save your ass, Herr Thompson? Which of course you would do, being a man utterly without honor. What is that American expression you quoted to Herr von Bursian? An honest man is one who stays bought. I do not think you are honest, Herr Thompson. No, we must get you out of here, pay you off and get rid of you. Then, after a short while, everything will die down. People will forget old Nazis for a while until some new fanatic surfaces. You should eat, Herr Thompson. It is possible you will need your strength."

"What are your plans?"

"Herr von Bursian has arranged for a safe house for you in the city. I will take you there and fix it for you to leave sometime during the next two days."

"Last time you arranged something I almost wound up at the bottom of the Spree."

Weber shrugged. "Things go wrong. I made the mistake of hiring incompetents. These days you have to do everything yourself. Even so the best plans can come apart. I remember a young officer when I was in the paratroops in the war. He had this thing he did to impress the troops. Harmless really. Very impressive to new men. You were a soldier, Herr Thompson. You remember how afraid they are before their first fire-fight."

"Yeah."

"Well, Guenter de Crecy, I think his family were Huguenots who came to Prussia when they were being slaughtered in France in the seventeenth century, had this little act he put on. He would line up the recruits and tell them all about the honor of dying for Fuehrer and Fatherland. All the time he would stalk up and down flipping this grenade up and down in his hand. Finally he would pull the pin and balance it on his helmet. Naturally everybody would dive for cover. He would stand there with everybody scuttling away until the fucking thing went off. Of course, as you know, nothing happened to him. The force of the explosion dissipated in the air, the helmet absorbed the downward shock and all he got out of it was a slight headache. He did it many times. Occasionally even at parties when he was drunk."

"What happened?"

Weber reached for another slice of ham and stopped to stare down at it. "One cannot take all contingencies into consideration, Herr Thompson. De Crecy had this dog, a beautiful animal. She loved him. A big Doberman. Very well-disciplined, normally. But for some reason, on this day, she raced across the parade ground and leapt upon him with affection just as he put the grenade on his helmet."

"And?"

"It fell off. He lost his left leg, his balls and, of course, the poor dog was killed. So as you see, one cannot think of everything." He glanced at his watch. "I think it is time to be going, Herr Thompson. We have very good contacts among the police. But so does your CIA. Sooner or later they will turn up here."

"I've got to tell the girl."

"No. You will tell her nothing."

"She saved my ass yesterday."

"True. And today she could turn you in. She is a woman, Thompson. Weak. Emotional. Why place temptation in her way?" He motioned me toward the door. "Your bill is paid. We will leave through the back."

Weber led the way through a long corridor toward a door opening onto the parking lot. His massive body blocked the view. As we went through, all I heard were two coughing sounds from the silencer, and his body slumped back from the impact, twisting against the wall as he fumbled reflexively for his gun. Cassierer's bodyguard elevated the nine-millimeter Beretta automatic and put another bullet between his eyes, motioning me out of the door ahead of him. Two others were waiting in the parking lot, pinning my arms and tying them with a length of rope. They pushed me into the back of a Mercedes, driving slowly through the deserted streets of the little village. A few people, mostly old, straggled toward the church to early mass as the sun came up over the Wall in the distance. Nobody spoke on the drive to Cassierer's apartment.

The old man sat in his study behind an antique Chippendale desk, empty except for an ancient, cracked leather blotter holder, an old-fashioned pen and pencil set, and a small Steyr automatic. He was wearing a pair of running shoes, unpressed corduroy pants and an ancient beige cashmere sweater with a brown leather patch on the left elbow.

"Sit down, Thompson. Get out, Leszek." He turned to me. "You're supposed to be a highly trained killer, Thompson. About the only chance you've got of leaving here alive is to jump me, take this gun and shoot your way out of here." He picked up the Steyr, ejected the magazine, cleared the breech and held up one cartridge, reinserting it in the empty magazine and arming the pistol once more. "I once won the pistol shooting championship of the Israeli army, and I assure you I will kill you with some satisfaction if you make the attempt."

He leaned back in his chair, rubbing his nose with the forefingers of both hands. "I should have realized that you were totally unreliable, Thompson. Your psychological profile is reasonably clear. A psychopathic personality with a thin veneer of civilization likely to crack under the slightest provocation. Such abstract concepts as honor or even willingness to carry out contracts are clearly alien to your vocabulary."

"Maybe you didn't pay enough."

"How much is von Bursian paying? A million? Five hundred thousand? It would be cheap at the price.

211

However, Thompson, my price is a good bit higher now. It's the information you've got against your head."

"You're going to have to get in line to collect. The competition is getting stiff."

"I'm indifferent to your executioner, Thompson. You have information I want about the Orpheus Circle. I intend to have it. One of the men who brought you here is an expert at extracting it. I hope you don't force me to use him."

"You want the names of the Orpheus Circle?"

"Yes. All of them."

"Then you've got to figure out a way to get me into the archive. I've got a process which will break them loose but it takes time. I need access to the computer."

"You have one name. Von Bursian. Who is he?"

"He uses the name Grundig. He runs a small machinery business in Erlangen."

"You're blackmailing him?"

"I'm trying. He says he's got to liquidate a lot of assets to come up with the money."

"How much?"

"A hundred thousand dollars."

"You're a fool, Thompson. In addition to being treacherous, you're stupid. You could have gotten more. Much more."

"Or dead."

"What is his address?"

"Grundig Maschinenbau. Goethestrasse 15, Erlangen."

Cassierer picked up the phone and barked orders into it. "Now the others. How will you get the names?"

"It's fairly simple. You compare the SS files with the Displaced Persons files. On the computer you can do this fairly rapidly."

"Don't play games, Thompson. If it were that simple we would have done it already. We don't have any place to start. You have obviously come up with some sort of shortcut."

"Yeah. But I'll have to show you how it's done on the computer. It's too complicated to explain."

"You're lying."

I shrugged. "You use that." I nodded toward the little gun. "And you get nothing. Go along with me and you may lay your hands on two hundred ex-SS men."

"At least one of whom is a high-ranking East German intelligence officer, no?"

"Tumerius thought so. I didn't have time to find him."

"You realize he was working on his own? Nobody realizes he is missing yet. Even East Germans have weekends."

"Makes sense. His career would have been made if he could put the finger on a former SS man in a top job."

Cassierer shook his head. "He wouldn't have fingered him. He would have used him as a milk cow and an insurance policy, squeezing him dry over the years. A beautiful setup. His victim would have had an urgent interest in keeping him not only alive but happy. His career would have flourished. And if he died," Cassierer shrugged, "his protector would immediately be revealed."

"And you won't reveal his identity and punish him either, this 'victim.' You'll use this former SS man to seed Mossad agents throughout the STASI and the East German police until you know every time Honecker goes to the john."

"You are a crude and vulgar man, Thompson, utterly lacking in refinement. However, you do have a certain quick and primitive understanding. Yes. We will use him, whoever he is, and use him well. It will be a classic setup."

213

"And you'll sell what you get piecemeal to the U.S."

"We are a small country, without resources or real power. All we've got to survive on is our wits and nerve. We will sell to whoever pays the right price. Who is he?"

"I told you. I didn't have enough time to winkle him out."

"How much time do you need?"

"For one name? Depends on what you give me to start with. If you've got a set of names of East German intelligence types whom you suspect, it would cut the process radically. Otherwise, it means running every file through the computer for the age groups in question and comparing them with the DP files."

"That would take years."

"Weeks. Less if you had more assets. A couple of computer specialists and another heavy-duty machine wired to the archive."

"And with this you could over time discover all the names?"

"Maybe not all. Ninety percent. Like I said, some of the SS files are missing. The system isn't foolproof. Also some leads would help."

Cassierer stared at me thoughtfully. "You know, Thompson, it occurs to me that we have all tended to underestimate you. Weber. Von Bursian. Xerxes. Tumerius. Me. I wonder what you are planning now."

"How to get out of this in one piece. I'm wanted for murder, treason, assault and God knows what else. At least four counterespionage organizations are trying to either kill me or put me on the rack. Look, I'll find your goddamn Nazi antiques for you. Just guarantee me a way out of this rathole."

"Very well. You produce the names, and I'll see that you get wherever you want to go."

"Leszek." He had hardly raised his voice when the

bodyguard appeared. "Take him to the plant. If he makes any attempt to escape, kill him instantly. Goodbye, Thompson. I doubt that I'll be seeing you again. You have my word. Come up with the names, and you'll go free. Otherwise." He shrugged. "A pity. You have a certain Odyssean charm about you. I wish you luck."

They tied my hands with the length of nylon rope and led me out to the Mercedes, blindfolding me in the car. It took half an hour. We seemed to be moving in circles, so it was hard to tell where we were. The car stopped at what was obviously a gate and moved a few hundred feet farther. They pulled me out and led me across a cobblestoned courtyard into a building, taking off the blindfold as the door closed behind me. We were in a warehouse, a new concrete block building with low steel rafters and open insulation on the walls. The place was spotless, stacked high with cardboard boxes, leaving aisles in between. A slender man wearing thick glasses and a white laboratory coat stood in front of me.

"Dr. Thompson. My name is Klaus." He spoke German with a heavy Israeli accent. "Obviously that isn't my name, but if you have to address me, you can use it and I will answer. All right?"

"Sure."

He led the way into a smaller room at the back of the warehouse. It was lined with computers of all kinds, from linked industrial machines to children's toys. In the center a Hahn computer identical to those at the Document Center was set up.

"Have you worked it out, Dr. Thompson? What we've done?"

"You've accessed the Document Center files."

"Yes. I've been trying for about a week, and we finally managed to crack the codes today. Are you a computer expert, Dr. Thompson?"

"No."

"Pity. One of my young assistants finally came up with the solution." He was grinning.

"How'd he do that? He must be a mathematical genius. It's supposed to be impenetrable."

"He seduced LeRoy's secretary. Anyway, the machine is yours. It's a duplicate of the one you were working on at the archive. Cassierer insists that I follow your research, so I suggest we get started. They have a system for detecting unauthorized access. We've shorted it out electronically but their technicians will notice it fairly soon when they run their normal systems check. However, from what I hear, it shouldn't take you long."

"It won't work."

He stared at me. "What won't work?"

"I need more than the computer. I run the SS files and sort out those in the right age group with the appropriate rank and background. Then I run this list against the DP files and come up with men who could be substituted. Once I've narrowed it down, I need to compare the SS files with the DP records since the computers don't show pictures."

"You're kidding. You mean they used identical pictures? They wouldn't have been so dumb."

"Why not? There weren't any computers in 1944. Who was ever going to check two million DP files against a million SS records? Also, they were in a hurry. It was quick and easy. But I can't guarantee anything unless we can see the files."

"We can get into the files on Monday. Cassierer has another scholar assigned to the Center doing legitimate research. But he'll need names to work with."

"It would help if you've got some suspects."

"Try this one."

He handed me a card with 'Hans von Torta' listed on it. I ran the name through the SS files and came up with a page and a half of biodata. "He was born in

1918. I think Orpheus tried to stick with the guy's original identity as much as possible. Torta is 5'10", 160 pounds, blue-eyed, ruddy complexion. He's got a high-school education and was in the artillery. I'll abstract this and ask Fritz here to list everybody in the DP files with similar characteristics."

"Fritz?"

"The computer. I call it Fritz after Frederick the Great."

The Israeli grinned. "You mean because he's so arrogant."

"And always thinks he's right." I ran the program. It took some time. One of Cassierer's thugs came in with coffee.

"How'd you wind up in Germany?" I asked the Israeli computer expert, watching the green screen flood with files, dissolve and flood again as the search went on.

"My father was a German Jew. I swore I would never come here. But I am a mathematician, and the Germans are superb in the field. I swallowed my hatred." He shrugged. "I got here and found they were much like Israelis. Intelligent, hard-working, arrogant. Also not like Israelis. Conventional, pompous, know-it-alls without much passion. But, then, one can't have everything. Israel offers little to computer specialists. Here, you've got everything." He waved a hand at the crammed laboratory.

"It's state of the art. The Germans are clever as hell. They've decided they can't compete with the United States and Japan at the research cutting edge, so they let you spend gigantic amounts of capital developing new technology and then buy it from you for peanuts. Or they buy people like me with doctorates from Berkeley. A new batch every five years. The Soviets are doing the same thing. Only instead of buying the technology, they're stealing it."

The screen had suddenly gone quiet. "Let's see the

217

printout." He tapped a couple of keys and the high-speed Japanese printer began to spit out a roll of paper. He studied the comparisons for three or four minutes without looking up, eyes intense behind his thick glasses.

"It's very rough, Thompson. There are a hundred and thirty or so possibilities for Torta. That means we'll have to compare his file picture to a hundred and thirty DP files."

"Yeah. Well, I never promised you a rose garden. It'll take your new guy in the archive a while, but he can gradually work through the names."

"We know Torta disappeared, and we suspect he was part of the Orpheus Circle. We don't have any starting point for the others."

"Take everybody born between 1910 and 1922 with an SS officer's file. There can't be that many. Run the same search on them. Check their pictures against the same DP profile. In six months you'll have most of them."

"If we had unlimited access to the files, yes. Unfortunately, that's going to be increasingly difficult, given the fact that everybody and his cat and dog will be looking for the same thing. However, I must say your idea is ingenious."

Cassierer's bodyguard came into the lab and loosed a torrent of Hebrew at the young scientist.

"The old man wants to talk to me. Excuse me, please."

I sat down at the computer and began to scan the hundred and thirty Displaced Persons files, comparing them to the Torta profile, rejecting the unlikely ones, saving the possibles. Intent on the job, I didn't notice the Israeli enter and stand behind me watching.

"How are you doing it? I mean, what are the criteria?"

"Start with social class. All these young SS men were *Abiturienten*. Otherwise they could never have been officers. So you reject anybody who didn't go through the incredibly rigid and demanding German high-school system. The people we're looking for belonged to either the petty Prussian nobility, the junkers, or at the very least the professional classes. So you reject anybody who isn't the son of a landowner, doctor, lawyer, government official or member of the intelligentsia. That eliminates about sixty percent. Then you move on."

"Sasha." The bodyguard spat a phrase in Hebrew at the young scientist.

"I'm afraid you're going to have to leave with our friend here, Dr. Thompson. Something has come up. Something urgent. I must bid you goodbye." He didn't offer to shake hands, and Cassierer's bodyguard had one again looped the rope around my wrists and drawn it tight.

"Grundig?"

The young man nodded. "It was foolish of you to lie to us. We checked, of course. Grundig is a Protestant cleric, a man of impeccable antecedents who spent the war in a concentration camp. Why did you do it?"

"Playing for time. I didn't think you could run a make on him quite so quickly."

"You lost, Dr. Thompson. Time has run out for you, I'm afraid." He nodded toward the bodyguard.

219

# Chapter 14

THEY DIDN'T BOTHER WITH THE BLINDFOLD. THE bodyguard got in front and the other two crammed me in between them in the back seat of the Mercedes. We were in Kreuzberg, a dilapidated area of the city which had been taken over by Asian and Middle Eastern minorities, mostly Turks. The Germans had imported more than four million of them in the sixties and seventies to man the economic miracle which had outrun their war-depleted manpower. Two hundred thousand remained in Berlin. Now, with unemployment at eight per cent and the growing problem of accommodating an unassimilable Moslem minority, resentment of the so-called guest workers was intense. Driven back into ancient ghettos, living on unemployment, unwilling to return to the poverty of Turkey, totally alienated from the sea of Teutons around them, they hunkered down and hoped for an economic upturn as their children learned German and broke with the rigid traditions of family and religion. Neither German nor Turk, they drifted in a racial purgatory, unwanted and without hope.

The Turks imported into Germany all the political divisions of the home country. The Gray Wolves, fundamentalist Moslem fanatics à la Khomeini; conventional Marxist leftists and violence-prone anarchists; young men with no program other than vengeance on a society which treated them like subhumans.

The Mercedes turned a corner and found itself in the midst of a milling crowd of Turks with banners proclaiming some cause in long sentences terminating in great red exclamation points. The crowd surrounded the car, laughing through the closed windows, dancing around it. Then the Israeli driver made a mistake. He tried to bull the big car through, and the mood outside shifted instantly. The smiling faces were suddenly snarling, hands began to rock the car, the right door was ripped open and the thug on my right pulled out. I rolled out behind him, shaking off the hand of the other guard, landed on my shoulder, spun off into the crowd and started to run, belted occasionally by one of the Turks who had swarmed over the car. Behind me the crowd was a dense mass pummeling the Israelis as I turned a corner and headed down a side street, cutting into one of the doorways leading to an inner courtyard, climbing a set of steps smelling of cabbage and stale urine to the top floor.

The rope was cutting into my wrists, and I could feel the blood wet on my hands where it had rubbed through. A female head, covered by a bandana, appeared in a doorway, large dark eyes surveying me. I turned and showed her the bloody ropes. The door closed, and I leaned against the wall, listening to the distant sounds of the street demonstration. The woman opened the door and came out carrying a large serrated bread knife. She sawed through the rope and stepped back, expressionless. Then, motioning with her head, she led me into a spotless room furnished with worn overstuffed furniture and half a dozen colorful kilims. She led me into a small kitchen and turned on the water, handing me a towel. I washed off the blood and accepted the fruit juice she offered me. Two small children appeared at the door of the kitchen. The mother said something to the older, who must have been about eight.

"My mother asks if you are escaping from the police." His German mimicked the guttural working-class Kreuzberg dialect perfectly.

"Tell her, yes, but I am not a criminal."

"She says you must leave immediately. If the police find you here, they will send us home to Turkey. She says she is sorry, but she cannot help you."

I nodded, bowed slightly and left the apartment, moving down the steps into the courtyard and onto the now deserted street. A television set flickered in the window of a video shop, showing an afternoon news show. Suddenly my picture appeared on the screen. The same old passport picture the cop had carried at the library. The soundless image held for a few seconds and cut back to the anchorman. I turned right, rounded a corner and came up against the Wall. It curved here, indenting into East Berlin. The twelve-foot expanse had been irresistible to the artists who shared the Kreuzberg slum with the Turks. Every inch was covered with modern Expressionist masterpieces. Imitation Nolde, Grosz and Schmidt-Rottluff marched across the wall, an endless stream of cultural soldiers in a war against white space.

I moved along the wall and pushed open the door of a gasthaus, walking into a Berlin which had ceased to exist in the inferno of 1943–45. The old Kneipe had somehow survived not only the war but the plastic revolution. Its ancient marble tables and bentwood Thonet chairs, the bar with the big brass beer pump handles, the boar's head, *Auerhahn* and deer antlers interspersed among photographs of long-dead soccer teams, customers in vests and watchchains lined up in front of the turn-of-the-century facade and soldiers home on leave from the war.

The place reeked of dope. The clientele, barely visible through the cloud of smoke, was self-consciously blue-jeaned and long-haired, ten years after the style had died in the United States. The old workman's bar was an artsy-fartsy hangout for German yuppies and the budding artists and writers of the quarter, specializing in roast chicken and superb beer served in liter mugs with the *Zur Henne* chicken imprinted on them. In shirt sleeves, slightly dirty, unshaven, I looked right at home. You sat wherever there was a free place. I moved over to the wall where a couple of beards and three young women were in deep conversation.

"Eric, you are perverse. What you are suggesting is the extinction of the movement."

The young beard looked weary. "Gisela, you are a hopeless romantic. We have an opportunity to exhibit. All of us. In a major gallery, not in that rathole Bielicki runs, taking sixty per cent of the price of a painting. Fischer is willing to put on a real show. A hundred pieces on the Kudamm. We'll get reviews. People will buy. And he takes only forty per cent. We can eat for a change."

"I don't object to the exhibit. I object to the censorship." She was pretty in a dark, unkempt sort of way, with a thin, driven face and luminous blue eyes contrasting with a mop of uncombed black hair. She wore paint-stained overalls over a cheap plastic blouse and the inevitable running shoes.

"All he's asking is that the cunts be taken out. Jesus, that's five pictures, Gisela. Everything else he will show."

"What's he got against cunts? Is he a faggot or something? I notice he didn't object to the Priapus sequence Elke did. What's he got against my cunts?"

"No. He's not a faggot. He's a businessman. A lot of his clientele is middle-brow conservative. He's leading them in our direction. Gradually. I explained it all to you. He likes your cunts. Only if he hangs them in the gallery it's going to offend a lot of people."

"Why?" Another of the women, a blonde with long stringy hair hanging down her back, dressed in a granny dress, demanded. "Nobody will know what they are. They don't look like cunts."

The young beard lit a hand-rolled cigarette and passed it around. "Because Gisela insists on titles. 'Cunt after fucking.' 'Cunt before fucking.'"

"I'm making a statement. You male assholes think it's only something to stick your prick in or for us to sit on. It's something society hides, refuses to look at, as if it were dirty or evil. Well, it's beautiful, and I'm bringing it out in the open and that fat capitalist on the Kudamm isn't going to keep them out of the show."

The waiter brought me a beer and half a chicken, deep-fried, the crust crumbling as you touched it, a paradigm of a roast chicken, an open insult to the genre in fast food joints and most restaurants. The beer, heavy, alcoholic, and cold, mixed with the grease, cut it and cleaned my palate for another bite. German chickens scratch around on the ground instead of living out their lives in wire cells. The meat is stringy with muscle and flavor, in contrast to the solidified oatmeal of American chicken.

"Look," the beard said. "The problem is simple. We're all broke. Nobody has money to buy paint, much less food. Either we start selling or we're going to have to go to work as soon as Gisela's unemployment checks stop."

The prospect plunged the little group into depressed silence. The dark girl leaned on her elbows and pushed an empty beer stein in small circles around the table. "God, I wouldn't have believed you could be so fucking materialistic, Eric. You wrote our manifesto. Art as the last purity in a world corrupted by materialism. Political nihilism as the only defense of art in a polluted society. Freedom from societal constraints designed to imprison us in bourgeois values. Now I can't paint cunts? You sound like some," she groped for a sufficiently contemptuous word. "Some American."

"Don't be stupid, Gisela," the blonde said. "Americans would laugh at us."

"So now you are pro-American? One year there and you are corrupted."

"No. They are stupid, violent, materialist pigs with no culture and less history, rootless mongrels without a past or a future."

"Well?"

The blonde shrugged. "You could still show your cunts there and they would yawn. Only in Germany are we so stupidly conventional."

I ordered another beer and one of the two beards glanced at me. "Speaking of the devil, you're American, aren't you?"

"Yeah."

"You speak German?"

"Yeah."

"Do you agree? Could one exhibit cunts in America?"

"*Penthouse* and *Playboy* do it all the time."

"No. No." He waved this off. "I mean in a cultural setting, not pornography."

"You mean artistic cunts?"

The blonde grinned and winked at me.

"Yes. Of course. Gisela is making a statement."

"Artistic or political?"

"Both."

"Yeah, well, I don't think you'd have any trouble exhibiting them in the States in a big city. It would depend a little on how specific they are."

The dark intense girl was staring at me. "Haven't we met before? You look familiar."

"Maybe. I come often to Berlin."

She turned and whispered something to one of the

beards. There was a small conference as I finished the beer and tried to catch the waiter's attention.

"Excuse me," the first beard said. "We've been having a debate about censorship and art. Maybe you heard?"

"A little."

"We would like you, as an objective foreigner, to look at Gisela's paintings and tell us whether you think they are pornographic."

"Why me? I don't know anything about art. Anyway, I'm American. An uncultivated barbarian."

"You're exactly what we want. Sophisticated critics are enveloped in bourgeois intellectualism and cultural prejudices. We want a clean, fresh, primitive look. If you like the paintings, if you are not offended, then Gisela is right. If you are turned off, then perhaps we should reconsider."

" 'Lo, the poor Indian,' " I muttered.

"I beg your pardon?" The beard had on a black turtleneck sweatshirt, black corduroy pants, and black suede shoes. He had a round black earring in his left ear. He looked like a banker in drag.

"Sure, I'll look at them." Anything to get off the street, get a little breathing room.

As we left, the beard asked for ten bottles of beer. "You don't mind paying, do you? We're a little short at the moment." I cracked my last hundred-mark note and followed them out into the sunlight. We walked down a street which curved away from the Wall for three blocks and then turned an abrupt left into an alley, moving to the end which was blocked by the twelve-foot-high concrete barricade of the Wall. They lived in a sort of commune in the five-story building's attic, a high-ceilinged room criss-crossed with twelve-by-twelve beams under a tile roof. Gisela's paintings were hung in a dense mass on the wall facing the door. Swirls of abstract color around oblong scarlet centers vaguely resembling rare roast beef. Another wall had been taken out and replaced by a huge plate glass window overlooking the killing ground between the two walls. Watchtowers like toy children's houses rose at intervals. A large German shepherd prowled back and forth on a long lead attached to a wire, ranging across the central stretch.

"You ever see anybody escape?"

"They shot one about six months ago. He didn't quite make it to the second wall. He had a funny little metal ladder, the kind that opens up. He got one of his feet caught in it, and they shot him."

One of the beards opened three bottles of beer and passed me one. The slender blonde fiddled with a machine for rolling cigarettes, pinching dope onto the thin paper and rolling it carefully, licking the paper and twisting the end. She lit it, took a deep drag, holding it, and passed it around.

"You don't smoke?" one of the beards asked, incredulous, as I passed it up.

"Reminds me of the war."

"What war? Vietnam?" The dark girl stared at me, fascinated. "You were in Vietnam?"

"Yeah."

"Why?"

"They put you in jail if you didn't go."

"Then you should have gone to jail."

I shook my head. "Too dangerous."

The joint came around again, and this time I took a deep drag, tasting the sickly sweet odor on my tongue, leaning back on the cushions, feeling the tension drain out, taking a pull on the strong German beer.

"What was it like?"

"Vietnam?"

"Yes."

"Dangerous."

"I know that." She was impatient, her dark, slightly

227

pointed face close to mine. "I mean how did it feel? When you killed somebody? You know. What happened to your mind?"

I took another drag on the butt which was almost gone. It was high quality dope, some sort of Middle Eastern hash with the faint smell of manure about it. "Nothing much. Relief. Depends on how close you were. With a rifle or a machine gun, it's all sort of abstract. Up close, with a knife, when you can feel the blood run down your hand." I shrugged. "You notice it more."

The first time it had been bad. There were three of us. A redneck sergeant on his last patrol before being rotated and a loopy kid from the slums of Newark with long stringy blond hair and no front teeth. "Look, lieutenant," the sergeant had said, his pale skin glistening in the jungle heat. "This is my last gig. I'm out in two days. I got a real bad feeling about it, so no heroics, huh? We go out a couple of hundred yards beyond the perimeter, smoke a few and come back, okay? You can get your medals after I'm gone."

Things were quiet at Dong San. The slopes had attacked a couple of weeks before and the gunships had caught them out in the open. Some of the bodies were still there, draped like rag dolls over the wire. A burial party had gone out a couple of days after the firefight and the gooks had knocked off one, so the colonel said to hell with it, let the fucking vultures take care of them. The birds had gorged for a few days, leaving nothing much but the black pajamas and skeletons. But the Cong was still there, beyond the wire. Once every hour or so a mortar round would wing in and everybody would dive for cover. And every night the three-man Special Forces patrols would go out headhunting. We were supposed to be looking for prisoners, but it was all a little pointless. The gooks wouldn't tell us anything even if we brought them back. And there was no way we could hold them prisoner inside the perimeter. Once in a while we'd take one and send him back on the chopper which came in with ammunition and replacements every third day. Battalion would question him and write reports. But mostly we went out to kill.

"Okay, Thompson," the colonel had said. "Take it easy, will you? The last two second lieutenants lasted about three days and one of them cost me my best sergeant. So forget all that shit they taught you in the Rangers, SF, and jump school and just do what the fuck Lester here tells you, all right?"

We'd moved out through the wire single file on our bellies, going under on our backs, lifting the wire and sliding through. The sergeant rose ahead of me in the dark and started to run as we cleared the wire. It was two hundred yards across the clearing to the jungle. He dropped ten paces before the trees, motioning us alongside.

"The slopes are spaced out about every hundred yards. Two in a kind of little hooch. They don't like the fucking dark any more'n we do, so they don't go out much. There's one over there." He motioned to the right. "About three yards in. See the little hump?"

There was an almost imperceptibly darker blur against the heavy blackness of the trees. "We go off to the right maybe twenty yards, we'll be in their hooches. We can lay low for a couple of hours, rumble on back to the perimeter. And old Lester is out on the first chopper for home."

Problem was, Lester's luck had run out. We moved in a couple of hundred yards, crossing a footpath leading to one of the Cong foxholes. "They got a mortar," Lester said, feeling the footprints in the wet path. "Feel how deep the prints are? Cong are real light folks. They're carrying something heavy like mortar shells to sink like that."

"Shit, sarge. Let's waste the bastards," Newark

229

said. "Only take a second. Get us a couple of scalps.
You can sell 'em back at battalion."

"Colonel said he gonna court-martial anybody he
catches selling scalps."

"Yeah. Bullshit. You can get twenty-thirty bucks for
one in Saigon."

We moved about ten feet from the path and settled
down on the wet jungle floor to wait. I'd almost
nodded off when the young pimply-faced soldier
gripped my arm, pointing down at the path. His pale
face shone in the dark as if painted with phosphorus.
"They're bringing in mortar shells." Six pajama-clad
figures moved single file on the path, each balancing
baskets on a pole across his shoulders. "They gonna
dump on us tomorrow, sarge."

"Shut up, kid," the sergeant said. "Where are their
guards?"

They came on top of us by accident, two small
figures carrying Kalashnikovs as big as they were.
Lester caught the first one by an ankle, twisted him
viciously and drove his face into the dirt before he
could cry out. The kid was slower. His knife went up
and into the belly of the following Cong but not before
the Kalashnikov had begun to chatter. I could feel the
small-caliber bullets whisper across the jungle floor
around me, hear them thump into Lester who gasped
at the impact, slumping on top of the Cong who
struggled to free himself.

"Get the motherfucker, Loot."

I'd been frozen, but now the knife came out, and, as
the Cong shook loose from the dead sergeant's grip, I
grabbed him by the hair, pulling his head back, slash-
ing the knife across the exposed tendons.

"Are you okay?" The dark girl was leaning over me.
"Yeah. I'm okay."

"Have some beer. You went pale and started to
sweat. Then you sort of spaced out."

"Where are the others?"

She shrugged. "Georg and Harry went to the gallery to arrange for our exhibition. Marlise is meditating. She always meditates in the afternoon. Was it bad? The war I mean?"

I shrugged.

"Were you wounded?"

"Huh?"

"Wounded. Were you wounded?"

"Oh. Yeah.

"Show me."

"Look. Thanks for showing me your paintings. They're," I groped for a word, "a new perspective."

"I used a mirror."

"I beg your pardon."

"To see what it looked like. You know, I stood over a mirror. Otherwise I couldn't have gotten a really good look."

"Yeah. I see what you mean."

"Show me?"

"Huh?"

"Where you were wounded."

My hand moved toward the right side of my groin instinctively. "Is that where you were hit?" She ran a hand over the area, pushing me back onto the cushions. "I've never seen a wound before. I'd like to paint one." She undid my belt and unzipped my pants, pulling them down, staring at the angry red gash and the faded remnants of the hasty stitching. She stroked it and then started to laugh, pushing my shorts away.

"My God, he's big." She stared at me speculatively for a moment and shrugged inwardly, standing up, stripping off the T-shirt with a picture of Prudhomme on it and stepping out of her blue jeans. She knelt astride my chest and bent to kiss me, tongue exploring my lips, cheek, neck. "You want to see what I painted?" She lifted up over me and brought herself down over my face.

"Oh, Jesus. Jesus. Jesus. Don't stop."

I must have dropped off. I mean she was fairly athletic, and the beer, dope and general exhaustion combined to put me under. The cop was shaking my arm when I woke up. Gisela was dressed, leaning against the wall, hugging her breasts. Two other cops with the stubby Heckler and Koch submachine guns the Germans use were on either side of the door. An officer was talking to the two beards.

"It's him, isn't it? We weren't positive. Gisela said she saw him on television, but we weren't certain. When we saw his picture in the newspaper, though, we were pretty sure."

The officer nodded. "It's him. I congratulate you on doing your duty as a citizen."

"Fuck that. We want the reward. Five thousand marks it said in the paper. Where do we collect it?"

The officer took out a notebook and wrote an address. "It will take several weeks. Give me your names. I will write them in my report. Then the prosecutor will make a decision."

"Look. We need the money now. Can't you speed it up?"

The officer closed the book, motioning to his men to move me out. "No."

"Hey, American."

I turned. The girl was grinning at me. "Don't look so down. I'm going to paint your wound. I'll call it 'Revenge of the Viet Cong on the American Pigs.'"

"What will you call yours?"

# Chapter 15

LUDWIG VON WRANGEL SAT BEHIND A MASSIVE OAK desk in a corner office of the Berlin City Hall, a huge brick building taken over by the city government from the district of Schoeneberg after the war. You entered the building through large wooden doors leading onto an immense hall built in early railway station style. Von Wrangel's office, part of the unofficial presence of the West German government in Berlin, was down the hall from that of the mayor. The city wasn't part of West Germany legally, but money talks and the Bonn government subsidized 55 percent of the beleaguered former capital's budget. This gave von Wrangel's office a virtual veto over the actions of the city administration.

He met me halfway across the big, high-ceilinged room, holding out a slender hand. "Good to see you again, Thompson. I trust the police were correct?" In a three-piece suit, tassled loafers and a silk Countess Mara tie, he looked infinitely more at home than he had in black turtleneck and leather jacket at the Einstein cafe.

"They didn't beat on me, if that's what you mean."

233

He motioned me to an ancient, slightly cracked leather chair, one of half a dozen scattered around a heavy oak cocktail table.

"Coffee?"

"Sure."

"I must say, you're a man of some ingenuity. We've been looking for you for days."

"Why?"

He stopped in the middle of offering me cream and grinned. "Kathy said you had a sense of humor. Let's just say that you have aroused more animals than I thought inhabited our local zoo. Cream?" His Cambridge accent was almost perfect. Only the slightly rolled R's occasionally betrayed him.

"Black." The coffee was superb. Thick, strong, bitter.

"Good, isn't it? I make it myself. The Arabica beans come from a *finca* I discovered in the Colombian mountains during my last tour. Oh, but do forgive me. Perhaps you'd like something stronger? A brandy perhaps?" He hauled out a triangular bottle from an antique cabinet and poured me a generous slug in a crystal snifter. "Duque de Alba, the best of the Spanish brandies. I think you'll find it much more honest than what the French are foisting off on us these days."

I sipped the brandy and waited.

"You're wondering why you're here. Or, rather, who I represent among all the players." He stared down into the amber liquid, swirling it gently, letting it warm up, inhaling the fumes from the narrowed top of the glass. "You are a specialist in the Nazi period, Dr. Thompson, and you know the German character about as well as any foreigner ever will. So what I'm about to say should not shock you too greatly."

"Try me."

"Yes. Well, as you know after the war virtually all former members of the Nazi regime, even minor party

234

members, were excluded from public life. However, your people, the military government, quickly realized that this deprived them of the help of just about anybody who had any experience in public life. After all, ten million out of ninety million had been party members. And there is no question that they were among the most ambitious and energetic, if not the most morally scrupulous."

He was putting me to sleep belaboring the obvious. His precise English, impeccably inflected, was monotonous. He was clearly enamored of the mellifluous sound of his own voice.

"In any event, very shortly a large number of former Nazis became quite influential members of the government, academia, industry, the intelligentsia. They were mostly not criminals, you understand. Not concentration camp guards or SS murderers. Just former party members and government functionaries. Still, they represented a powerful minority who tended to help each other out."

"Sort of one big dueling fraternity without the scars."

Von Wrangel forced a smile. "If you like. At any rate for some time, perhaps into the seventies, they exercised quite a lot of power. They were, for example, able virtually to halt the pursuit of Nazi war criminals. Not, I might add, out of a sense of loyalty to them, since quite a few of these people were repelled by the crimes committed, despite their nominal party membership. Their reasons lay elsewhere. Essentially they, and all Germans at that time, sought to put the past behind them. A continuing series of trials and publicity spreading the stain of German guilt even further was the last thing we needed as a nation. So more or less everybody agreed, tacitly, you understand—there was no conspiracy—to let the whole thing drop."

"You haven't been having much luck lately."

"Quite. The Mengele story was a most unfortunate revival of the whole sordid business. Even worse was the nonsense about your president visiting Bitburg. It has opened wounds that we thought were definitively healed, and our diplomacy is going to have to spend a few more years sewing them back up."

"And Barbie will spill his guts in France if they put him on trial."

"I don't think they will, Dr. Thompson. Remember the Charlemagne Division?"

"The French fascists who fought to the last man defending Berlin from the Russians?"

"Yes. There were some survivors, of course. They and an association of former members of the French *Milice*, the paramilitary French police established by the Germans, have infiltrated the prison where Barbie is held. We understand he was very nearly poisoned last year. Sooner or later they will kill him in a way that makes it seem a natural death. He is, after all, a sick old man. And the French government will be grateful. I seriously doubt that it is in anybody's interest in France to put him on trial. Even some members of the resistance would just as soon see him quietly disappear. There was definitely a major betrayal of one of the networks. Barbie will certainly be able to implicate some French heroes in that betrayal."

"Or lie enough about the dead to destroy their reputations."

Von Wrangel shrugged. "Surely you do not wish to debate truth versus its appearance? Not a man of your subtlety, Dr. Thompson. What difference does it make what really happened? One is dealing here with perceptions. Unfortunately, the paradigm of the evil German is seared in the minds of whole generations. It requires no more than a phrase, a key word to call it forth once again."

"What's all this got to do with me?"

"We have a marvelous expression in German, Dr. Thompson. 'Intelligence runs after me. But I am faster.' Please do not play the fool with me. Obviously, the discovery and unmasking of fifty to a hundred influential Germans as members of the Orpheus Circle would lead to extremely unpleasant worldwide publicity for the German nation. You can see that?"

"Yeah. How are you going to stop it?"

"For Germany alone, it might be quite difficult. But, of course, there are other interests at work here which make the problem somewhat more amenable to solution."

"You mean somebody else is willing to do the dirty work?"

"In fact, we are embarrassed by a plethora of collaborators, Dr. Thompson. Your head is devoutly wished by Mossad, the CIA, the STASI and, I suspect, by one of those obscure French intelligence organizations which specializes in political murder. The Mossad because you betrayed them. The CIA because the Americans share our view that it's time finally to put the Second World War to bed, as it were. The STASI because they do not wish to have any of their top officials revealed as ex-Nazis, and the French because they fear that, on trial, these former SS men could implicate French collaborators now in high places. And, of course, there is the Orpheus Circle itself. You have managed to acquire a rather impressive circle of enemies, Dr. Thompson. Including my own government."

"Which one are you going to turn me over to?"

Von Wrangel grinned. "It's a pleasure to deal with intelligence, Dr. Thompson. Obviously the solution to our joint problem is to eliminate you. No?"

The brandy was superb. It had seeped into me, loosening the tension. The atmosphere in the room was that of an old British club, slightly musty, smelling vaguely of leather and Cuban cigars. "So who gets the privilege of making the hit?"

"You seem a little too eager to die, Dr. Thompson. I would have thought a man of your proven ingenuity would have, how do you say, an ace in hole."

"If you want to see my hole card, you have to bet."

Von Wrangel smiled and reached into a briefcase at his side, extracted a gray envelope and flipped it across to me. I recognized the papers proving von Bursian's identity which I'd mailed to myself what seemed like a year ago.

"Rather clever of me, no? We checked out the possible places you could have hidden the documents. Your apartment was taken apart. So was Kathy's. You do not have a safe deposit box. Then it occurred to me. Your post box. Quick, safe and beyond reach. It isn't, of course. We picked this up last night after some discreet negotiations with the postal people."

"How do you know I didn't mail another set to the States?"

"I don't, Dr. Thompson. But one of our agents will regularly burglarize your mail box there for the next month on the off chance you did."

"You know von Bursian. Otherwise you wouldn't have known about the papers."

Von Wrangel stared down at his impeccably manicured nails. "He is my uncle. But please do not draw the wrong conclusions, Dr. Thompson. My father thoroughly disapproved of his brother-in-law. Until he died several years ago, he refused to have any contact with him. I do not know him personally and have absolutely nothing to do with the Orpheus Circle. When he called on me for help I was repelled."

"So why save his life and protect the rest of the murderous bunch?"

"I serve my country, Dr. Thompson, not personal values or abstract morality. It's time to, as you say, get

Germany off the hook. We simply cannot afford the scandal of discovering dozens of people in high places who are former SS men. It would tear the regime apart and perhaps the country. Think of the ammunition it would give our enemies on the left." He shook his head. "No. My uncle is not protected by blood ties but by geopolitics."

"It's not going to work. You can't stop it."

"Oh? Why not?"

"I've described in general terms how I got von Bursian's name. Anybody with a little patience, time, and computer skills can match up the files and eventually find the Orpheus Circle."

"If I were you I wouldn't concern myself with it, Dr. Thompson. We have made arrangements to deal with that possibility. Your primary problem right now should probably be saving your neck. I confess that I shall watch you try with somewhat the same feeling I have at a fox hunt when the dogs, fooled repeatedly, have finally worn the quarry down and are closing in. Have you ever seen the end of a fox hunt, Dr. Thompson?"

"No."

"Yes. Well, it's probably just as well." He glanced at his watch. "I'm afraid I'll have to cut this short since my next appointment is due. Was there anything else?"

"You've told von Bursian?"

"Not yet." He looked momentarily puzzled. "Why do you ask?"

I stared at a spot on the wall beyond his head. "No special reason."

"Of course. How stupid of me. You were blackmailing him. And now, of course, he needn't pay." He stood up and extended his hand. "It's a pleasure to have met you, Dr. Thompson. Sergeant Kuckler will show you out."

"You mean I'm free?"

Von Wrangel shrugged. "In a manner of speaking. I, at least, have no further interest in you. And the police have been told to call off the search. It's now between you and your . . ." He smiled. "Friends. I'm giving you what the Brits call a sporting chance." As I left I heard him ask his secretary to place an urgent call to SOFOL GMBH in Frankfurt, and a hundred thousand dollars began to slip through my fingers.

The cop escorted me down the massive marble stairway, through the lobby and out onto the street. The sun was shining, a pale pastel northern sun. I started walking. The city was bathed in a beige-pink light filtered through thin cirrus covering about half the sky, transforming the grim soot-stained buildings, momentarily blurring the hard edges, giving the scene the soft unfocussed texture of an old photograph. It had rained a lot during the summer and the small parks were deep, lush green, folding in the sun and giving it back.

I stopped at a street stand for a beer and one of the superb German sausages, served on a paper plate with a glob of mustard and a thick slab of bread so brown it was almost black. Across the way, in a construction site, a bulldozer backed up and dug in, lifting bricks, ancient wood and the detritus of a building bombed to oblivion in the war. The old man behind the counter leaned on his arms and watched. "They found a bomb in there yesterday. American five hundred pounder. I remember when the building burned. In February 1945. I'd lost a leg. They'd sent me back here to the hospital." He spat on the ground at my feet.

"I'd rather have been at the front. There, at least, you died like a man with a gun in your hand. Here you were a rat in a hole waiting for the planes to kill you."

"They find many bombs?"

"Every week or so one turns up. Then they call in the bomb squad to unscrew the fuses and detonators."

"Sounds like interesting work."

240

The old man glanced at me. "You're American, aren't you?"

"Yes."

"You think what you did to us was any different from what we did to the Jews? Killing women and children with bombs while the men were away at the front? You think that was any better than what those young SS men did? The ones your president turned his back on?" He shook his head. "If we had won the war, my friend, we would have tried and executed the people who ordered our cities bombed just like you did our generals. There wasn't any difference."

I threw five marks on the counter and started toward the center of town. There was no point in arguing. In pointing out that the Germans started it all with the carpet bombing of Rotterdam and Coventry. The sense of guilt was gone. Their self-confidence was coming back and with it the dogmatism, stubbornness and nationalist pride.

It took me an hour to reach the bar. The dark interior smelled of last night's beer and sweat. A Turkish woman, head wrapped in a scarf which was half a veil, swept among the tables which were filled with upended chairs. Behind the bar the weight lifter with the Rastafarian hairdo filled the brand name scotch bottles from half-gallon jugs of mass-produced skull buster.

"We closed, Jack," he said, concentrating on not spilling the amber liquid on the labels as he filled the funnel.

"Scottie around?"

"Be back soon. Can I help you?" He spoke a precise English, enunciating every word like an elocution lesson.

"How about a beer?"

He wiped the counter and set up a glass, opening a bottle of Beck's and placing it alongside. "Five marks." He rang up the sale and went back to filling

241

the bottles. "You in bad trouble, man. You know that?"

"Yeah?"

"They after your ass. They catch you in here, man, Scottie can kiss his license goodbye."

"I need a ride out of town."

He finished the last bottle and capped it. "Ain't no way. You in real big trouble, man." His enunciation had suddenly degenerated. "Why don't you get your ass out of here? We got enough trouble on our own without some fucking honky asshole bringing more." The door to the street slammed shut behind me. I forced myself not to look around.

"Shut up, Clyde." Scottie put an arm around my shoulders. "Clyde's nervous. Fuzz busted some dope heads in here last night. And his wife's pregnant. Can't get his ashes hauled." He leaned across the bar and retrieved a beer from under the counter, flipping off the top with an opener hanging from a chain. "I thought you'd be in Timbuktu by now."

"I'm trying. They've got the place buttoned up like a whore's heart."

"What you gonna do?"

"Does the duty train still run?"

"Yeah. Leaves about seven-thirty in the evening and gets into Frankfurt the next morning."

"What do you need to take it?"

"Same as always. Uniform. ID card. Orders."

I waited. Scottie tipped back the beer and drank about half of it. Sweat glistened on his forehead. The weight lifter rubbed the bar and watched.

"Yeah. I guess it could be done. What you think, Clyde?"

"I think your ass is in a sling and you just about to hoist it up a little higher. They put your balls in a wringer, Scottie, you fuck with them."

"You got any scratch?"

"How much?"

"Five hundred would usually do it. But you got lots of people pissed at you. Might run up to a thousand."

"I can handle that."

"Lemme make a call."

Clyde opened another beer and raked in another five marks. Scottie came back after ten minutes. "Pressure is on real bad, man. Gonna cost you ten bills."

"Where do I go?"

"Man's got a photography stand out at Green Week. You know. Where the krauts pig out every year? He'll know you. Old guy. He's got a source for ID blanks. The real thing. He'll take your picture, fix up the card and close it up in plastic like they do out at the caserne."

"How good is it?"

"Hell, man. It's the real thing. His daughter works in the army ID office. She pretends to fuck up four or five cards a day. Slips the sergeant a bill here and there. Been doing it for twenty years. Half the people in the PX got their IDs from her. He'll throw in the flag orders for the train free."

"How about the uniform?"

"No problem." He sized me up. "Forty-two regular, huh? You ought to be a major by now. Shoe size?"

"Nine."

"I'll have it dropped off at the photographer's by six."

It took me an hour to walk to the Kempinski, an elegant old-fashioned hotel catering to the unobtrusive rich. The doorman was looking the other way or I would never have gotten in. Kathy and Stein were alone in the big main lobby, sunk into leather chairs around a massive cocktail table covered with a heavy tea service discreetly embossed with a scrolled Kempinski initial. Stein watched with a smile as Kathy came into my arms.

"Where were you? My God, I thought you were dead. What happened?" I looked at the old man. "He knows everything, Alec. I had to tell somebody."

"Don't be concerned, Dr. Thompson. I'm not going to turn you in. Which doesn't mean that I find your actions anything but reprehensible. You seem to be a singularly amoral young man. And almost equally incompetent."

"Then why not give me to Mossad?"

"Would you care for some tea? It's excellent." He motioned to the waiter for another cup. "Perhaps because I regard the whole thing as none of my business."

"The Orpheus Circle is none of your business?"

"The Orpheus Circle. The whole distasteful concentration on crimes which are now lost in the mists of history. The search for vengeance, one of the more disagreeable aspects of a primitive desert religion to which I never adhered and for which I have no sympathy."

"You're not Jewish?"

The old man shrugged. "Obviously, if you consult my aryan *Nachweis,* that marvellous Nazi invention for tracing your ancestry, then I am, although both my parents converted to Catholicism well before I was born." He paused. "And always, of course, with the caveat that it's a wise man who knows his own father. But I am, sometimes to my own despair, certainly culturally a Jew. That does not mean that I must condone the actions of that nasty little Sparta which Israel has become nor aid its highly efficient and murderous intelligence services." He sipped his tea, holding cup and saucer near his chin.

"Do you know Cassierer?"

"I have met him. Had Hitler not been so stupid as to antagonize the German Jews, Cassierer would have made a superb German officer in the Second World War. Disciplined, courageous, unimaginative and utterly ruthless. Today he, and others like him, are consumed with hubris. They are leading Israel to destruction by a mindless militarism. And they will eventually find everyman's hand against them."

I looked at Kathy. "He thinks there might be a new wave of anti-semitism when the Arabs develop enough diplomatic and economic clout to pursue their interests intelligently."

"They already have the money. Western banks are stuffed with it. Our universities are full of their young men learning the intricacies of Western public relations, finance and the other arcane skills of modern imperialism. Soon they will begin to persuade the populations of the Western democracies that support of Israel is not in their economic self-interest. Then," he shrugged, "as always throughout history, the West will turn on its own Jews."

"Maybe. But what alternative is there? Hunkering down and hoping the latest pogrom will blow over hasn't helped much either."

"Use our brains, Dr. Thompson. Jews have supplied three of the most important political con men of all time. Do not look so stupid. I refer, of course, to Christ, Marx and Freud. Each of them formulated patently ridiculous ideologies which have taken hold of mankind's imagination and revolutionized human thought and behavior. Often for the worse, I might add. We might be a lot better off without that Pentecostal preacher, St. Paul, and with the harmless pagan superstitions of Dionysius and Aphrodite."

Kathy caught my eye and winked. "Introduction to Cynicism 101. Prerequisite for Advanced Cynicism 404."

The old man was in full flight. "Let us take Christ. As nearly as I can figure out from the confusion of his supposed teachings, he was an itinerant magician who promised life everlasting to those who became his acolytes. For two thousand years people have espoused this nonsense, although there exists not a shred of proof for it. Then there is Marx, an eccentric old lecher with bad digestion who discovered something everybody had known about since man climbed down from trees, the class struggle, which postulated that those with money would try to keep it and those without would try to take it away from them. After formulating this momentous insight in some of the most opaque prose ever written, he then, of course, went completely bonkers and announced that such perfectly rational behavior could be controlled by his nutty theories. When the Russians tried to put them into effect they originally thought they could develop the socialist man in thirty years, then three hundred. Last I heard they were working on a thousand."

"And Freud? What's political about Freud?"

"Everything. He is the father of fascism. His domination theories underlie all modern concepts on thought control. His insistence that patients submit wholly to the will of their master, the psychoanalyst, is simply another manifestation of the *Fuehrerprinzip*. One misses the point with Freud if one concentrates on his peripheral obsession with sex—which was, after all, only a pathetic attempt to rationalize his own strong incestuous desires, first for his mother, then for his daughters. Out of this inner struggle came his adherence to that idiot Fliess's theory that women's sexuality was located in the nose. What it was really all about was domination, a natural preoccupation for an ambitious young Jew in anti-semitic Austria-Hungary. He couldn't even get himself appointed to a professorship. He, as my students say, 'didn't get no respect.' These feelings of frustration sublimated themselves into his crackpot theories converting the natural and normal friction between aging males and resurgent youth in any animal society into a political theorem embossed with a Greek name to give it legitimacy. You smile, Dr. Thompson. But I am right."

"I'm still not sure what it's got to do with anything."

The old man leaned forward. "It has this to do with the Jew, Dr. Thompson. Instead of succumbing to the instant gratification of superficial domination, intellectual or otherwise, he should put his talents to the task of coming up with a tactic which will save his hide. Just, I might add, as you are going to have to do when you walk out of this hotel." He glanced at his watch. "And now, my dears, I really must be going. I wish you both luck." He pulled himself erect and walked out of the lobby, legs moving with the puppetlike stiffness of the very old.

"He's wrong."

Kathy looked at me. "In what way?"

"Power is everything. Without it you're nothing. Hiding out doesn't work. You've got to fight. Just like the Israelis are doing. Even if you lose."

She put her hand on mine. "What are you going to do?"

"Try to survive. Have you got a car?"

"I rented one."

"Take me by my place. I've got to pick up my clothes. Scottie's going to work it for me to get on the duty train."

"Alec, that's nutty. They'll be watching your place."

"Yeah. I know. But they won't be expecting me. Anyway, like I say, there's a time to quit running. I just did."

She drove the small Fiat with the same vicious confidence as she had the Morgan, weaving in and out of traffic with a fine eye for the last couple of centimeters of clearance and leaving in her wake a horn-blowing mass of enraged Germans.

"You in a hurry?"

"Alec, you're a macho moron. They're sure to have the apartment staked out."

"If it is we'll forget it." She was approaching the

turnoff. "Slow down and drive past the door." The quiet suburban street was deserted except for the slow-moving figure of a German cop ambling up and down in front of my building.

"Okay. Let me out and park facing the other way." The cop had stopped to watch us. He was an older man, in his fifties, with a large paunch and a fringe of gray hair cut too long, dripping out from under his uniform cap. "Excuse me. We're looking for Koenigsallee. It's supposed to be near here."

"Koenigsallee? Never heard of it. But I'm not from the neighborhood. Here, let me look." He pulled out the little book of maps every Berlin cop carries and fumbled for a pair of wire-rimmed glasses. As he slipped them on, I gripped his right wrist in my right hand, put my left under his elbow and spun him around and up against a parked car, jamming his arm up behind his back.

"Don't make me break it. Just keep quiet and nothing will happen to you." I extracted the 9-mm automatic from its holster and pulled back on the arming pin as I let him go. No cartridge entered the breech. I examined the gun and saw the hole where the magazine should have been. The old cop had turned now, sweat popping out all over his face.

"I don't keep it loaded. I'm afraid of the damned thing. A colleague blew part of his foot off once by mistake." He reached in his pocket and handed over his metal cylinder. "You are this Dr. Thompson, no?"

I nodded.

"They say you are a killer."

"When does your replacement come on?"

"In an hour."

"Okay. Come on. We're going in the house." I motioned him ahead of me, sticking the gun and clip in my pocket. Frau Waldeier kept a spare key tucked under a loose brick in the banister around the entryway. I retrieved it and entered the house. It took me ten minutes to pack, the old cop standing in the middle of the floor mopping his face.

"What are you going to do with me?"

"You're in bad trouble if they find out what happened, no?"

The thought had not occurred to him. "My God, they will take away my pension. I've got only a year more to go."

I picked up the suitcase and my portable typewriter and motioned him out. On the street I handed him the disarmed automatic. "When your relief comes on in an hour tell him nothing. Just forget I was here. Act as if it was a quiet tour. By the time they find out my stuff is gone they'll never figure out who fucked up." I ejected the ammunition from the clip and threw it into the woods across from the house.

# Chapter 16

"WHERE TO?"

"The bank. We can just make it before it closes. I've got to con the manager into cashing a check for a thousand dollars."

She threw her purse over to me.

Two fat bundles of five-hundred-mark bills, still in the original bank wrappers, were stuffed in among the usual female detritus.

"How come?"

"I knew you were going to need money. It's one thing I've got plenty of. Don't act like a damn fool. Take it."

"How much is there?"

"Fifteen hundred. It's all I had in my account. I can get more tomorrow if you need it."

I stared at the two thick sheafs of pink bills, riffling the clean new money.

"What's the matter?"

"I was just thinking of the hundred thousand von Bursian was going to give me. Look, I haven't got fifteen hundred dollars. I may have a thousand in my account back in the States. I'll give you a check and send you the rest. Okay?"

"Sure. Where do we go now?"

"Green Week."

"You're kidding."

Green Week was an orgy of Teutonic gluttony, a week in which the whole city flocked to an immense complex of exhibition halls and ate itself into a catatonic daze. Everything from fried Sri Lankan grasshoppers to crocodile filets were served in a series of pavilions set up by a hundred of the world's nations eager to cater to the Germans' insatiable appetite for the novel. Whole families moved down the concrete aisles gobbling down tacos, pita, pickled Chinese snake, Tibetan yak liver and poisonous-looking fruits from New Guinea or the mountains of India.

"Scottie's forger is the official photographer."

We parked about a mile away and walked alongside the immense grounded spaceship the Berliners had built as an exhibition hall. It is another kraut Beaubourg, all glitz and glass, a Lego collection of bulbous parts stacked on top of each other, the final Bauhaus degeneracy. In front, a pair of immense wrought-iron figures, looking like Martians dressed up for a jousting tournament, dominate the landscape.

After walking for a half hour through German beer halls, a fake Tivoli and miniature New Yorks, Hong Kongs and Haifas, we found the photographer's office. It was off the Spanish exhibit, a bullfight scene awash in pictorial blood and real Fundador.

"I've been waiting for you, Dr. Thompson. You're late. Do you have the money?"

I showed him a stack of five-hundred-mark bills. He was about sixty, with a fringe of white hair around a brown, liver-spotted skull.

"I would like to count it, please."

I passed over the bundles, and he counted, thin

bony fingers moving in a blur. He nodded. "Very well.
I must tell you, if I had known who you were I would
never have agreed. Not for this price. It's too dangerous. If they bust you and you spill your guts, one of the
sweetest little hustles in Berlin will be over. However,
I owe Scottie, so I will do it."

He led me back into a combination darkroom and
studio, and threw me a plastic garment bag with a new
American Army officer's uniform inside. "Put it on.
Pray that it fits. The general here is a stickler for
neatness. If it doesn't you're in trouble with the MPs."
It was a little tight through the shoulders and loose in
the waist, but it looked okay.

"Are you all right?" The photographer looked at
me, a sudden anxiety in his face. "You've gone white
as a sheet."

"I'm okay."

"Ah, the uniform. You were in Vietnam, no? I know
the feeling. I was in the war, the big war. On the
Russian front. You don't forget." He turned abruptly,
loading the camera with a blank ID card. "This is a
Polaroid. It won't take long. Make a name plate for
yourself." He waved toward a collection of white
plastic letters in a felt box. "You're wearing a major's
rank. They abbreviate. Make it read Maj. Use this
phony ID number. It's at least in the right series and
I'll enter it on your flag orders as well. Only a check
with your supposed unit could get you in trouble.
You're attached to the 305th Signal Battalion at Nuremberg. On TDY with the MLM here in Berlin."

"MLM?"

"Military Liaison Mission. They do overt intelligence patrols in East Germany. The Soviets do the
same thing in West Germany. It's a relic of the Second
World War. There are only thirty or so of them, so
you're unlikely to be challenged. Nobody bothers
intelligence people, and they tend to stick to themselves."

It didn't take long. A half hour later we emerged back into the flowing mass of humanity, a young American Army officer with his handsome young wife on his arm.

Kathy stood back and looked me over. "It could stand pressing, but you look . . ." She hesitated. "Natural. Like you were born to it."

"Yeah. Well, don't get carried away. It's no life for little kids. You keep moving around all the time. And the schools are terrible."

She took my arm in both hers, the softness of her penetrating the thin summer uniform. "Shut up, you crude insensitive male beast. Now what do we do? We can't go to my place. And every hotel in town is sure to be watching for you."

"Harnack House."

"The officers' club?"

"Yeah."

"You're wacko."

"Remember Poe's short story?"

"Which one?"

" 'The Purloined Letter.' "

"Oh. Yeah. If you want to hide something, put it in plain view and nobody will look there. So you think the officers' club in Berlin is the last place Xerxes will be looking?"

"That, plus I can't see spending the night in the car."

"Why not? What do the historians of the twenties say? Half the population of the United States was conceived in the back seat of a Model A Ford." Her face suddenly crumbled, and she came into my arms, ignoring the masses of chewing humanity flowing past us in determined gluttonous rivers. "I'm scared, Alec. It's no fun anymore. I don't want them to kill you."

I kissed her gently, inhaling the Chanel 22 mixed with a whiff of fear which came off her skin, and pulled her into a corner of the corridor, out of the mainstream. "Look, we'd better split. I can con my way into the club, hole up until tomorrow night, catch the train and be out of here in twenty-four hours."

"I'm coming with you. Pretty young redheads distract attention. Besides, nobody is going to be looking for me. I'm camouflage."

"What about Xerxes? He'll hang your ass when he finds out."

She shrugged. "I was a contract employee. On probation. They won't bother me. It was a lark. You know? Life was getting dull for the mousy little academic. Being a spy was fun and games. But it's . . ." She shivered. "Too brutal."

"Somebody's got to do it."

"Let's go," she said, taking my arm.

She tooled the little Fiat out of the fair area onto the Avus, a long stretch of autobahn built as a racetrack before the Second World War. It's now a strip of concrete leading fifteen miles to nowhere, ending at the border of East Germany and the city. Berliners use it to "clean their sparkplugs," opening up their high-powered Mercedes and BMWs on its almost curveless length, reaching speeds of a hundred and fifty miles an hour before having to slow down as they near the border. Kathy floored the gas pedal and the little car sat back on its rear wheels and took off. She glanced over at me and grinned. "For a hero, you're a godawful coward."

"I'm also alive. Slow down. You've got to get off at Huettenweg." She turned off the aborted autobahn and drove through the lush greenery of Berlin's main park, a forest covering a third of the city, replete with wild boar and deer and, on Sundays, half a million Germans determinedly trudging through it. We crossed the main thoroughfare of the American ghetto, Clayallee, and a minute later parked outside Harnack House, an imposing villa, named after a prewar German theologian, which had once housed a learned society. In 1945 the American Army had confiscated it for an officers' club and generations of young warriors had lived and loved in its imposing Visigothic splendor.

The desk was manned by a bored German who glanced at my ID card and flag orders and riffled through dog-eared room cards before coming up with an empty. "You're lucky, major. We've got a double but only for one night."

"That's all I need."

"Twelve dollars, please. You have to be out by eleven. Dinner is from six to eight. There is a dinner dance in the bar tonight from nine to two a.m., so you have to eat early unless you want to pay the seven dollars and fifty cents cover charge for the dance. Do you want me to book a table?"

"No, thanks."

The room overlooked an immense tree-shaded garden, with three tennis courts in the distance, miniature white-clad figures dancing after the invisible balls. Kathy came into my arms. "Hold me, Alec. Just hold me. I'm scared."

I held her in the dying summer light, her tangled red hair flared across the pillow, body trembling in my arms. "You know something? For a passing fancy you're beginning to grow on me. Alec, what are you going to do once you get out of Berlin? They're not just going to let you go. They'll come after you."

"Who? The CIA? You've been reading too many bad novels. They can get away with this crap in Berlin because we're here by right of conquest. It's almost a war situation. There are virtually no legal restraints. In the States they wouldn't dare touch me." I'd been trying to suppress the natural course of events as she lay against me, legs entwined in mine. But one thing was leading to another.

255

"I don't want to make love. I'm too tense."

I kissed her. "Ignore him. He's a mindless animal, lacking in finesse or sensitivity."

Her arms encircled my neck in a compulsive grip, her mouth on mine. "Okay. Let's see what we can do for the poor fellow," she said, giggling. She flipped me over on my back, crouching over me, running her hands up and down my body, letting her tongue slide over my stomach. "No. Don't move. Let me do it."

It was dark when I woke up, arm dead from the weight of her head. I reached across her for my watch, making out the faintly illuminated dial. It was almost ten. Kathy moved beside me, burying her head in my shoulder. "What's the matter?"

"You want to eat?"

"God. Men. All you think about are your stomachs. Are we too late?"

"We can go to the dinner dance."

"Oh, shit. That's all I need." I ran my hands down her back, stroking the taut roundness of her behind.

"Hey. I thought I'd defused you."

"What about you?"

"Well, there is that," she said, coming awake as I moved my hand down over the slight rise of her stomach, holding her. "My God, you're so gentle," she said, suddenly turning away, onto her stomach. I kissed her back, running my tongue down her spine, running my hand over her behind, spreading her legs, stroking her. "Do it this way," she said, arching herself up toward me, guiding me through her legs to her. As I entered she clamped her legs around me, burying her face in the pillow.

Our bodies moved together in slow unison, speeding up as she tensed beneath me. "Now, now, now, Alec, now." She turned her head and grinned. "Good stuff, huh? Might even replace chocolate ice cream some day."

"You're about as romantic as a crocodile."

"You mean I roll over and smoke a cigarette and turn on the television set after we make love?"

"That or something equally crude. Let's eat before they close the kitchen."

"You're gross. You know the old joke."

"Which one?"

"What does the British girl say after making love?"

"Feel better now, dear?"

"The American?"

I reached back in my memory for the old joke. "Do you still love me?"

"The Austrian?"

"Can we eat now?"

"The Greek?"

"Now will you leave my little brother alone?"

She leapt out of bed, her big muscular body moving like a cat. "Come on. Suddenly I'm starving."

The Harnack House dining room and bar were in the cellar, a dimly lit, low-ceilinged cavern with a raised stage occupied by a combo of drums, piano, bass, clarinet, horn and electric guitar. They were playing some respectable forties swing when we came in. The room was about half full, most of the men in civilian clothes with a sprinkling in uniform. The headwaiter led us to a table over near the bar.

"Weird."

"What?"

"The ambiance. It reminds me of a forties movie."

"That's probably when the room was designed. You could have any woman in town for a pack of cigarettes or a can of Spam. Kids lined up behind you for the butts you threw away. Garbage was fought over. It was a city on the verge of starvation, and we were the conquerors after a righteous war."

"But forty years later?"

"It all ended in 1955 in West Germany. But Berlin is like something preserved in amber. It's a military city. The commandant, a major general, is God."

"What would you like to drink, sir?"

"I'd like a Campari and soda," Kathy said. Before I could order, a voice behind us at the bar boomed out.

"Send the little lady a bottle of champagne, Hans. Compliments of Howard Morgan."

He was about fifty, a full bull with Ranger, paratroop and combat infantry badges and a chestful of fruit salad. His uniform jacket was open, revealing the beginnings of a paunch. He was drunk.

"No, thanks," Kathy said, forcing a chilly smile. "I'd rather have Campari."

"Oh, well, little lady, pardon me." He turned back to the bar, commenting to a captain on his left. "Snotty little bitch."

"Take it easy, Colonel."

"Easy, my ass. Gimme another scotch, barman."

We ordered roast beef and a bottle of the superb Bordeaux the club got from the French PX. The beef was overcooked and tough, accompanied by soggy French fries and green beans covered with greasy bread crumbs. Kathy dug in. "My God, I haven't eaten so badly since high school. Do they do this deliberately or don't they know any better?"

"German cooks trying to keep the Americans happy."

Behind us the big voice boomed out. "You hear that, Sam? Goddamned snot-nosed major knocking our club. Hey, you. Yeah, you, Major. I'm talking to you. When a colonel talks to you in this man's army get on your fucking feet."

"Take it easy, sir."

"I'll do what I fucking please, Sam. They're throwing my ass out in the street next week after thirty years and three wars and you want me to take it easy?"

"Sir?"

It had been ten years. I was trying to remember how you bent your back.

"You don't like the food, asshole? Is that what I heard?"

Before I could answer, Kathy had turned in her chair and stared at him. "I wouldn't feed it to pigs."

The colonel, staggering a little, slid off the chair and came over to our table, leaning on it, looking down at her, sweat dripping off his forehead, face red, small burst veins in his nose standing out.

"Well, now, little lady, we're real sorry you're not happy, you and the major. Only it occurs to me the reason you aren't happy may be the major here. I mean he's just a snot-nosed kid. What you need is a real man, honey. Somebody who knows his way around." As he spoke he lifted one ham-like hand and began to stroke her arm.

"Take it easy, Colonel," the captain said, climbing down from the bar stool.

"Mind your own fucking business, Sam. Why don't you join us for a drink at the bar, honey? You and the major. I got a real weakness for redheads. My second wife was a redhead. She was a pistol, I'm telling you."

"No, thanks. I'm tired. We were just going up to our room."

As she stood up, the colonel stepped back, licking his lips as he stared at her, up and down. "Yeah. Well, you can wait a little, honey. You come on and dance with ole Howard here. And you." He stabbed a finger at me. "You sit down at the bar and put yourself a beer on my tab."

I moved around the table as Kathy pulled away from his grip and stood between them. "Thanks, Colonel. But my wife is tired. We're going up to bed."

The big hands gripped the lapels of my uniform jacket and pulled me aside. He lunged past me, reaching for Kathy, and stumbled over a chair, sprawling on the drink-stained carpet in front of the bar.

"I'd get my ass out of here, if I were you, sir," the captain said. "He's bad news when he gets like this."

"Aren't there any MPs around?"

"He commands them, sir."

"Alec. Let's go."

The colonel was on his feet now, weaving. "You. Cocksucker. What's your unit?"

"MLM."

"I shoulda known. Goddamn cocksucking Russian-speaking intellectuals. What's your fucking name, kid?"

"Wilson."

"Wilson what, soldier?"

"Wilson, sir."

"Asshole is your name, Wilson, sir. You better tell your wiseass, little redheaded cunt some of the facts of life, asshole. Like how it's right and proper to suck up to superior officers in this man's army. You hear?"

"Yes, sir."

"Get me another drink, Sam." He turned back to the bar, and we moved out of the restaurant. The waiter followed me through the door, presenting a bill on a silver tray.

"My apologies, sir. He's not a bad fellow when he's sober. Just can't handle his whiskey. He's being forcibly retired. Didn't make general."

"Yeah." I leaned back against the wall, willing the rage away.

"You're something else, you know that?"

"Why?"

"You can take an immense amount of crap and nothing shows on your face."

"My Indian ancestry. You know that old Indian saying?"

"Which one?"

"Don't get mad. Get even."

She shivered and took my arm. "Let's go to bed."

She awakened me the next morning in the most effective manner possible. "He wakes up before you do," she said, giggling as I struggled up from sleep. "Lie still." She moved on top of me, her big body concentrated on the task. "He's big and she's little. Be patient, lover." She lowered her body on mine, stretched out full length, letting him inside bit by bit, moving almost imperceptibly against me.

"Be still. Don't move. Let her do it." It went on forever, moving me to the edge, pulling back, her body moving against me, offering her breasts to my mouth, then the sudden gasping wrenching frenzy as I turned her on her back, an uncontrollable spasm. She buried her face in my neck, wrapping her arms around me.

I disengaged finally, groping for my watch. "We have to check out."

The afternoon went by in a blur. We checked my bag at the main railroad station and had lunch at a kneipe across the way. "Let's walk through the zoo," she said, taking my arm. "I've never seen that new lizard they just got in."

"The Komodo dragon?"

"Yeah."

The Komodo dragon turned out to be a young one, about three feet long, lying unmoving and asleep in a sand-and-rock-filled cage. "Not very impressive, huh? I thought they were twelve feet long and man-eating. Is nothing ever what it's supposed to be?"

"Not much. You want to go watch the monkeys screw?"

"Don't be gross. Let's go to the Einstein."

"In this?" I indicated the uniform.

"You're right. They probably wouldn't serve you. Okay, the Moehring then." We ordered thick German chocolate with whipped cream and watched the city pass before us. Turks, Africans, Moslems in flowing robes seeded into the grimly scurrying crowds of pale Central Europeans.

"It's a great city. If it were reunited, it would rival Paris as a magnet for Europe. They're really a great people, the Germans, despite all the trouble they've caused."

"Things are changing, Kathy. The Germans are no longer the power they were. There aren't enough of them. And they don't have the geography to survive an atomic first strike. You need big populations and a lot of space to play the great game these days. Only Russia, China and the U.S. have both, at least right now. Maybe in the future Brazil and Australia, if they could put together the people and the economy necessary to support a military establishment. Everybody else is second-rate. That's what pisses off the Europeans. The British, French, Germans, Spanish. All world empires once and now nothing. Obviously they're anti-American."

"And us? How long do you think we'll last?"

I shrugged. "Not seven hundred years like the Romans or four hundred like the Brits. Fifty, maybe, if we're lucky and nobody pushes the button."

"And us?"

"You and me?"

"Yes."

"You want us to last?"

"I'm not sure."

I leaned across the table to kiss her. 'When you are, let me know. Come on, I'm going to miss my train."

The taxi dropped us at the small station in Lichterfelde where the American military train left each day for Frankfurt. It was all done by rank. The enlisted men rode in cattle cars and the generals in private compartments. A major shared a four-bed compartment. I went through the processing without incident.

The forger's daughter had reserved the space for me using the fake numbers on my flag orders. It was all routinized. Kathy and I sat in a waiting room packed with wailing babies and soldiers' wives, surrounded by mountains of luggage until the train was called. She walked with me alongside the track to the seventh car, turning toward me as we reached the entrance, taking me in her arms, burying her face in my neck.

I was pushing my bag onto the train when Xerxes appeared, followed by O'Brien and two of their thugs, fanning out to box me in. "Sorry to interrupt this touching scene, Thompson, but the fun and games are over."

"How did you find me?"

Xerxes gestured over his shoulder. "Thanks to Col. Howard Morgan. He checked out the unit you were supposed to be with and found out you didn't exist. Remembered the signal we'd put out on you. Put it all together. Brilliant police work."

Morgan came out of the darkness, strutting. "Hung your ass, huh, kid?" He turned to Kathy. "You're going to need a ride back to town, honey. I know a real good French restaurant you'd like. French fries are real crisp."

# Chapter 17

XERXES WATCHED THE COMPUTER SCREEN FLOOD with data, erase, flood again, the electronic signals merging with each other, disassociating and clarifying like some living thing. "What's going on?"

"Something's fucked up. I can't get a reading."

"What are you trying to do?" He, O'Brien and LeRoy hovered over me in the basement of the Document Center as I played the keys.

"I had isolated five names before the manure hit the fan. Checked them against the Displaced Persons files and found the identities they'd taken. There wasn't time to find any more. These are the names." I called up a list on the screen.

"So, what's wrong?"

"I can't find their files. Either those of the SS men or the DPs whose identities they took."

"Try again."

I typed in "Wilhelm Guenter, Freiherr von Allenstein" and punched the "enter" button. The screen flooded with data as the computer scanned the files and rejected.

"There's nothing on him. No party file, no SS file,

no marriage application file. The files are wiped clean."

"Whose name did he take?"

I typed in Michael Prange, a German from Temesvar in Hungary. Again the screen worked and came up with nothing.

"Try the others."

I punched in the names watching the Hahn patiently scan the files with no result.

At the end Xerxes leaned back against the wall and stared at me. "You're pulling something. You're holding out."

"Holding out for what? You've got me cold. For murder one if you feel like using it. Why would I hold out?"

"Then what's going on?"

"Somebody's erased the files from the computer. Whoever did it has probably also taken them out of the file cabinets."

"Give me the DP names they assumed."

I wrote out the five names from memory and passed them to Xerxes who gave them to O'Brien. "Check them against the DP files." He turned back to me.

"How would they know who to look for? Did you give this to anybody else?"

"No."

"Then how would anybody know these five names?"

I didn't answer. There wasn't one.

Xerxes turned to LeRoy. "Is there any way you can trace these names? Is there a duplicate file? Another listing other than the SS and DP files?"

LeRoy frowned. "Yeah. We've got a set of alphabetical listings in notebooks upstairs. Sort of an index. It gives the name and SS number. We could try that."

We moved up the iron stairs to the main floor and started down a hall. Nathan Cassierer met us halfway. "Good evening, Mr. Xerxes. Thank you for your invitation. I see you have recovered the elusive Dr. Thompson."

"Yeah. There's a glitch, however."

"A glitch?"

"He can't seem to find any of the names."

Cassierer smiled a frosty smile. "Really? How surprising. I suggest you turn him over to my people for a few minutes, Mr. Xerxes. We have lost patience with Dr. Thompson. I'm reasonably sure we could obtain the information we all want."

"Maybe you wouldn't mind waiting in LeRoy's office? The others will be here in a few minutes."

LeRoy extracted a key ring and opened the file room. Black notebooks covered all four walls. He selected one and flipped through it to the B's, halting abruptly.

"What's the matter?"

"The page where Boelling's name should be has been ripped out."

"Try the others."

I called off the names and he went through the folders. Every page was torn out.

O'Brien came in and handed Xerxes the slip with the names of the DPs, shaking his head. "No trace."

"Okay, Thompson. Cut the crap. Obviously you wiped the computers clean, stole the files and cleaned out the folders. You had time that night when you were here with the STASI officer. Somewhere you've got a stash. Where is it?"

"No way. You're talking about a minimum of six hundred thick files. You'd need a truck to get rid of them. Plus it would take hours to wipe the computers. All that's assuming I knew the identities of all the Orpheus Circle, which I don't. It took me a couple of hours to find each one of these, and they were the easiest. The tough ones could take a week." I shook my head. "Somebody with a complete list of the Orpheus Circle had to have been here. Somebody who knows the archive and can work the computer. One of your people, Hugh."

"Bullshit. You figured out some quick way to isolate the names." LeRoy's voice was rough with aggression. "You've been nothing but trouble, Thompson. Ever since you got here." He turned to Xerxes. "Cassierer's right. Hang his ass, then he'll crack."

"Maybe. In a week. Or a month. Meanwhile, what do we do with our friends upstairs?"

"What friends?"

"Thompson, you have caused a series of major diplomatic incidents. First, the Israelis see us as having fucked up a major operation of theirs. The West Germans are enraged that we're digging up ex-SS men they'll have to prosecute, without bringing them into it. The East Germans, with whom we and the West Germans have been trying to develop somewhat better relations, figure we're trying to blackmail them by isolating some SS men high up in their government." He grinned. "Which is partly true. And the British and the French, with whom we share the governmental authority of this town, are pissed that we have not consulted them."

"Sounds like you have a problem."

"Not half as big a one as you do, asshole," O'Brien said. "Murder one draws life in Germany. Parole after twenty-five years."

"Come on. Let's go down to your office, Hugh. No point in keeping them waiting."

LeRoy's spacious office was filled. Cassierer shared the couch with a British colonel, resplendent in Sam Browne belt, ribbons, and a swagger stick, and a small dark Frenchman in a double-breasted suit, wire-rimmed glasses and a day-old beard. Von Wrangel lounged in one of the big leather chairs, sucking on an unlit pipe. Across from him a pallid man in a plastic-looking tweed jacket, unpressed trousers, and the East German equivalent of penny loafers sat with a large worn leather briefcase on his lap, toes pointing inward. His multicolored tie came only halfway down his shirt, the thin end extending beneath the larger by another couple of inches. They all stood as we entered.

Xerxes crossed over and extended his hand to the East German. "I appreciate your coming, Herr Stronk." The man bowed and sank back into his seat. "Please be seated, gentlemen. I believe you have all been introduced? Good. Then we can get down to business. You know why we're here. Dr. Thompson." He nodded toward me as I leaned against the row of file cabinets along the wall, flanked discreetly by the two thugs and O'Brien. "Has made some interesting discoveries here in the archives. He has, we believe, been able to discover as many as two hundred former Waffen SS men, some clearly war criminals, who arranged for their false deaths at the end of the war and took the identities of Germans displaced from eastern nations. They selected doubles of the same age with roughly similar physical characteristics from among the displaced persons who had been killed in action and substituted their photographs and, indeed, their identities in the files. As the war ended, they arranged their own 'deaths' with the help of Gestapo colleagues, assumed new identities and, presumably furnished with negotiable valuables such as gold and jewels, sank from sight in postwar Germany, building new lives. The name of their organization was the Orpheus Circle. It came to light during the interrogation of Adolph Eichmann."

"You have the names?" The East German spoke in a soft tired voice with the elided accent of the south.

"Dr. Thompson was able to isolate some of the names." Xerxes hesitated and Cassierer broke in.

"Before deciding to use the information to blackmail one of the murderous swine."

"May we be allowed to see the names Dr. Thompson has found so far?'' the East German asked, his voice not much above a whisper. "If any are to be found in the German Democratic Republic, they will be tried and punished.''

"We have a problem,'' Xerxes said. "When I asked you to come here I assumed that we would be able to persuade Dr. Thompson to reveal those names he has already found and explain in detail the system he used to do so. Given the fact that all of us here have a direct interest in the results of such an investigation and probably some interest in coordinating our efforts to arrest and punish these people, it seemed a sensible idea. However, we now discover that the pertinent files are missing.''

Cassier interrupted. "Stolen, undoubtedly, by the slippery Dr. Thompson.''

"Excuse me,'' the East German said. "Am I to understand that you have called me here as a representative of the German Democratic Republic to inform me that you are unable to identify the members of this Nazi group?'' He looked a little incredulous. "If that is the case, I will excuse myself. You will receive an official protest from my government in due time.''

"That's not what he meant at all, Stronk,'' von Wrangel said. "The object of the meeting was to coordinate the arrest of these people so that they would not escape if we went about it piecemeal. What Mr. Xerxes is telling you is that our researcher''—he smiled faintly—"has not been able to come up with the names.'' Von Wrangel hesitated. "I should point out to you gentlemen that my government is concerned that this operation be conducted with the utmost discretion. While it is true that all of these men were members of a reprehensible organization, I should point out that the mere fact of membership in the Waffen SS is not a crime in Germany. There must be proof of the commission of a criminal act before proceedings against them can be brought.''

269

"True. Herr von Wrangel," Cassierer said. "However, the publication of a list of prominent West Germans, people famous in academia, politics and the professions who are former SS men, would be devastating for your nation's public image."

"Precisely," von Wrangel said. "Devastating and unnecessary."

"My government will not be a party to protecting the reputation of criminal fascists," the East German protested.

"Not even, Stronk, if it turns out that some of them are high-ranking members of your government?"

"We will attend to that if such is the case," the East German said, voice stiff.

"If we can come to no agreement to do this discreetly you can be assured that my government will give the East German names worldwide publicity," Xerxes warned.

"You're assuming that we can be brought to accept such a deal," Cassierer said. "Why should Israel avoid washing your dirty linen in public, gentlemen? After all, it was Jews these swine killed and incinerated."

The two Germans looked at each other across the length of the long polished cocktail table. "I believe our governments are already making arrangements to give yours satisfaction, Herr Cassierer.

"The Leopard tank and Zeiss optics," Cassierer said under his breath, smiling his old man's smile.

Xerxes cleared his throat. "I think we're getting a little ahead of ourselves, gentlemen. There are no names as yet which we can reveal. At least not with any proof. We remain unable to find the files which seem to have disappeared."

"You think this"—the Frenchman indicated me with a flick of a small hand—"individual has destroyed them?"

"That's what we are about to find out." He turned to me. "What have you got to say, Thompson?"

270

"A couple of things. I may have an idea how to retrieve the names. But before we go any further, I'd like to know what kind of a deal I'm being offered."

"Deal?" Cassierer stared at me, an old hawk studying his prey before pouncing. "Deal? Nobody is offering you any kind of deal. You give what you have, and we will decide your fate."

"In that case I suggest you find the Orpheus Circle yourself. And it'll be interesting to see how the world press reacts when I begin to describe this meeting at my murder trial."

The Frenchman looked down at his fingernails. "You are very unlikely ever to stand trial, Dr. Thompson. I would, however, like to suggest to my colleagues that if you can come up with the names, we agree to free you and deport you from this city. Should you ever return, it might have unfortunate consequences for you." He looked around the room.

I watched the reluctant nods. "Well, Dr. Thompson?"

"Herr Cassierer supplied me with the name of an SS officer, Fabian von Bursian, who had participated in the massacre of Jews in the Ukraine during World War Two. This officer was listed as killed in action during the Battle of the Bulge late in 1944. Obviously, if alive, he was using another name. He was seen but not identified at an international conference in London. Using a list of the Germans attending that conference and the personal data in von Bursian's SS files, I ran through the computer comparisons of every Displaced Person file for people within a certain age range and with characteristics similar to those of von Bursian."

"What made you think he had taken the identity of a displaced person?" the Brit asked, high-pitched voice larded with Oxbridge arrogance.

"It seemed a logical place to look. These people were uprooted, without family or connections. The chances of being found out were close to zero, especially in the chaotic conditions of postwar Germany. And I'd already tried everything else."

"And you found him?"

"The Orpheus Circle made it relatively easy by using the same pictures as those in their SS files."

"And who is he, this von Bursian?" the East German asked.

I looked at Xerxes who shrugged.

"Erwin von Kollwitz."

"Oh, I say. That's a bit thick," the Brit said. "He's in partnership with Wolverhampton Industries in Sussex. I know the chap well. Had dinner with him at the ambassador's in Bonn last month. Really, old boy, you must be mistaken."

"Check him out."

"Who else?" Cassierer asked.

"General Wilhelm Brosius." The East German's head snapped up from the pad he had taken out of the ancient briefcase.

"Impossible!"

"The commander of the Volkspolizei?" The little Frenchman stared at me incredulously.

"His name is Christian, Freiherr von Erlangen, born Breslau, June 11, 1919. Hauptsturmbahnfuehrer, Das Reich Division. Former commander of Einsatztruppe B. He's had plastic surgery but he's still recognizable."

The East German's pallid complexion had turned chalky. "You are sure?" His low voice was almost a whisper.

"Positive."

"Where are the files?"

I shrugged. "They were here. I saw them. Somebody has lifted all of them."

Xerxes turned to LeRoy. "It's your archive, Hugh. Who could have done it?"

LeRoy frowned. "The only one possible was Herr Ludwig."

"The one in the pay of the East Germans?" Xerxes looked at Stronk.

"Yeah. He had access, knew the computers and nobody would have checked him going and coming."

"It couldn't have been Ludwig, Hugh."

"Why not?"

"The files were still in place when he was killed. Tumerius and I had accessed them. It's got to be somebody else."

"Is there any other record? Any file we've overlooked?"

LeRoy shook his head. I leaned against the cabinet watching the scene.

"There is one, Hugh."

He turned, face thick with hostility. "Yeah. Tell me about my archive, you treacherous son-of-a-bitch."

"The visa files."

LeRoy's face, tanned from endless rounds of golf, nose a matrix of red veins, paled.

"What are those?" Xerxes asked.

"Anybody who is old enough to have been a war criminal, who applies for a visa to travel to the United States, is automatically checked against the Document Center files to see if he has a Nazi criminal record. Like a good bureaucrat, Hugh maintains a card file cross-referencing all such requests. Helps justify the budget."

"Well, Hugh," Xerxes barked. "What the fuck are you waiting for? Let's see the visa file."

"He didn't apply for a visa," LeRoy said, meeting my stare, mouth tight, rage mounting within him.

Xerxes looked puzzled. "You mean you've already checked?"

"No. No. I mean I don't ever remember his applying." He moved to one of the cabinets containing alphabetically arranged drawers of cards, unlocked it and pulled out the K's, riffling through them rapidly, pushing the drawer to. "Nothing, like I said."

"Shit." Xerxes turned away as Hugh started to relock the drawer.

"Mind if I have a look, Hugh?" I asked.

"Yes, I mind, asshole. I don't want you going near my files."

Xerxes turned back, watching the scene. "What's the problem, Thompson?"

"Nothing. I'd just like to double-check."

Xerxes stared at LeRoy who moved away from the file. I found the card, a three-by-five, under von Kollwitz, Erwin, and slipped it out of the drawer. "You must have missed it, Hugh."

"Yeah, well, why shouldn't von Kollwitz apply for a visa? That doesn't prove he's von Bursian." He turned to Xerxes. "He's a phony, Frank. All this crap is a hustle he's built up to con money out of Cassierer. Only it got out of hand."

"There's an SS file number in pencil in the upper left hand corner, Hugh. Your writing, no?"

He glanced at it. "Yeah. So what?"

"It's von Bursian's file number."

Xerxes took the card. "Are you sure?"

"It ought to be. I've lived with it for a month." I turned to LeRoy. "You, or more likely Herr Ludwig, stumbled on von Bursian when you checked out von Kollwitz for a visa. Probably somebody remembered the similarity of the pictures. Anyway, you had in your hands a leading German industrialist, a former war criminal who was using a phony name. You couldn't resist, Hugh. It was too good an opportunity for an underpaid bureaucrat to get rich. How much have you taken him for?"

"You're nuts, Thompson. I don't know what you're talking about."

"You saw me getting close and saw the golden goose about to get slaughtered. So you passed the word to von Bursian. He sent Weber and his goons to eliminate me. When he realized I had him identified and a file

274

stashed away which would surface if he eliminated me, he paid me off. But to be on the safe side, he told you to get rid of all the Orpheus files. He gave you a complete list, and you didn't have any choice. He had you trapped just the way you had him. If they caught him, he'd give you up. And vice versa. Two rats in a cage with the water rising."

I turned to von Wrangel. "But von Bursian doesn't trust LeRoy, so what does he do? He contacts his nephew, whom he hasn't seen in thirty years. He presents his case. It's not in Germany's interest to have him and his group exposed. The publicity would be devastating to the new Germany, especially after Bitburg. The files in the Document Center have to be destroyed. He asks you to arrange to have the Bundesgrenzschutz special commando in Berlin, the SEK, come in and burn it. Not something a lot of people would have been unhappy about in any event."

Von Wrangel moved in his chair and shook his head. "Not quite. One of the senior officers of the Grenzschutz is in the Orpheus Circle. He gave the orders. All they needed from me was logistical support and information. However, you are essentially right. I helped my uncle because I did not believe, and do not now believe, that forty years after the war we should pursue these people and continually reopen old wounds."

"Yeah, well, I picked the same night to come here and the manure hit the fan. It was up to you then, Hugh. And you came through. Where are the files? They can't have been destroyed. You haven't had time."

His eyes flicked to the row of cabinets I was leaning against. Xerxes followed the look. "Open them, Hugh."

LeRoy took out a key ring and opened the cabinets one by one. "The SS files are in these. The DP files at the end." His tan had faded. The anger drained away.

"Why, Hugh?" Xerxes asked.

"Money. What else?"

Xerxes stared at me across the desk, his coarse face sagging with weariness. "We managed to get a deal, Thompson. No thanks to you. Instead of having an East German police general, a politburo member and a couple of high-ranking executives on the party secretariat in our pocket singing like canaries, all we get is a pledge of silence on our own villains."

"When does the balloon go up?"

"Tomorrow. The Germans will sweep up the really bad ones at dawn. East and West. In the East, they'll handle it quietly. No public trials. We agreed to go along. In West Germany there will be a lot of resignations and retirements. Five members of parliament. Two undersecretaries in major ministries. A general. Some top industrialists, including your von Bursian."

"Von Wrangel?"

"He's retiring from the foreign office for health reasons."

"Trials?"

Xerxes rubbed his eyes. "Some are inevitable. There are some bad people on that list. But they'll be spaced out. No big scandal."

"Cassierer will go along?"

"Yeah. The Israelis have wanted the license for the Leopard for years. They've got it. A couple of submarines. A billion-dollar loan. Some other small items, whatever they can shake loose."

"The East?"

"Stronk is still in there with the old boy. A negotiating commission will come up from Israel to finalize things. They want restitution, upkeep on old cemeteries, rebuilding of synagogues, some trade concessions. And fibre optics licenses from Zeiss, of course. The East will go along."

"Not much choice."

"No. Not much choice. Looks like everybody comes out of this with something but you, Thompson. Poetic justice."

"Yeah. Plus cutting off my research by barring me from the archive."

Xerxes stared out the window. "Well, apply again in about five years. If I'm around, I'll see what I can do." He stood up and held out his hand. "Meanwhile, if you're ever looking for work, give me a call. We need freelancers occasionally. Here's your ticket out of town. You're on the ten o'clock plane. You can just about make it." As I reached the door he stopped me. "Kathy's waiting for you outside. She'll drive you to the airport. There will be a couple of my guys behind you to make sure you leave."

O'Brien came in as I was about to leave. "You were lucky this time, Thompson. Next time you get in our way we'll hang your ass." He wasn't expecting it. The punch caught him just below the breastbone and doubled him up on Xerxes's carpet. He opened his mouth like a fish, sucking for air.

I walked out of the archive, listening to my heels on the marble floors of the empty corridors, and into the glare of the lights illuminating the perimeter, put up after the Grenzschutz attack. She was waiting in the little Fiat. I slipped in beside her.

"O'Brien called me. He said they were throwing you out of Berlin."

"What about you?"

She shrugged. "Male chauvinism has its uses. A woman in the throes of passion is unreliable. They've forgiven me. I might even get another offer from them sometime. I'm supposed to take you directly to the airport. They've got some thugs behind us." She indicated the car.

"Let's go."

"Are you okay?"

"Yeah. Aside from being dead broke, cut off from

277

my research, and probably on some government blacklist which will eventually be discreetly revealed to the powers that be in Santa Cruz, I'm in great shape. Stop by the *Postamt,* will you, Kathy. I'll check my box for any mail." She drove through the darkened streets to the small post office, and I collected a mass of letters and magazines. I went through the pile. An invitation to give a lecture at the University of Texas on the correlation of Nazi sports training and the building of a military esprit. A bill for thirty dollars for books from the University of Michigan. A postcard from London from my ex-wife. And a deposit slip from the Bank of Bad Godesberg for three hundred thousand marks.

"What's the matter, Alec?"

I passed the thin sliver of paper over to her, and watched the grin spread across her face. "He deposited it a day early. On Monday. Before von Wrangel talked to him. How about coming to Paris with me? I know a little hotel in the Seventh near the Musée Rodin. Overlooks the garden of the Hotel de Matignon where the French prime minister lives."

"I've never been to Paris in June."

# Epilogue

Paris (AFP) June 15. A leading German industrialist, Erwin von Kollwitz, died today when his Mercedes crashed at high speed into the stanchions supporting an autobahn bridge outside Frankfurt. Police officials speculated that von Kollwitz, one of the leading architects of the German postwar economic miracle, had fallen asleep at the wheel.

Bonn (DPA) June 16. A wave of resignations hit the West German political community today, led by the Christian Socialist Party's top specialist on defense, Franz von Boelke. Four other parliamentarians and two undersecretaries of state, as well as Bundeswehr General Heinrich Lummer, also retired under mysterious circumstances.

Sources close to the government refused further comment.

Berlin (ADN) June 16. A purge among the upper echelons of the Socialist Unity Party (Communist) appears to have taken place over the weekend. The commander of the Volkspolizei, General Wilhelm Brosius,

Politburo member Michael Walkowski and several lead-ing members of the executive secretariat of the Central Committee are rumored to have resigned.

Informed sources close to the party leadership indi-cated that the purge was a result of differences between the hard-liners supporting Moscow's policies and the so-called "Germans" seeking closer relations with the FRG.

Frankfurt (AP) June 20. German newspapers have reported a mysterious wave of suicides among leading academics, professionals and politicians in the country over the past week. At last count some twenty people, most in their sixties, are reported to have taken their lives.

Suicide is on the rise in Germany, but epidemics such as that which took place over the past week are virtually unheard-of, even in this society saturated by stress. Several investigative reporters have attempted to estab-lish some connection between the deaths, but they appear to be totally unrelated and coincidental.

Paris (AFP) June 29. Count Guillaume Henri d'An-gouleme, former officer in the infamous Charlemagne Division, was arrested in Strasbourg today and accused of the murder of ten French resistance fighters on May 15, 1944 at Dreux.

D'Angouleme, believed to have been killed in Berlin in April 1945 while fighting with the French fascist unit, assumed the identity of Pavel Becker, a German dis-placed person, and lived quietly in Strasbourg for the past forty years.

He has protested his innocence of any crime.